Unspoken Destiny

Erin Silva

Unspoken Destiny

This is for all those lovely souls damaged by trauma, who hide their hurt with a smile to protect others.

This is to bring awareness to sexual assault and suicide, hoping to give a voice to all those affected by these tragedies that the world has to offer.

I never truly imagined that I could publish a book. Doing so is harder than I ever imagined, but rewarding in the same breath. I would've never made it this far without the love and support from family and friends.

I'm eternally grateful for everything, and can't fathom life without all of you.

I'm especially grateful to my three beautiful children and husband. Without them pushing me to follow my dreams, I'd never be able to say that I'm an author.

Thank you.

DEAR READER

Please remember that your mental health matters! Below you will find a detailed Trigger Warning list, broken up by chapter to prepare you for what's to come in the chapters ahead. Ensure that the Trigger Warnings listed are not something that will trigger you, so you can fully enjoy reading this novel. In addition to the extensive list, each chapter containing major Trigger Warnings will also have a warning along the top of the chapter.

I hope this story resonates with you, as these subjects mean to bring awareness to the serious traumas occurring in the world today.

Ranging from mental abuse to SA and suicide, trauma comes in all forms, and this story brings real-world issues to life—how it affects not just the victim but everyone surrounding them. Thank you for picking up my book. I want to make sure that you maintain your mental health, so I ask that you not skim this list but process it thoroughly.

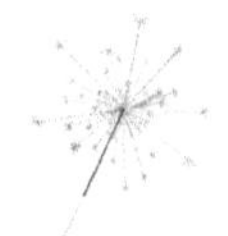

<u>Mental Abuse:</u>
Chapters: 1, 3, 6, 7, 17, 26
<u>PTSD & Depression:</u>
Chapters: 2, 16, 17, 18, 19, 23, 24, 25, 31, 34, 35, 36, 37
<u>Cancer/Death of Loved Ones:</u>
Chapters: 2, 36, 37
<u>Graphic Depictions of Child Sexual Assault:</u>
Chapters: 4, 5
<u>Graphic Depictions & Suggestions of Adult Sexual Assault:</u>
Chapters: 21, 33
<u>Graphic Depictions of Suicidal Death:</u>
Chapters: 36
<u>Graphic Depictions & Suggestions of Homicide:</u>
Chapters: 21, 32, 33, 35, 36
<u>Violence:</u>
Chapters: 4, 5, 20, 21, 23, 26, 30, 32, 33, 34, 35
<u>Suicidal Ideation & Self-Harm:</u>
Chapters: 16, 25, 31, 36
<u>Alcohol & Drug Addiction:</u>
Chapters: 4, 5, 19, 21, 23, 26, 27, 30, 33, 35
<u>Infidelity:</u>
Chapters: 27, 29, 32, 35
<u>Domestic Abuse:</u>
Chapters: 26, 30
<u>Consensual Sexual Content:</u>
Chapters: 15, 32

CHAPTER ONE
CHILDISH MEMORIES

SEVENTEEN YEARS BACK

"You can't play with trucks! You're a *girl*! You'll make 'em gross with germs!" Walker shouts at Sadie. She's only a few years younger than him, but it doesn't matter. He finds her annoying, tiny, and clingy. He upturns his nose, yanking the toys from her grasp.

They always seem saddled together against their will. Both their fathers are lawyers, and through work, they became close.

This gathering is the Thomas family's famous Fourth of July party. Her mother, Diane, has been buzzing around all morning, ordering workers around and curating everything to ensure the party's perfect. Large decadent tents are hoisted, tables and chairs meticulously arranged, and decorations placed flawlessly. The catering staff is in a frenzy, attempting to achieve the impossible: pleasing Diane Thomas. Upset at Walker's rejection, Sadie runs into the house searching for comfort. She stumbles upon her mother in the hall, primping her face.

"Mediocrity isn't acceptable in this family." Diane Thomas stands in front of the hall mirror as she adjusts her breasts.

Sadie stares as her flawless mother nitpicks her own invisible imperfections.

Diane is a perfectionist on the outside, despite her wicked nature. Her involvement in the community is unmatched, and the fact she comes from old money is another major contributor to the reputation that she maintains. The expectations for her child seem even higher than those placed on her as a young girl.

Finishing the adjustments of her dress, she turns her sights on her daughter. Sadie is wearing her fluffed-up, firetruck red Fourth of July dress. With the stiff, heavy fabric weighing her down, she spends the day constantly tugging at her neckline. Diane kneels to her and smiles apologetically.

"I know that beauty isn't fun, but when we have it, the world demands us to use it. You're a beautiful little girl, Sadie Thomas, and the world will chew you up and spit you out if you don't use what your Momma gave you." Diane doesn't realize that Sadie is seeking comfort from Walker's torment. Instead, she absorbs her own compliment with a chuckle.

Sadie trudges back to the party. The scraping of her pinching black shoes as she drags them across the concrete is barely audible over the band playing in the distance. She isn't like other kids. There's no playing on the grass or running around. She must sit carefully and look pretty, with her blonde hair half up, pinned just right with firecracker glitter bows. Baby hairs falling into her bright green eyes force her to constantly blow upward and clear them.

It wouldn't matter if her mother let her play, considering Walker refuses to play with her anyway. She doesn't understand why he's so mean. His sarcastic sense of humor and midnight blue side-eye are always accompanied with sly comments about her frilly dresses and how much of a shame it would be to get them messy.

She wants nothing more than to be friends, even with his

constant teasing for being so pale and tiny, for her loud, goofy laugh, or most of all for being younger. It's only three years, but to him, that makes all the difference in the world. It's not her fault she's so pale; she's not allowed to go outside and play with the other kids. She *must* focus on schoolwork and extracurricular activities.

Walker acquires his own sun-kissed skin tone from participating in every sport imaginable. He could be picked out in a sea of eight-year-old boys with his curly, light honey brown hair and a bright white smile.

Sadie's dad, Richard, notices her sitting in a white folding chair away from everyone. Yanking at the collar of her dress, her face scrunches in disapproval. She grunts as she fidgets with her dress and aggressively pushes back at the hair that frames her face. Shifting his stance, Richard stretches his back out. The movement is much needed after standing in place for so long listening to other lawyers talk shop. He heads toward his daughter, fully anticipating the disappointment that paints her face.

"What's wrong, Sweet Girl?" he asks, sitting down in the chair beside her. He glances back and forth between her and Walker, knowing precisely what bothered her.

"Why's he so mean? I don't get it," she asks. Richard tugs at the collar of his button-down shirt. Diane chooses outfits for the entire family, ensuring everyone is picture ready.

Although the Fourth of July party has always been a Thomas family tradition, Diane took over the responsibility as matriarch of the home. She extended the event, increasing the invite list from the law firm families to every group she's in charge of. It represents her as a person, and she relies on its success in building her own self-image. To those who attend the party, it appears lavishly overdone, with not a single piece of décor out of place. To a trained eye, an undercurrent of chaos flows among those who run the event.

"He's a little boy. Someday, he'll want girls to pay attention. He'll be crushed when he gets older and wants you to notice and you don't. It's a circle; sadly, you're stuck on the curve that makes you feel unwanted. Just remember how special you are…. You want to come with me? I need to talk about boring things to more boring people." He chuckles under his breath. It makes her smile, knowing it's true. The people there are all over-dressed and lack any interesting qualities.

"No thanks, I'm having more fun sitting here," she says, smirking at her father. He shrugs, nudging her arm with his elbow encouragingly before standing and rejoining the sea of people talking endlessly about nothing. Social gossip among the women and business gossip among the men. Her father almost disappears within the group of men, all dressed similarly.

On the other hand, her mom couldn't contrast more. Anyone could pick her out in a room no matter where she goes. She's stunning, not because she dresses to impress, but because of her many unforgettable features. Soft brown hair and piercing green eyes are her two most identifiable attributes, as well as skin akin to a porcelain doll. Those qualities aside, she appears ten years younger than her true age. Her figure is that of a swimsuit model, but she does nothing to maintain it. She's unequivocally beautiful, and though she needs no reminder, it's the first comment anyone ever makes.

Sadie stands, determined to play with the other kids at the party. Turning to walk toward them, she hears a disapproving *tsk* from her mother. It's almost like Diane waits for Sadie to leave her designated spot and dirty her perfect dress. She turns to her mother, who stands with Melony, Walker's mom, and a few other women that Sadie doesn't recognize.

Melony Harris is an average-looking woman, especially amongst swarming socialites. She's curvy but seems to pull it off rather well, even with her pregnancy. You'd think that Walker's looks come from just cloned himself in looks and personality.

Melony is quiet and self-conscious, unlike the men in her family. James, Walker's father, is both boisterous and comedic, a stark contrast from Melony. Walker runs up to Sadie, who had returned to her seat after being told to do so. "You know why your **mom** won't let you play with us? She knows you would embarrass her for being such a **baby**."

Sadie's tears build. She always feels her mother dislikes her. Although she wants nothing more than to be accepted and loved by her mother, she doesn't believe she can achieve it. Always feeling subpar to everyone and everything else in Diane's life, she equates herself to *the mismatched little misfit forced by birth*. Even at age five, Sadie feels inadequate, stemming from a lifetime of subtle disapproval. Though she tries to fight back the tears, they still come.

She turns in her seat, attempting to quiet the sobs and hide her face from the crowd. Crying would only confirm what he said to be true. Diane would surely tell her to stop fussing and grow up. Her mother's voice echoes in the back of her mind; *'Only women who are pathetic, and want to put on a show, cry in front of others.'* Or another famous phrase *'Tears should never leave the waterline; it's a waste of money and time when you smudge your makeup.'*

With tears too heavy to choke back, she jolts up, shoving past Walker and running into the house. Once she reaches the threshold, she sprints past the living room and her father's den into the bathroom, slamming the door shut behind her. She trembles, standing on her tiptoes to reach, and glimpses into the mirror to find tears streaming down. She flushes with embarrassment, making her cheeks red. A knock at the bathroom door startles her.

"Someone is… um… someone's in here," she stutters, hoping the stranger will go away. Turning the water cold, she splashes her cheeks to wash away the tears and heat.

"It's me. I'm sorry I made you cry. I was trying to be funny,"

Walker says, the door stifling the volume of his voice. She doesn't respond, continuing to rinse her face. Fearing he might hear her heavy sobs; she sniffles to choke back tears. "Sadie… can you hear me?" Struggling to balance on the line between rage and sorrow, erratically teetering from one emotion to the next, she takes a deep breath and dries her face.

The door swings open violently, nearly causing Walker to fall forward. Smirking, she stands an arms-length from him. The forced smirk is unsettling.

In a calm manner, little Sadie straightens and responds to him, "Don't talk to me ever again. Your jokes suck… just like *you*." The detachment between her emotions and her words creates an uneasy feeling in his stomach.

All the comments Walker made over the years effectively constructed a wall between the two of them. The constant pushing away, bit by bit, until he finally accomplished it. She's done chasing his friendship.

After that day, she continues to avoid him, entirely ignoring his existence during holiday parties and small gatherings alike. Avoiding him becomes less troubling when his parents' divorce. Sharing custody means that he lives half his life with his mom on the other side of Lexington.

As Sadie grows up, the parties continue, but the Harris family's attendance dwindles away. Being teased by Walker Harris turns into a not so fond childhood memory.

Chapter Two
Walker Harris: Let's Talk Trauma

EIGHT YEARS BACK

"When did you realize your parents weren't staying together?" The lady in a frumpy sweater leans forward in her seat with a clipboard in one hand and a pen in the other. She readjusts, glancing at her watch frequently enough to tell me that this visit's almost over.

"I think… I was about eight… at one of Dad's work parties we had to go to." I trace the veins on the back of my left hand with my right pointer finger. Talking to a grief counselor about this stuff feels like an enormous waste of time. Clara needs to talk about her feelings, not me.

"What makes you think that? Was there an incident?" I nod but don't volunteer information. These visits usually follow the same pattern. She asks personal questions, and I respond with the bare minimum, if anything at all. "I see. If you're uncomfortable, we don't have to continue."

"My dad overheard a girl tell me she never wanted to talk to me again. He asked what happened and grabbed my shoulder, but I pretended it wasn't my fault." I become silent as I visualize what happened years ago.

"It's nothing. Sadie can't take a joke," I say to Dad and shift my stance. I attempt to shrug off his clenching hand. Mom happens to walk into the house.

That's my chance to get away!

I furrow my brow a touch and wince. "Dad, you're hurting me!" I whine, hoping Mom will interject so I can make a clean getaway.

"What's going on?" Mom says in an accusatory tone, waddling over to us clutching the sides of her stomach. Dad releases my shoulder and turns his focus to Mom. With the newfound freedom, I clear out of the room. An argument was bound to erupt between the two of them, might as well take advantage of it.

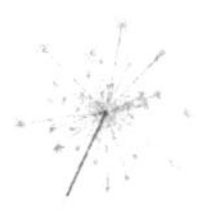

A few moments of silence fill the room between us. The counselor, Christine Cox, nods like she's listening to the memories playing in my head. I break the quiet. "They always argued… It was never really about me, even if they acted like it.

They always ulterior motives." I clasp my hand over the arm of the chair, cracking my knuckles.

"That makes a lot of sense. You were a very observant little boy to discern that," she says, nodding and taking notes. I shrug the compliment.

People think kids don't know what's going on, but they pick up feelings that never become words. They definitely thought that Clara would be their marriage's saving grace, but since when did having more children improve a marriage?

Their separation wasn't an amicable one. Although Dad was naturally a nice guy, Mom's self-conscious. The number of women constantly attempting to hook up with Dad created a lot of trust issues between them. It's an insane thought that loving someone so much could still result in divorce. The issue was Mom didn't love herself and projected that onto Dad.

"That was before your sister was born then? How did the things change after that?" The questions she asks are personal but feel nonchalant and stock. Questions that most people would avoid. I sigh and push back further into the couch cushion.

"Fine, I guess," I mutter. The memory of them returning from the hospital forces itself to the forefront of my mind. They were exhausted, but genuinely happy to be around each other. Clara was so little and content, she hardly cried. They didn't argue again until Clara started crying more and sleeping less. She was about three months old.

In those first few months, Dad would take me to baseball games and the arcade. We went out almost every weekend, letting mom spend time with Clara and rest. It reminded me of the time I spent with Dad before the arguing started. He was the life of the party, wherever we went.

When they fought, I found myself with Clara, protecting her

from the yelling. She seemed calmer when we were together. The yelling made Clara cry, and I hated hearing her cry.

After Clara's first birthday, divorce was inevitable. Mom insisted that her delusions were right all along in that Dad didn't love her. It made the divorce process not only lengthy, but more painful, especially for two people who still loved each other.

I had to grow up fast. By the time it was finalized, I was ten years old. Watching Mom lose sleep and crying about Dad was hard. They were unhappy together, and unhappy apart. Between two parents who worked overtime and were emotionally strained, I took it upon myself to ensure my little sister hardly noticed the struggles our parents so obviously endured. I played with her and kept her happy. I even dropped sports for a short time to be home so I could help Mom with Clara.

"Fine? Something must have changed. There was a year before the divorce happened. Did the fighting stop?" Her eyes were burning into the side of my head. The fight or flight wrestling inside causes my eyes to shift to the door, begging me to bolt for it.

"I guess… they were happy for a few months."

"Happy how?" she rapidly responds with a question, pulling for more details that I don't want to share.

"I don't know… *happy*." My heart rate elevates, thudding in my ears.

"Happy, like they didn't fight?" She lobs the conversation back into my court aggressively fast.

"No—"

She cuts me off. "No, they didn't argue; or no, they still argued?" She appears so calm while interrogating me.

"Yes, they argued! Okay?! What do you want from me, lady?" I snap, the hostility breaking free.

Anger is an emotion I bury deep. In the past, I would cover it up with humor, but nothing seems funny lately.

Ms. Cox purses her lips, placing the clipboard on her lap. She nods her head again in a, '*I understand everything you're experiencing*' way.

"There it is. *Anger*. I was wondering when you were going to let that show. Anger is a stage of grieving, and based on what your mother said about the funeral, I expected this... I thought it would've come sooner though."

I've been having these weekly visits with the therapist for two years now.

Dad spent the end of his life in denial. Refusing to accept the fact that he was sick, he didn't go to a doctor until it was too late.

My emotions twist and turn, hopping from anger to grief. I shoot up from my seat.

"Fuck yeah, I'm pissed... I'm *furious*! It just doesn't make sense! He was healthy... lectured me on eating right *and* exercising!" Pacing the room, I watch her intermittently to ensure she's paying attention. "He *never* smoked! How can someone that healthy *get cancer*? How's that even fair? He was my dad... *my fucking dad*! He *got* me! He was the one to make me laugh...." My voice cracks as I attempt to force down the sadness that boils out of me. "I have every right to hate the fucking universe. It took my dad away from me. Away from Clara. She won't even remember him like I do! She won't remember him goofing off and juggling eggs before cracking them for breakfast! She won't remember his pretending to call the police when we didn't laugh at his jokes! She won't remember him playing air guitar as he brushed our teeth! She was too young!" My eyes well with tears, but I wipe them away before she sees.

Moving to the door, I grip the handle tightly, hesitating long enough to take a deep breath.

"Walker... do you feel you have to fill your father's shoes for your sister's sake?" She stands half a step behind me.

My sigh comes out shakily as I attempt to keep composure.

I've bottled these feelings up for two years, keeping a smile on my face just as Dad would've. Turned every sour situation into a joke, an ill-timed bit that made everyone awkwardly laugh until it turned genuine.

I force a smile and turn to Ms. Cox. "Of course… who else will? Clara deserves a father figure, even if it's just her big brother." I sit back down on the couch and relax in the armchair. She returns to her seat, crossing her legs. Picking up her clipboard, she begins scribbling.

"Masking isn't good for anyone. Nobody understands the hand that distributes the depravity that is loss. No one knows what dictates the decision of whom to take and *when*. We must accept that this life is not eternal."

"For some of us, it's not even partial," I sneer to the hallmark bullshit everyone spews when they don't have anything else to say. No different from *'I'm sorry for your loss'*. It's something someone says to relieve their own discomfort with the situation.

Ms. Cox nods and scribbles some more, making my sarcastic quiet chuckle shake loose. She glances up. I shrug and re-position myself, leaning on the arm of the chair.

"Are we done here? I have to go to work." I don't have to be there for another hour; I'd still be at school right now. She smiles at me and looks down at her watch. When her eyes trail back to me, her smile fades.

"We can sit here in silence if you'd like… but you have another twenty minutes. Would you like to stop talking… or maybe you'd like to just listen?" Leaning back in the seat, I huff.

"If you want to talk, I won't stop you," I respond, unintentionally more hostile than I usually act. She stands and walks over to a filing drawer. Her hands drag down to the second drawer, selecting a manila folder stuffed with a fat stack of papers. Ms. Cox returns to her seat, searching through the papers.

"You came to me shortly after your father's eulogy incident… cursing the world for taking him… correct?" She eyes me from over the rim of her glasses. I nod, and her eyes return to the page. "You told me your Aunt Rachel was making inappropriate jokes, which reminded you of him." She looks up for another non-verbal confirmation. I nod, and once again, her eyes return to the paper she holds. "You saw many people that day you hadn't seen in years. One particular example you noted was the Thomas family."

Flashes of grown-up Sadie flicker in my mind. She was thirteen at the time and looked like a blonde version of her mother. The change was drastic. She was growing up and not the frilly, annoying little girl I knew. Our families stopped getting together when the divorce was announced, like they didn't want to pick sides and instead, decided to choose neither.

I stare off into the distance.

"Many told you that you resembled him… that you could've been his twin." My jaw tenses, the topic of looking and acting like my father is almost like a shadow I can't shake.

Living up to the expectations set by him is a crushing weight. She pauses, probably notating my lack of response, and then places the pen back down atop the clipboard on the table next to her.

"I would love to continue to see you, but you recently turned eighteen. I do have a list of recommended adult therapists and strongly encourage you to review them." She hands me a sheet of paper with a list of therapist's names, addresses, and office phone numbers. She stands to put back my file. Placing the folder under her arm, she juts her hand out to offer a handshake. "It's been a pleasure meeting you. I wish you well, Walker Harris." She pitifully smirks and turns toward the file drawer.

This is the last time I will be forced to participate in therapy again.

Chapter Three
Sadie Thomas: Unhappy Coincidence

FOUR YEARS BACK

I *know* I'm destined to be great; there *isn't* another option. I'm expected to be perfect or experience a form of exile that is so much worse than being forced away. A backhanded form of exile that requires my presence, accompanied by a low humming of constant disappointment. Diane constantly gives passive-aggressive suggestions or, as she calls them, "compliments".

Yes, my mother is on a first-name basis with me. This isn't by choice, though her actions cause me to have a coldness toward her that would deem calling her by her first name fitting. She doesn't want me to refer to her as *mom* because she doesn't want strangers to think she's "old".

An audible clicking sound reverberating down from the air vents interrupts my train of thought. Rolling over in bed, yawning, I reach for my phone. I still have twenty minutes to lie around until my alarm goes off. Wiggling my legs under the feather down quilt, I reveal one to the cool air. I huff as I fidget with the amount of leg exposed to the air—searching for the perfect balance. Flipping my pillow, allowing my cheek to press against the cooler side, provides the most comfort.

'Oh my! I thought you were her older sister!' The sound of strangers' comments rattles through my brain. Becoming a teenager hurt our relationship. The older and more mature I look, the more my mother makes it a point to make me feel inferior. If I retaliate against the comments she makes, then she breaks down, and it's *my* fault for having hurt feelings. Over the years, I've learned to shrug off as much as possible.

As ugly as she is on the inside, she's twice as beautiful on the outside. I've heard that pretty women are crazy and temperamental, which can't be more accurate in her case. Dad is such a kind, warmhearted person. He's so laid back and accepting. For every snide comment my mother gives me, my father follows up with a long conversation dismissing it. It's a shame that I've developed so many insecurities that no number of outside comments could remedy them.

Sitting up in bed, I rub my eyes as they adjust to the darkness. I sling my legs over the side of the bed and stretch my back. Might as well get up since my mind will not allow me to sleep. I stare at my reflection in the full-length mirror.

'You're such a pretty girl.' I sneer at myself. Normally, this would be considered high praise from a stranger. But it's hard to take any compliment when my mother always follows it up with, *'Well, duh! She has excellent genes.'*

Nowadays, I spend most of my time avoiding the house. Thanks to our local community college offering summer courses, I'm far ahead of schedule in my schooling. I'm also in just about every club that my private school has to offer, which isn't a short list. My main focus is to build up my college resume. I plan on applying to Johns Hopkins in Maryland in the spring. You'd think she'd be happy that, at seventeen, I'll graduate early and attend a prestigious school. Instead, she responds with phrases like, '*You're abandoning me*' and '*You're going far away on purpose to get away from me.*'

She's not *entirely* wrong. Part of it is genuine, but I mainly work hard because it's ingrained in me that I *must* do great things. I want to be successful for myself as well. I'm proud of the accomplishments I've made so far.

I sit at my desk, opening my laptop. Different volunteer options pop up from my research the night prior.

Shortly after beginning my browsing, my mother enters the room. "It's your first day of senior year! How exciting! Get in the shower, you lazy bum. You can't show up looking like you just rolled out of bed!"

I sigh quietly and close the laptop. She walks over to my window, yanking open the blackout curtains. My hands shoot up to shield my eyes.

"Jesus Christ! Why you up so early, anyway?" I ask as if I don't already know the answer.

She's up to ensure I look *"decent"* on the first day back at school. She knows other mothers at school and doesn't want the possibility of gossip. The thought of hushed comments about, '*Diane's daughter looks homely*', is a serious fear of hers.

She bustles around my room. "You know me, always up early.... My to-do list is long! I have a hair appointment and a nail appointment." Her eyes trail down to my plain, stress-bitten nails. They brighten, and a broad smile grows on her face. "How about I rearrange my day, and I pull you from school to have a girl's day, just the two of us?"

"I can't ditch school," I respond in an unconvincing, disappointed tone. She purses her lips with narrowing eyes, turning away to continue fidgeting about my room.

"Well, it'd be too much work to rearrange my day anyhow." Huffing the words out and continuing to discuss every minuscule detail of her mundane upper class housewife's day.

With the nonstop droning, I almost miss her question about

when I'll be home. A mischievous-looking grin stretches her mouth in an unsettling way.

"Why…. What's happening?" I ask hesitantly. She wants something; it's clear. She never cares whether I'm home for dinner or not. Most nights, I'm gone until six or seven, doing anything to keep me out of the house. Between volunteer work and going to the local hang-out areas, I always find something to occupy my time.

I don't have any friends, mostly just acquaintances. When you're the youngest kid in the class, especially by an entire year, friends are difficult to come by. Most of my class thinks I'm stuck up, and those who know I'm shy consider me strange.

"Well, your father is having one of his work friends over, and I saw they have a son around your age and—" I hate when she uses Dad to get me to do things. She knows that I'll never disappoint him.

I interrupt her. "Why is the coworker having his family come? Dad rarely invites families over to the house." Honestly, since the Harris family, Dad refuses to get close to coworkers at all. Dad struggled with their divorce. I, however, was glad to be rid of Walker Harris. The last time I saw him was at his father's funeral. He seemed more reserved and not *as* rude, but that was several years ago.

I shudder at the reliving of the childhood ridicule I had to endure. I catch her analyzing me and stretch my arms above my head, yawning forcefully.

"Well actually, *I* invited them. His wife is on the Country Club committee with me. She never supports what *I* want."

There it is! She probably wants me to keep their son entertained so this poor lady will stay long enough to be ambushed by Diane's negotiation tactics. I wouldn't necessarily call it a negotiation… more of an inquisition.

"As fun as that sounds… today is the first day of school. I have a lot to prepare for the first week back. I'm student council president, and you know our school always does back-to-school week with a lot of flair." I have nothing to do after school, but the thought of keeping some random guy entertained sounds awful. My father and his coworker will most likely have dinner in his office. Partially to avoid the women, but also to discuss business they could discuss while at work tomorrow.

Her disappointment takes hold. "It doesn't surprise me that you'd have to do something, seeing how you're *so* popular.... How come I never see you with any friends?" She offers a snide comment on her way out.

The only good part about her comments is that they're usually followed by her leaving the conversation.

Walking into my attached bathroom, I begin preparations for the day. Last night, I selected and hung my clothes. I flip on the light, nearly jumping out of my skin when I catch my bedhead in the mirror. I quickly grab a brush to tame my hair while I wait for the straightener to heat.

I put a headband on, wash my face, and brush my teeth. Staring into the mirror, I assess for any impurities my mother will point out if I don't hide them. Acne isn't an issue, but my eyebrows are unruly and need shaping; putting on some mascara couldn't hurt.

My everyday outfit usually involves jeans, a pair of plain tennis shoes, and a tightly fitted dress shirt that accents what little curves I have. I'm relatively thin, so wearing tight clothing accents my smaller curves.

After I get dressed, I stash lip gloss in my pocket for after breakfast. Flicking off the lights, I lean back into the room to grab my crossover bag and cell phone before going downstairs.

Lydia dusts the foyer at the bottom. She looks up and smiles. "Good morning, Ms. Thomas," she chimes, never breaking pace in her cleaning.

I respond with a respectful "good morning" and continue through the dining room into the kitchen.

Diane sits at the breakfast bar eating her daily grapefruit breakfast. She glances up and rolls her eyes.

"Why do you dress so plainly? We pay a great deal of money for you to dress to our family *status*." She hesitates on the last word, her eyes darting toward me and then back to the paper. She pulls her eyes up when I don't respond, as if she's calculating my emotions to interpret a response. I rarely respond to her anymore.

"Are you saying I don't look pretty?" I ask, trying to trip her up. She hardly ever admits to making negative comments toward me, so confronting her with a question tends to stop the conversation faster than ignoring her. She rolls her eyes again and sighs with distaste.

"You're pretty. Of course you are. You look like your mother! Heaven forbid I suggest something to help improve how others see you." She sighs again. There must be a lack of oxygen in the room.

Setting the paper down as if to better evaluate me, she continues, "You look *fine*. At least you're not dressing like half the sluts at your school... I *suppose*...." I proceed with my morning, getting my to-go coffee and a muffin, as she ends her rant. The muffin is still warm and smells freshly baked. The chocolate chunks glisten, making my mouth water. I walk to the garage door as she shouts at me, "At least put on lip gloss!"

"Ah, leave the girl alone, she's a gorgeous gal inside and out!" Dad states as he walks past her to the coffee machine on the counter. Prior to grabbing his travel mug, he leans in and gives me a kiss on the forehead. "Besides, I don't want guys staring at her shiny lips! Leave them plain, Sadie-cat... capture hearts with your mind." He taps atop my head like I'm a young child. I giggle and take a bite out of my muffin. With my free hand, I rummage through my pocket to pull out the lip gloss and wiggle it in the air toward her. When she realizes I planned to put some on all along, her face softens. Dad pours himself a cup of coffee as she returns to her seat.

"At least you have enough forethought to bring it with you," she grumbles under her breath as she pulls the seat.

"Oh, Sadie-cat, don't listen to your mom... probably cut something out of her diet again, and it's making her angry," Dad whispers to me with his hand up, blocking his words.

"You know I can hear you! And there is nothing wrong with my helping her!" With furrowed brows and crossed arms, she tilts her nose up in the opposite direction.

"Aw, honey, I didn't mean anything by it." He walks over to her, beginning the typical groveling that happens after she gets annoyed. I head for my car, hoping to avoid hearing any more of the conversation.

Pulling into my assigned spot at school, a wave of anxiety washes over me. My jaw tightens as I think about going to homeroom. I pull down the car visor to look into the mirror, making sure I don't have chocolate on my face or in my teeth.

Before I leave my car, I put on the lip gloss. As I head into the school, a guy I've never seen before waves at me from across the parking lot. I wave back, but he's waving at a group of students behind me. My cheeks grow hot as I rush into school. Walking with my head down, I push past the mass amount of students socializing in the halls. Sara, a girl whose locker is next to mine, smiles at me.

"Morning," she says as she takes off her backpack, pulling out her planner, notebook, and pencil bag. I proceed in the same manner with my crossover bag.

"Good morning. It's good to see we have lockers next to each other again this year!" My eagerness must have deterred her from the conversation.

She leans back away from me as if I'm being too loud. I lower my voice to a whisper. "Oh, I get it...." I grab my coffee and take a swig. "I am a grump without my coffee too!" I awkwardly laugh as I take another sip.

Her lips pull taut, and eyes widen as she slowly backs away, nodding. It's clear I make her uncomfortable. I'm always gawky. Other students are nice to me, but no one asks me to hang out. I was only elected Student Council President because no one ran against me. It's just easier to keep to myself, no possibility of rejection. I guess I never stopped being the sad little girl that all the other little kids refuse to play with.

I progress through the day with minimal interactions, outside of answering questions posed by teachers.

Walking into the house, the smell of dinner makes my stomach grumble. "Oh, Lydia, you outdid yourself," I say as I pull my shoes off and toss them toward the stairs. As I walk toward the kitchen, I get stopped by Dad, who's sitting at the dining room table.

"Don't bother. Your mother is in there hovering over Lydia… as if *she* knows how to cook." Dad snickers to himself, turning the newspaper page. Diane always skims it at breakfast, and Dad reads it in the evenings over dinner.

"You're right, I don't wanna be in the middle of that." Dad smiles.

"How was school, Cupcake?" I huff as I plop myself into the dining room seat. "That bad, huh? I bet high school is *not* your time to shine. I was a college guy myself. You'll find your place." He brings the paper back to his face, concluding the conversation.

Leaning my face into my hands, I press my elbows onto the table. It's about half past four and the tension from the kitchen is palpable. The doorbell rings, beckoning Diane, who rushes from the kitchen.

"They're early!" She pauses to glance at her makeup in the small decorative mirrors hanging in the dining room. She turns to me, now standing tall in preparation to greet our guests, and mouths the word *behave*. The front door opens to reveal none other than the guy I waved at in the school parking lot this morning. Remembering the incident, my face turns beet red. He smirks, looking me over with his mahogany brown eyes.

"Hey, you're the chick from the parking lot." He crosses his arms, one eyebrow raising.

"You know each other? Perfect, then you can keep each other company while us gals chat!" Diane declares as she grabs the lady's arm and hurries off to the living room.

Dad shakes his work friend's hand and leads him off to the den. Which leaves me standing there across from this guy I've never met and thoroughly embarrassed myself in front only hours ago.

"You going to invite me in or should I sit out here?" he asks smugly.

Before I can respond, he pushes past me into the house. I step back, avoiding physical contact.

"Uh... I'm sorry. I was just shocked. My name is Sa—"

"Sadie, yeah, I know. Remember the people I was actually waving at? Yeah, they told me about you. I'm Dave. Nice place." He walks down the main hall, looking around at the walls and ceiling as if he's inspecting the house.

"Thanks, my Dad picked out all the—"

"Do you have anything to eat, or do we have to wait for whatever that smell is?" He scrunches his nose, as if the smell churns his stomach.

"Well, Lydia made food for us, and we always eat right at—"

"Oh, you're one of *those* stuck-up trust-fund girls, huh? I was hoping my buddies were wrong. Too bad... you got a pretty face." The cocky, condescending act that he puts on as he insults and compliments me at the same time is ludicrous.

"What's your problem, *Dave*?" I hang on his name, making it sound like an insult.

"What's my—"

"I *said*, What's. Your. Problem. You heard me right," I interrupt him just as he did to me. "You've been acting like a douche since you walked in… to be quite honest, I'm jealous of everyone in the world who hasn't met you!" Diane and Dave's mother walk into the hall at the end of my insult.

"Sadie Rose! Apologize! Now!"

"No, this arrogant prick is the one who should apologize. I am done entertaining for *you*." I storm out of the house in a fit of rage.

Going to the closest fast-food place, I buy a cheeseburger combo, and chill in my car for the rest of the evening. Ignoring all the phone calls from Diane, with angry voicemails pinging reminders on the screen.

She'll never accept what I did. Only time will smooth this into a topic that gets brought up when she's mad and needs extra fuel for her existing fire.

CHAPTER FOUR
SHATTERED INTO SILENCE

**Trigger Warning: This chapter contains graphic depictions
of child sexual assault
SEVEN YEARS BACK**

On the other side of Lexington at a different time entirely, lives eighteen-year-old Walker and his family. After the divorce, they moved to Duncan Park, a significantly cheaper side of Lexington. His mother, Melony, works the midnight shift as an emergency room nurse while the children sleep. Hours are strenuous, and she often finds herself working sixteen hours straight.

To make ends meet, Walker works evenings at a local fast-food establishment. Without his extra income, they can't afford groceries weekly. Most of his free time goes to helping financially. Clara spends a lot of time at home. Being only ten years old and having no ride doesn't provide much availability for extracurricular activities. Not to mention, the finances can't support the cost of joining sports and clubs.

She, unlike her brother, is introverted and shy. Which is good in his eyes—the protective big brother. Her growing up creates a lot of tension. She constantly reveals her preteen hormones with attitude and pushing to grow up faster.

Like both of their parents, Clara has blonde hair and blue eyes. She's thin, but still healthy-looking. The thought of puberty being right around the corner makes him uneasy, because he knows that hormones lead to one thing that he certainly is not ready for... boys.

As her big brother, the once pleasant conversations have turned into debates about what not to wear and how she should play with toys instead of makeup. Being a boy himself, he knows that sex is at the forefront of teenage boys' minds.

Between the constant work and never-ending stress of raising a family single-handedly, dating is not a priority for Melony.

Fate changed that narrative when it sent Karl and other patrons of a bar fight to the emergency room where she worked during one cool night in March. Karl couldn't keep his eyes off her. As he received his stitches for his busted left eyebrow, he was lectured continuously for moving to catch a glimpse of her.

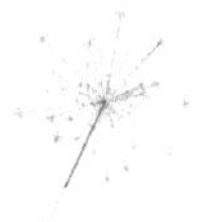

"Who's that beautiful woman over there?" Karl points past the curtain to Melony as she walks by his bay to get to her own patient. She's not his nurse, but her curvy, innocent looks catch his eye. The emergency room doctor pauses mid-stitch to turn and see Melony walking past the bay again.

"Oh, you're talking about the nurse? Her name's Melony." The doctor lifts his finger to point at her.

"Is she single?" His grin grows to a full smile. The doctor huffs and turns back to Karl's bleeding eyebrow.

"Hold still, this is an emergency room, not a bachelor show."

As the doctor resumes stitching his face, Karl winces. Surprisingly, not numb from all the alcohol in his system, the pain throbs. After applying bandages, the doctor leaves the curtain bay. The moment the doctor is out of sight, Karl rips out his IV. Blood runs down his arm as he exits the bay to confront her.

"Oh God! Sir, you're covered in blood! Did you take out your IV?" she exclaims, directing him back to his hospital bed and placing gauze over the site. Her eyes trail up to meet the amazement gleaming in his. He smirks at her, making her question his insanity.

"Are you single?" he blurts out, not breaking eye contact. She chuckles and blushes as she turns away from the intense eye contact.

"You're drunk and—"

"No, I'm not. Are you single?" Interrupting her, he reiterates his question. She smirks, blushing sheepishly. Visibly flattered, but uncomfortable.

"I don't know what to say… We aren't supposed to fraternize with our patients…." She checks behind her as if she's breaking the law.

"Say yes. Besides… I'm not *your* patient. That poor soul over there… *he* can't date you." He grins as he meets her eyes again, slowly dragging his gaze up her body. "His loss." The vigorous flirting makes her cheeks burn with heat. She hasn't felt this way in a long time, and it's a deeply satisfying experience.

"Yes." Pulling a sticky note out of her pocket, she steps back away from the bed. She writes her number on a torn piece of paper and places it on the bedside table.

Flowers and small trinkets were regular occurrences before Karl lost his job. As his financial security dwindles, the gifts that were once bought are now homemade items and handwritten notes. He never hesitates to make her feel like the most important person in his life. With his savings account draining, the visits transformed into moving in. Being able to smooth-talk Melony assists in maintaining the relationship. He's very persuasive, and in his case, helps him to be an excellent liar.

Stemming from years of child abuse, his lying is a defense mechanism to protect himself from worse punishments. As an avid smoker and drinker who is also addicted to pills, he checks all the stereotypical boxes of a product of abusive addicts. His beer gut is prominent with a thin, tall stature. With greasy, unruly hair, he looks like a grease-ball and smells worse—musky, as if he prefers not to shower. He believes that poreclogging fragrances are bad for the skin. He avoids deodorant and soap at all costs to 'maintain his health'. Never mind the sense of smell for everyone else. Melony didn't take notice of his particular scent; being blinded by love can have that effect.

"Get a fucking job—" Walker mutters as he shuffles past the recliner toward the hall after getting off work. Karl leans forward in his seat, head lobbing with the motion.

"What's that? Ya' got somethin' to say to me, boy, you say it with your chest." Placing the bottle on the side table, he grabs a cigarette and lighter. His movements exaggerated from intoxication. Melony leans forward from the couch and grabs the cigarette from his hand. Turning her attention to Walker, she interjects.

"You know that Karl is working from home. He's so close to figuring out the logistics of that secret project he's working on! Let's not fight guys, I've had a long couple of days." Trying to keep the peace, Melony encourages Walker to back down.

Returning the cigarette to the pack, Karl fidgets with his nicotine gum, forcing a piece loose from the aluminum.

"Where is this *secret project*? He's been working on it for months now, and no progress." Walker air quotes while bobbing his upper body side to side as he spews each word.

"If I speak about it, someone will overhear it and steal it! Even you!" Karl sneers, grabbing the liquor bottle and taking a swig. Walker scoffs. Standing up in a stagger, he faces Walker, standing over him only a few inches.

"What are ya' gettin' at? Ya' think you're tough, till you fuck around and find out."

"That a threat?" Walker squares up to him, preparing himself. Melony jumps from her seat and shoves herself between them.

"Walker, apologize. Stop this now." She places her hand on Walker's chest, pleading eyes turning downward as her lips stretch tight over gritted teeth. Throwing his hands in the air, Walker grunts loudly. Dismissing Melony, he turns toward the hall.

As he walks away, he mumbles under a heavy breath, "Sitting around drinking away our money."

The house is tiny, leaving little room for escape. The kitchen, dining, and living room are all in one section, with a compact dividing wall between them. A slender hallway starts in the living room and stretches to one full bathroom and three cramped rooms. The largest room can hardly fit a queen-size bed and dresser.

The house is overflowing with people. Adding the boyfriend, who never leaves the house other than to drink, makes quarters feel claustrophobic. Once Walker clears the room, Melony turns to Karl, who acts wounded by Walker's words.

"How am I supposed to work when we have a beautiful young lady getting off the school bus every day? Who's gonna make sure she gets home safely," Karl whimpers, acting concerned for Clara's well-being. Melony wraps her arms around him.

"I know babe, someone should be here for her. You're so good to us." She kisses his scruffy cheek.

He isn't wrong; if he started working, Clara would return to an empty house. Walker works straight after school most days, and Melony starts work at three in the afternoon. Though, Clara isn't coming home to much.

Most days, he passes out in the recliner covered in chip dust, surrounded by empty beer bottles and some infomercial blaring in the background. The smell from cigarettes, alcohol, and lack of showering coats the living room so strong Clara runs straight to her room and shuts the door every day.

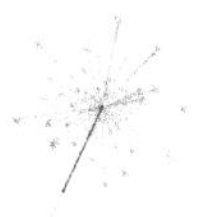

After finishing her homework, Clara comes from her room to find something to eat. On her way to the kitchen, she pauses in the living room entryway, offering the sleeping lump of a man a sandwich. Dinner's not in the refrigerator, which is uncommon. Usually, Melony will cook something to reheat, before going off to work.

"Hey, sorry to wake you, but you want a sandwich?" She hesitates as she approaches the recliner. Thinking he didn't hear her; she clears her throat. She often gets ignored because of her soft-spoken voice. "Karl?" she asks, stepping closer. His hand shoots out from the recliner and grabs her inner thigh. She squeals, jumping in the air.

He lets go of her and stretches in the recliner. "Sorry, Darlin', having a bad dream. What did ya' say?" Lighting a cigarette, he shifts.

Melony always emphasizes that he's only allowed to smoke outside or in the garage, but she's at work. With her gone, he can do whatever pleases him.

Uncomfortable with the exchange, she hesitates. "I... I... I, uh... do you want a sandwich?" she asks with a shaky stutter. Heat burns her cheeks. Taking several steps back, she builds space between the two of them.

He senses her discomfort and catches her avoiding eye contact. His mouth curves, revealing an evil, bone-shivering grin. "Did I make ya' nervous, Darlin'?" She shakes her head too quickly to maintain a cool composure. Feeling exposed despite being fully clothed, she wraps her arms around herself. As she angles her body away from him, the sense of danger radiating off him is palpable. With a last-ditch effort, she forces her fists down to her side, attempting to appear confident.

"I'm going to make a sandwich. Let me know when you finally decide!" she exclaims, mustering up all the courage she has.

The uneasy sense of dread grows into a pit in her stomach. She wants to end the conversation, partially to escape him. Straightening herself, she walks to the kitchen. Karl, who rarely gets up, enters the tiny kitchen behind her. He watches her in a calculative way. The feeling of being stalked by a predator makes the hair on the back of her neck stand on end.

His eyes bore a hole into her back. Afraid to look and potentiate a conversation when he is acting so strange, she picks up the jar of peanut butter. An unsettling moan is released from behind. Without hesitation, and not thinking, she looks toward him. He's no longer grinning but wears a sinister smile from ear to ear.

She abruptly slams down the jar of peanut butter. "You know what, I changed my mind; I'm not hungry."

She attempts to walk past him. Grabbing her arm forcefully, he prevents her from passing. He lowers his lips to her ear. Clutching a small amount of her hair in his free hand and twirling it, he inhales as if to smell her fear.

Her breathing hitches and speeds up in a disheveled hyperventilation. Shaking quickens and takes root deep in her bones. Goosebumps prickle up her skin as the unease dissolves into sheer panic, stealing the air from her lungs. Terror grips her at the eerie, unspoken future that her body senses. He transforms from the disgusting pig who sleeps in the recliner to a horrifying, drooling monster.

Her heavy breathing arouses him even more. "Oh, sweet girl, I can tell I make ya' nervous… ya' must know how beautiful ya' are." His eyes trail down her slight frame. "Ya' have me so bothered… I can't hardly stand it. I'm bursting here." Dropping her hair, he caresses his fingertips down the side of her rounded cheek.

She flexes away from his touch. The grip on her arm grows tighter, preventing her from running off. "Oh, don't try to fight… I know ya' want me."

She pulls with all her strength, throwing her body in the opposite direction.

It's futile.

Tears stream down her cheeks. Screaming would only anger him, as they're the only two in the house. Even though it's pointless, she has to try.

She shrieks for help, but his hand smothers her shrill cries, clasping over her mouth.

"Oh, ya' want to role-play, huh? Am I the burglar who just walked in?"

He navigates her to the couch and sits her down, his body crowding over the top of her as he frantically kisses her forehead and cheeks. Pushing at him with one free hand, she desperately tries to shove him off, kicking his legs with all her might. His entire weight presses against her, trapping her thighs, rendering her strikes powerless.

With her mouth still covered, he utilizes his other hand to gather her arms together and pin them above her head. Nestling his face in the crease of her neck, his kisses migrate south of her face. Releasing his hand from her mouth, she immediately screams.

A husky, ominous chuckle emanates from him.

"Hush now, don't be a bad little girl. I would hate to have to punish you." Using his free hand, he yanks her shirt upward.

Her screaming and crying makes him cover her mouth again. In a breathy tone he whispers, "I know you're excited, but squealing will make me bust faster."

Her drawstring shorts made gaining access easy for him. Realizing that she's not getting free, her body falls limp, and she mentally shuts down. It's been a long time since she last dissociated. The last time, her dad passed away.

Once he felt the struggle creep to a halt, he releases her arms. They remain limp above her head. He hovers over her almost bare body, pausing for a brief moment. Acknowledging that the fighting is over, he releases her mouth. She stares through him, utterly detached. Undoing his pants, he forcefully spreads her legs to allow his large body to strenuously crush between her now-limp legs.

Shattering to pieces, her soul leaves her body. In its place, a numb, detached version of herself. Unfortunately, she isn't numb enough to prevent the burning, ripping sensation of him destroying any residual innocence that she held onto up until this point.

The sheer weight of his upper body presses down, making it difficult for her to breathe. When she does take a breath, all she can smell, and taste, is the cigarette stench and the alcohol on his breath. He kisses all around her mouth, her lips ajar in the dissociated state she maintains.

She feels this moment will never end.

As if time is running slow… almost at a standstill.

CHAPTER FIVE
WALKER HARRIS: ANYTHING FOR FAMILY

Trigger Warning: Chapter contains graphic depictions of child sexual assault, domestic abuse, and depictions of violence

SEVEN YEARS BACK

Shuffling down the short hall toward a snoring Karl in the recliner, I pause only to knock on the bathroom door to get Clara. Over the last year, her interests have shifted from Barbie dolls to primping.

In my opinion, a ten-year-old shouldn't wear makeup. "Hurry up, it's not a beauty contest," I grumble quietly enough to avoid the beast at the end of the hall. Her responding sighs of frustration could rattle the door. The attitude of this girl… you wouldn't believe she's shy with the huffs and puffs she throws at me. The door swings open, and an annoyed blonde-haired, blue-eyed pre-teen stands in the doorway, staring at me through furrowed brows.

"You wouldn't understand, you're a dumb boy." If her eyes

roll any harder, they'll get stuck in the back of her head. I grin at her, and a soft chuckle escapes my lips.

"A man." Her confusion grows, staring awaiting clarification. "I'm a dumb *man*. Not a boy... man, continue."

She sighs, rolling her eyes more vigorously as she shoves past me. Her hair bobs side to side with the drama that she puts into each step.

"The two of you knock it off, you'll wake Karl. He has a big day today."

I scoff. "Sure, whatever would the liquor store do if he didn't come in for his daily twelve pack?" Sarcasm seeps into each word, and Mom turns to me with heavy disappointment.

"Please, for today, try to get along. He's a good man, give him a chance."

"When has he ever been a *'good'* man?" I snip back, throwing up air quotes. She winces.

I have a habit of being volatile, not *violent*, but Karl flip-flops. This makes her flinch easily at words even a decibel above normal. "I'm sorry, Mom... I didn't mean to—"

"Damn straight you're fucking sorry." Karl walks up behind Mom. "Had I talked back to my Momma like that, grown or not, I'd get a lickin' that'd sting for a week. Your mom's too fragile, but I'll step in if I need 'tah."

"I'd like to see you fucking try," I respond, eyes slit glaring back at his smug smirk.

"Walk away, NOW!" Mom's shouts are dismissed for a moment, her stout frame allows our eyes to never break contact.

After I center myself for a split second, I turn to Clara. "You ready to go?" My tone evens out after a hitched, trembling breath. She dips her head, agreeing. We step around Karl, who doesn't budge.

"Oh, Honeybee, I'm so sorry he was that way to ya'. I was just trying to defend ya'." Hoping for forgiveness, Karl sweet-talks

Mom. "Ya' know, I had a tough time growin' up. My dad beat my ma' and me. I don't want ya' to think low of me."

There's always an excuse for his behavior. You'd think Mom would see through it, but nope.

I shake my head in disgust as I lead my sister through the door to the car. It's an old beater, but I bought it myself. Traveling around using the city bus isn't something you want to do in this neighborhood.

Clara pops into the passenger seat, the visor mirror immediately flinging open, and she stares at her reflection. She smiles and closes it up.

"What's up? You've never been this big on looks. Now it's all you care about." I knew the day would come when she worried about looks, boys, and hanging out with friends... but I didn't think it would come so soon.

"I'll be in middle school next year. Everyone already thinks I'm weird. I saw Sarah doing her makeup in class, so I want to learn."

She wants to fit in. I feel for her, the outsider. That's how I feel having to work and maintain school. "Besides, Karl said I'd look prettier with makeup and if I leave my hair down. He even took me to look at different types of makeup the other day while you were at work. It was fire." She shifts in her seat, fidgeting with the keychain on her backpack.

A pit swells in my stomach. What would possess a grown man to offer that compliment to a young girl? It disturbs me, but I wait for her to feel the awkward silence and reveal more information. She peers at me out the corner of her eye, but I keep my jaw taut with narrowed eyes trained on the road.

"What else did Karl say?" I try to sound calm, but the angry bite in my voice seeps out.

"Gosh, you think he's a monster! We spend time together after school. He tells me all kinds of things." The hair stands on the nape of my neck. With my grip tightening on the steering wheel, I hold back my words. She turns from the passenger window at the sound of rubbing leather. "He's actually really nice. Yeah, he drinks and stuff, but at least he isn't mean all the time."

My poor sister and mom are both past the point of repair. He has them brainwashed. When we pull up at her school, she's already unbuckling her seat belt, preparing to race off to her classroom. I snag her wrist as I pull to a stop. Whipping her head back around, her eyes flash to mine. "Let go! I gotta—"

"Listen to me. Mark my words. You might think he's great, but if you ever feel uncomfortable, you go to your room, lock the door, and call the police."

"The police? Get real!" She grabs my hand, attempting to pull her wrist free.

"I'm serious. Please call them. Don't hesitate." The thought of my having to go to work and leave her at home with him is unnerving.

Seeing the genuine look of concern on my face, she slowly bobs her head up and down. Once I release her, she jumps out of the car and rushes off. I take a mental note of what she had said about Karl as I watch her enter the building. The conversation doesn't sit right with me. Why didn't I notice him treating her differently? I can't put my finger on it, but something is off. I should have noticed these encounters. Something's already started, and all I can do is pray it's not too late to stop it. The hairs on my arms stand, and chills race down my spine.

"I'll fix this," I growl as I drive off to my high school, glad I have ten minutes of drive time to cool off.

As I walk through the halls between periods, I can't help but think about the current events in my life. Being a high school senior is hard when you can't hang out with anyone outside of school hours. I'm kind of popular, even though I'm constantly working. I can thank Dad for inheriting his outgoing personality. He was always so personable and friendly. I'd love to be satisfied with keeping to myself, but it's not in the cards for me.

As I walk through the halls, I make it a point to nod and smile at every student I make eye contact with, throwing in the occasional wave to maintain my likable demeanor. Holding the door open for one girl in my class, I dip my head in respect and smile as she smirks back at me.

"Thank you!" she says with a high-pitched, sweet hum. I continue through the hall door, making my way to class.

Over the past few years, I've had to grow up way too fast. But growing up quickly *for* Clara… it's worth it. We have always been exceptionally close, especially with everything we've gone through. I helped her to understand what was happening, and how she wasn't at fault. She helped me laugh through things and keep my hopeful outlook on life.

Someday, I'll graduate from high school and go off to college for pre-law. It makes me sad to think of leaving her. At the same time, I'll help her have a better life by setting myself up. I'll get us out of the tiny house and be someone she can look up to.

My thoughts are interrupted as I walk past a girl getting peer pressured by one of the football meatheads. He's trying to get her to go out with him, but she's refusing, and he's giving her hell for it. Overhearing the conversation, I continue to walk a few lockers down, not slowing as I say aloud to the person next to me, "Maybe he'd have better luck with the mirror since he's obsessed with himself, anyway."

"What's that, Harris?" The hallway hushes and slows its river-like bustling current, echoing snickers from students surrounding us. "I know you aren't talking shit over there." Trey stomps over with exaggerated arm movements to emphasize what he plans to happen.

He gathers a crowd, signifying that a fight is about to go down. I face away from him, toward the locker where I originally planned to go, when he bunches up my shirt in his fist. Not being much bigger than me, and definitely not stronger, puts him at a disadvantage. Yet, he thinks he can overpower me.

It's too comical *not* to laugh. I chuckle, low and deep, letting free a slow exhale. I grin, glaring at him from lowered eyelids.

"Dude, this is why I didn't join football; y'all do too much of this grab ass foreplay. I ain't into it. I hate to break it to ya' buddy, but I like girls...." Bethany and a few others giggle off to the side, and I wink at them before continuing. "I know you don't take rejection too well; I saw that with Bethany." I can't contain my rolling laughter, so I turn toward him, only to be met by his fist. He rocks into the side of my jaw. The punch stings, but I would never let him see that.

Grabbing my jaw and rotating it around, I smile at him. "Dude, it's no wonder you're on the sidelines with a hit like that. If you're gonna be all handsy, I recommend a safe word...."

His eyebrows hint at pain for a brief second before shifting back to anger as he swings at me again. I lean to avoid the hit. "Geez, I know you don't like getting turned down, but you don't have to be aggressive about it...." Laughing at him angers him even more, and he swings. He shifts his weight so far forward that he falls when I move out of the way, dodging every swing.

"Fighting in the hallway? That'll be enough! Both of you! Office! Now!" My English teacher comes walking down the hallway, breaking up the crowd. This teacher hates me. She can never take a joke and always has a stick up her ass. My smile falls as she looks at me with hateful eyes, "It doesn't shock me that you're involved. Why are you always where there's trouble?" Her question is rhetorical, but I feel compelled to respond.

I shrug my shoulders and give her a boyish grin. "Just lucky,

I guess." Everyone around us laughs, except her. Shaking her head in disgust, she points down to the end of the hall, as if I didn't know where the principal's office is.

"Well, you can tell the principal just how *lucky* you are," she bites back.

I guess that's another reason she's not my biggest fan. She's quick-witted and always has a response. I help Mr. Meathead from the ground. Jokes aside, I consider myself a decent dude.

"Come on, big fella, I think we have a date after all…." He huffs, unamused after getting yelled at, and rolls his eyes.

The fight, if you can even call it that, is over. I never even swung at him. It figures that I'm going to get in trouble. Entering the principal's office, the secretary sees me and smiles.

"Oh, look who's coming to visit us. Did you make an inappropriate joke again?" she asks, lowering her glasses to look over the rim. She glances at Trey "Oh no, Trey! You can't be here; the big game is this weekend! What did you two do!?" She asks, shaking her head in disbelief.

I sit in one of the available seats across from her desk. "Well, beef-boy over here just can't accept the fact that I'm attracted to women." I say with a big smile. I can't help but continue the joke. I'm already in so deep, might as well continue the laugh.

"Dude, you're a jackass," he says, not clarifying anything, which makes the joke even better because the secretary looks extremely surprised.

"Trey, I'm sorry. I never realized… I mean… I didn't know. I don't blame you for liking Walker, he's quite witty." She pauses, writing something down. "Trust me, you're better off without him. He's trouble. You have football and college to think about." She attempts to be sympathetic.

He pushes his face into his hands, elbows on his lap. No matter how much he tries, he can't hide his angry red face beneath his hands. I laugh to myself, shifting in my seat.

The lectures in the principal's office bounce off the walls.

My displays have clearly and repeatedly exhausted the principal. The after-school detention is fine, but I could've done without him calling Mom. She's pissed but not shocked that I'm fighting at school. She's aware of my short temper and incessant need to comment on everything. I return to the main hall and continue with my day, avoiding Trey as much as possible. I have detention for an hour after school, but luckily, today I don't start work until four-thirty in the evening.

The last period bell rings. I have a few minutes to get to my locker before heading to the library for detention. On my way to my locker, Bethany stops me.

"Thank you for helping me out earlier with Trey." She pauses, looking down at her shuffling feet before she drags her eyes along my body and back to my face. "He's such a douche. I wouldn't go out with him again, so he's all butthurt. Such a jealous jerk…." Her eyes glance down the hall like she longs for someone. It could be Trey; they've spent most of high school yo-yoing between dating and not. Her head snaps back in my direction, as if she forced her thoughts to shift.

"Anyway, I just wanted to say… thanks." She smiles.

Bethany is a pretty girl, but I could never pursue her. I don't have time for a girlfriend. I'm not a half-ass kind of guy, so I won't commit to a relationship when I don't have enough of myself to give. Not to mention I can't afford to go out on dates.

"Don't worry about it. I can't stand him. He thinks the sun rises with him just because he's on the football team." She tucks a few stray strands of her long black hair behind one ear and looks down at her feet again.

"I really admire that you didn't fight back. It takes a strong person to fight back and an even stronger one to control themselves," she says almost sheepishly. Her bronzed cheeks gleam red.

"Eh, I'm not a great fighter. I talk a big game, though, don't I?" I ask rhetorically, attempting to shoot her down, hoping she would see it as a flaw instead of something to make her interested in me.

"I'm sure you're good at… *a lot* of things." Brushing my forearm with the tips of her nails.

The tracing of her dainty finger along my forearm makes my skin tingle. It's obvious that she's implying sex, and I'm intrigued.

She walks away, calling over her shoulder, "You know where I am if you ever want to… *talk.*"

The light touch on my forearm still burns, entrancing me. How do girls do that? They can say so little yet stop us in our tracks. It isn't fair how much power they unknowingly wield. Or maybe they know the powers they possess and mean to use them.

I shake my head, hoping to shake the goosebumps off my skin and focus.

Off to detention I go. Unfortunately, I'm late, so the librarian has me stay an extra half hour as punishment. Having to remain behind that extra half hour makes me late to work, and they terminate my position because it isn't the first time this has happened.

I wanted to quit that job, anyway. The pay is shit, and they require so much. Sometimes, I'd have to stay after I clocked out to help. I'd get in trouble for all the overtime if I remain on the clock. It takes me about an hour to clean out my work locker and turn in my badge, hat, and apron. Maybe the next sorry sucker to wear them won't have it as bad as me.

My drive home is emotionally charged, starting with anger and progressing to dissociation. It's mainly me preparing for the conversation I'll have with Mom. Maybe I'm lucky, and she's working today and won't be home.

I open the door to find Karl with his pants down around his knees, pressed between my little sisters bare legs. She's motionless almost like she's dead.

The shock leaves me frozen in my steps. The ice in my legs immediately thaws as my blood boils. My vision blurring with rage, I cleave Karl from Clara. Even through my pulsating eyesight, I quickly inspect my emotionally shattered sister. I reach for her wrists, checking for a pulse. Her eyes fixated on the ceiling as small, faint breaths spew out in a jagged pattern. They're hardly audible through the whooshing sound in my ears. Tears well and fall atop her as I frantically attempt to cover her bare body. Sobs hitch, rattling through my chest, heartbroken for my innocent baby sister.

Karl stumbling back into the window and getting caught in the blinds pulls my focus and snaps me back into reality.

She's alive; emotionally shattered, but *alive*.

My face relaxes, brows flattening. Turning my head slowly, my eyes meet Karl's face.

"She wanted it! The little whore was begging for me!" He staggers, still trying to grasp his pants. "I have a right, you know! As the man of this house!" Spitting out his words, saliva foaming at the corners of his mouth. My fists ball tightly, turning white, struggling to keep my focus on Clara.

I take a deep breath, balancing out my mind, and lifting her. Her eyes flicker to mine. Doing everything in my power to calm my face, I give my best reassuring smile.

"Don't worry. I'm here. You're safe," I reassure her in a hushed tone.

She wraps her arms around my neck tightly. The smell of alcohol and cigarettes grows stronger. I can feel Karl's breath next to my ear. Releasing my neck, Clara pushes off me and falls back onto the couch beneath us.

"At least let a guy finish," he says with a chuckle, holding his pants up with one hand.

In a blind fury, I spin, punching him with all my force. He falls back against the TV stand, too preoccupied with pulling his pants up and throwing the buckle together to defend himself. I knock into him again, letting my anger fuel me. Karl hits the ground, spitting blood as he falls.

I can tell he's disoriented, but that's not slowing me down.

Karl lies unconscious on the floor, but I don't stop.

I have well and truly snapped.

The only thing that brings me out of my fury is the neighbors banging on the door and the sound of sirens echoing off in the distance.

Blood is everywhere, and it's not mine. It takes me a minute to calm down and focus.

Clara is the first thought that crosses my mind; I need to see if she's okay. The banging is replaced with the door being kicked in by police. I look down at my hands, covered in blood and vibrating with adrenaline.

Several officers flood the house as I collapse to my knees. Disoriented, I look around the living room, realizing what just happened… what all *I* have done.

One officer rushes up to me and puts me in handcuffs without question. The EMTs put Karl up on a stretcher. Blood covers his face and swelling blurs his features.

Still in disbelief, I'm escorted to the police car. As I peer out the window, I can see our neighbors covering their mouths in shock. Blue and red flash across everyone's faces.

I watch as they load Karl up into the ambulance. The officers enter the front of the car and call into the station. A sinking feeling overwhelms me; it's probably a comedown from the adrenaline rush.

I think inwardly, '*I hope the motherfucker dies.*'

CHAPTER SIX
SADIE THOMAS: LOVE AT A WEDDING

THREE YEARS BACK

What's it like being nine hours away from home? An absolute *dream*. Though not a dream for my gas tank as I pull over to fill up *again*. A loose, empty water bottle falls to the ground as I open the car door. Huffing, I bend forward to pick it up. A stranger gets out of their car, smiling at me in a kind, curious way.

"Hey, where ya' comin' from?" He peers around the gas pump to see the front license plate. I must *look* like I'm from out of town.

"Johns Hopkins." I cringe at the thought of telling a total stranger that. His eyebrows raise.

"Woah! That's impressive. What brings you all the way out here?" He lifts his baseball cap and scratches his sweaty head. Letting out a puff of air, he turns to look at the beeping gas pump.

"I'm from here… just coming home for summer break." As the words leave my mouth, I realize how melancholy I sound, like I'm on my way to a funeral.

He nods politely. We both finish pumping gas and go our separate ways.

As with the school year, the semester is ending, and I'm returning to Lexington. Words cannot describe how excited I am for summer to be over.

I'm not overly fond of returning to my life back at home. However, I'm excited about one thing: being a bridesmaid in my cousin's wedding at Talon Winery and Vineyards. She's older than me, so I didn't grow up super close to her, but I've never been in a wedding party.

I have to wait a few short weeks, which works for me, considering I haven't picked up the dress yet. I'm happy it isn't a crazy monstrosity, like what you see in the movies.

It's difficult to consider marriage when I've never been on a date. My cousin may be older, but only by a few years. If I match her timeline, I should already be in a relationship. I know that no one is truly pressuring me to settle down, but the thought of being lonely for the rest of my life isn't particularly appealing.

Veering off to the right to turn into our estate, my fingers tingle with anxiety. Taking a deep breath, I straighten the steering wheel and continue mentally preparing myself.

Until I meet *the one*, I'll focus on studying for the MCAT and avoid my house like the plague. It's May, so Diane has started planning the Fourth of July party. The house is in constant disarray. Sounds of Diane debating dinnerware rentals, music styles, catering interviews, and so on.

Studying isn't my only avoidance excuse. I also volunteer. Not just to help with my future medical school application, but also because I genuinely enjoy helping others. It gives me much-needed peace. Typically, people my age get a summer job, but my father refuses to let me worry about money.

Bradford pear trees line each side of the drive, late in their blossoming. Even with my windows up, my memories allow me to breathe in their sweet scent. Speckles of white peek through the dark green leaves. I pull around the circular driveway, parking my car off to the side nearest the house. They painted the front door while I was gone... I wonder what else has changed in the past few months.

I finally get home a little after six, *coincidentally* right on time for dinner. I was supposed to arrive earlier, but I had to stop a few more times than usual.

"Here she is! *Finally*! We've been waiting for you to start dinner! She's here, Richard!" My mother opens the door wider as I walk up the front steps.

She practically jumps up and down before embracing me in a firm hug. It feels so earnest, like she sincerely wants me around. Pulling back, she scans me like she's looking for changes only caused by time. She gasps loudly, and I nearly jump out of my skin. "Seriously? Long drives don't excuse wearing sweatpants. Honey... how embarrassing. Surely, you didn't stop anywhere and let people see you like this!" My eyes roll involuntarily.

Oh no, I'm out of practice! I need to keep those responses internal, so I can survive here.

"Nope, Mom, you're *so right*. Did I stop? Absolutely not! Not during a nine-hour drive. I willed the car to continue driving without gas!" My sarcastic humor doesn't make Diane laugh, but Dad walks into the entryway, chuckling.

"Oh, Sadie, quit antagonizing your mother; she only wants what's best for you," he says, barely able to hold back a smirk. He pulls me into a big hug. "Hey, Sweet Girl, we missed you," he whispers in my ear.

When he steps back, I'm able to see the big smile that takes hold of his face. Jokingly, he punches my upper arm. "Are you gonna tell us what that school of yours is like?" I smile and start to tell him about my year, but before I can even finish a sentence, Diane interrupts.

"Guys, dinner is on the table getting cold. We'll have all

summer for you two to discuss her new life... *without us,*" she says, making something exciting seem tragic and awful. My father's smile fades, and he turns toward the dining room off to the side.

The twelve-seat dining room table sits nicely decorated and prepared for a formal dinner, but that's every night in this house. She displays everything like the Queen of England is dropping in for a surprise visit.

Dinner passes slowly. The conversation focuses on Diane's next event, while Dad repeatedly says *uh-huh* and *mhm*. I sit in silence, counting the minutes until it's over.

That's essentially how the next month will go. Counting the minutes till the day is over, quietly avoiding confrontation.

The alarm goes off prior to the sunrise in a not-so gentle reminder of how long the day will be. I groan into my pillow, wishing I hadn't stayed up studying for the MCAT.

My leg drops off the edge of the bed with an echoing thud through the cool dark room. Rubbing my eyes, I review the day ahead.

Everyone meets for hair and makeup, but before that, we have brunch. The bride wants to ensure that we're all accounted for and understand our wedding duties.

Gathering my necessities and clutch, I go downstairs for some coffee. The rising sun sends beams of light fragmenting across the kitchen floor. The serenity of the early morning hours make it almost worth getting up so early... *almost.* Leaving the house with enough time to get to the restaurant early is a priority for me. I want to mentally prepare myself for the large group of people and obligatory socializing beforehand.

Turning off the highway and heading into town, I realize I forgot my dress and shoes, which elicits a frustrated groan. After brunch, I'll have to rush back home to grab them.

The wedding colors are all shades of purple. The fact that she chose dark purple for me is a blessing; it won't wash out my pale skin. Also, it makes my emerald eyes pop.

The bridal party is large, so the morning turns to afternoon quickly as the hairstylist and makeup artist work on each of us. It's nice to be pampered and around other girls who are happy to participate. Although everyone is a few years older than me, I feel like I belong.

We take a limo from the hair salon to the Vineyard. One girl keeps hopping up to twerk to a hip-pop song you can hardly hear over everyone laughing and chatting. As we pull up to the Vineyard, my parents walk up the path toward the entrance of the main lobby.

I approach them smiling. I feel beautiful and had such a wonderful day.

"Oh, Sweet Girl, you look amazing! Look at you!" my father raves. I smile and give him a hug. He always knows how to hype me up.

"You look very nice, Sadie. Don't forget to touch up your makeup before walking down the aisle. Some of it looks a little smudged," Diane comments, reaching for my eye to fix the small imperfection. I lean my head back to avoid her fingers touching my face.

"It's a natural smokey eye; it's supposed to smudge a little," I say, leaning my head back even further to avoid her.

"Oh, that's a style now, smudged, cakey eyes? I didn't notice. I guess I'm behind the times," she says, sighing as she pulls her hand back to her side.

Feeling the slight fold in her tight dress, she grabs at the sides and tugs, making her breasts pop. If she pulls any harder, they'll pop out. I roll my eyes, and she catches it.

Stepping close to me and grabbing my upper arm, she hisses, "Sadie Rose! Don't you roll your eyes at me; I'm looking out for you! Don't you have somewhere to be, considering you're here for your cousin, not yourself? Run along." She releases my arm and pushes past me.

She and my father leave to find their seats. Although her comments are rude, she *is* right. I am supposed to be in the back room preparing to walk. I rush off, the bouquet rustling as I quickly step to the back.

Being underage, I don't get to partake in cocktail hour. I stand near the bar with one of the other bridesmaids when I ask for a soda. The cop working security comes up to me.

"Excuse me, Miss, but what's in your cup?" He's undeniably handsome, in a 1930's way.

Dark hair slicked into a tapered fade and disguising his baby-shaped face with a rugged, well-kept beard. Looking at him, I can't help but blush; he's so attractive. Much taller than me, with a stocky build, far from a six-pack but not fat. In decent shape, probably necessary for the job. Speaking of work, the uniform only adds to the level of attractiveness. In a daze, peering him up and down, I don't respond. One of his eyebrows raises, and a smirk pushes through his lips. This makes me blush more, heat radiating throughout my face.

"Soda, I swear!" I blurt, not even convincing myself.

The nerves most likely stems from being accustomed to people avoiding me. Most guys won't look twice at me. At college, I'm avoided because of the perpetual state of studying. Though I do my fair share avoiding social gatherings, prioritizing grades. *Why am I so nervous?*

He isn't even flirting with me. The guy is just doing his job and being polite while doing it.

He chuckles. "Are you sure you don't need a drink, Miss?" He laughs at his own joke. "I'm Garrett. I know you're only drinking cola, but I needed something to start a conversation with you. See… I mean no disrespect to the bride… but you're by far the most beautiful woman I have ever seen."

I break eye contact to look down at his hands, catching him fidgeting with his fingers. As if he notices he's starting to display the nerves he buried very well until now, he continues with an edge of gruffness in his voice. "I had to shoot my shot…." His hands grasp into a firm fist and his eyes shoot to mine. A rushed whoosh of breath flies out "Ma'am?" His smirk spreads into a full smile. The silence in the conversation flattens his smile. In slow motion, I attempt to gather my racing thoughts.

Okay, so he *is* flirting with me.

"Are you asking me out?" I ask before I can fully process.

I let my thoughts slip out in the space between, attempting to add up the compliments he was paying me. Covering my mouth to prevent anything else from unexpectedly pouring out, I turn away from him, hiding my reddened cheeks. My shoulders slump over, shrinking into myself from humiliation. He looks shocked, as if he didn't intend to ask me out.

He stutters out his response, "I… uhh… yes. I was getting to that… I would ask you to dance here, but I'm kinda working." Flashing a faint nervous smile, he points his thumb to the bar and grabs his badge with the other hand.

"How old are you? There's no way we're close to the same age," I half shout; word vomit again. I need to stop thinking out loud.

Being a police officer, I can't imagine he'd attempt to date anyone underage, though I do look older with how I'm dressed.

Something about my thinking out loud calms him. He

slackens his shoulders, his jaw loosening with a grin growing bigger by the second. We can't both be a ball of nerves with an inability to hold in thoughts.

"Well, that's a bit forward," he flirts in a playful, joking tone. "I'm twenty, going to be twenty-one this year. I'm assuming you're younger, considering you're acting like a deer in headlights. I know that, as a man, I shouldn't ask your age, but you're clearly younger than me. Are you ninete—" he guesses, but I interject.

"Nineteen!" As if that would scare him away. The volume I'm speaking at would probably scare off a sane person. He smiles and lets out a small chuckle.

"Man, I'm lucky you're legal. If not, that would've been awkward." He laughs again and I join him. "Now that we got that out of the way, can I get your name?"

Good God, I'm asking a question and didn't even tell him my name. Before I can answer, one bridesmaid calls me for the bouquet toss. I halfheartedly apologize and excuse myself. As I walk away, I overhear Garrett whisper to himself, "Beautiful inside and out." I glance back at him, but he's already looking away.

After the bouquet toss, I get distracted dancing and enjoying myself with the other bridesmaids. An hour before the wedding ended, they closed the bar, so Garrett was no longer needed. He left, and we didn't even exchange information! The one time a guy acts semi-interested in me; I don't even get his number. The guy doesn't even know my name! Oh well, better luck next time. At least, that's the attitude I want to have about it. Something about how his smile meets his eyes when he looks at me will haunt my dreams. Who knows, maybe destiny will bring us back together.

Diane walks up behind me where I stand by the bar, not quite ready to give up on Garrett. "Sadie Rose, have you been drinking?" Distaste drips off her tongue as she enunciates each word.

Even if I told her no, she wouldn't believe me. I shrug and walk over to where my father stands. The party is dying down, and some bridesmaids are long gone, so we head to the car. Dad would typically pull it around, but he's been drinking, and I am the designated driver. Diane pitches a fit to my father, stating I'm drunk and shouldn't drive. My father looks me in the eyes and smiles; he tends to get extra friendly when he's been drinking.

"Sadie Rose, have you been dipping your toes in alcohol tonight?" His smile grows, accepting the fact that I'm not the perfect child. Diane, however, comes up behind him with a disgruntled look and ensures that her huffs, puffs, and annoyed sighs are well heard.

"No, I met a guy. But it doesn't matter… I didn't get his information." Diane looks over at me with a peek of interest.

"Oh, a boy, huh?" she asks, and retorts without hesitation, "He probably just wants sex, don't feel bad about not getting his information." I roll my eyes at her. It's good she's sitting in the back seat and can't see. I'm so glad summer is halfway over so I can get the hell out of here.

Chapter Seven
Sadie Thomas: Meeting the Family

THREE YEARS BACK

Waking up the next morning, a humming sensation thrills through my body, exhilarated. Recounting the awkward flirting encounter makes my cheeks burn and my lips tighten against my teeth in a smile I can't wipe away. The birds chirping outside and the sound of vacuuming are things I normally ignore. The interaction brought on a new sense of self-confidence, which is something that I have always struggled with. I stretch, a slight groan slips out of my mouth, and I run my fingers through my grease-filled hair.

I must have a pound of hairspray in my half updo from last night, because what isn't greasy is stiff.

"Gross." I say, heading into the bathroom for a much-needed rinse. I was so tired when we got home that I didn't take a shower before crashing.

After turning the water intolerably hot, I check my buzzing phone that rattles on the bathroom counter. Diane's text reminds me I need to be at brunch at exactly nine-thirty. I sigh, the thought of going out to brunch with Diane sounds miserable. I'm just glad Grandma Rose is here to give Diane hell instead of nitpicking me. Steam forms a thick cloud in the bathroom, creating condensation on the mirror. Wincing as my body adjusts to the scorching temperatures, I gather my hair to prepare for the washing of a lifetime.

My skin turns bright pink from the heat. I step out of the shower, wrapping my hair and body in separate towels. I continue to sing the song residing deep in my brain from the wedding, bouncing around between the bathroom and bedroom as I prepare for the day.

My phone buzzes again from the vanity. I finish styling my hair and go to check the calendar notification from twenty minutes prior telling me that the brunch is in ten minutes. Panicked, I rush out of the house.

Accelerating the gas, hoping to make the difference in time up with driving. Minutes later, red and blue lights flash in my rearview mirror, sirens blaring over my workout playlist.

Slowing and pulling off to the side, I mutter to myself, "Oh, just great. Dad's gonna **love** this." I can't help but think of the cop from last night, wouldn't it just be fate if he was the cop pulling me over? Almost would be worth the ticket.

Eagerly, I peep into the driver's side mirror to see the officer that got out of the vehicle. Definitely not Garrett. This cop is a short and plump middle-aged man. He waddles up to my window.

"Ma'am, do you know why I pulled you over today?"

I glance at the clock; I'm going to be late. I look back at the cop. He stares at me awaiting a response.

"Yes. I was going a little fast," I say, impatient with the exchange. Giving a reason for being pulled over is precisely what my lawyer father taught me *not* to do. After telling the cop, I can hear Dad's voice in my head:

Even if you know why you're getting pulled over, always reply

'No'. They may catch you off guard for another reason. If you tell them now, you have more than one reason to get a ticket.

I stare off for a second, my father's voice in my head taking center stage. I shake my head when I realize I'm not focused. Seeing this, the officer steps back to view my face better. He's probably trying to determine if I'm intoxicated. Word vomit *almost* takes over to make me shout, *I'm sober*, but I keep control of my thoughts and stay quiet. He takes a few steps to the side to examine my car and returns to my window.

"Ma'am… thirty over the speed limit is more than a *little fast*. I'm going to need your license and registration."

I reach into the glove compartment to get my registration, napkins and loose paper fall to the ground as I rummage. Once found, I turn to look through my purse on the passenger seat to get my license out of my wallet. I hand them over and he returns to his vehicle. He's gone from sight for a few minutes before he emerges with a ticket in hand.

"It's your first offense… normally I would let you off with a warning. However, you're going too fast to do that. Here's your ticket. Please, Miss Thomas, for your safety and others, drive the speed limit from now on." He hands me the ticket, my license, and registration and gestures for me to drive along. He returns to his vehicle as I pull off to rejoin traffic.

I make it to brunch only fifteen minutes late. Luckily enough, it wasn't a far drive. My family was just getting seated, which didn't matter to Diane; late is still late.

"Seriously? You can't manage to be on time? What could possibly be so important that you had to be late?" Diane nitpicks my tardiness as my father's mom steps in.

Grandma Rose has a disdain for Diane that started before I was born and never eased. She holds Diane in such critical regard, I wonder if that might be why my mother is so critical of me.

Although Grandma is very proper, she respects those who

rely on themselves to get through the world. My mother has generational wealth and a lawyer for a husband. She's never had to work a day in her life, unless you count all the party planning that she does for her groups.

"Leave the poor girl alone. At least she's doing something for herself other than being a perpetual housewife." The direct attack on Diane, while still building me up, makes me smirk slightly. "Now, tell me why you're late. It's out of character for you." She cups my cheek before pulling me into a firm embrace. I reciprocate, grasping her tightly. She drags the empty chair next to her out for me to sit.

"Honestly, I don't have a good excuse for being late. I over-slept. I rushed to get here on time and then got pulled over." I hold the ticket up as I sit. My eyes dart to Diane, whose furrowed eyebrows hang over her tense, squinting eyes. Her lips purse, disgust radiating from her.

"Look what you've done! This girl is so fearful of not meeting your standards now she's risking life and limb to make you happy! *You're* lucky that it was a mere ticket and not an accident!" Eyes gather on our table as Grandma Rose builds a scene, screaming at Diane. "So-help me, Diane, I would *never* forgive you!" My grandmother's contempt for my mother seeps out with every well-placed word, making it clear that even though it's *my* ticket, Diane is ultimately to blame.

My father, who's sitting across the cloth-covered table quietly in the leather high-backed seat, takes the ticket from my hand to examine it closer. The lawyer in him is surfacing, and as he reads through the ticket, you can see the gears turning in his head.

"Seventy-five in a forty-five!? Sadie Rose Thomas! You're lucky that this is just a speeding ticket and not an arrest for reckless driving! What in the world were you thinking!?" I can always tell Dad's emotions; his eyebrows give it away. They quiver between upturned and furrowed, worried and angry.

I reach forward and take a sip of water, attempting to avoid eye contact with him. The decorative engraved crystal feels unexpectedly smooth between my fingers. He clears his throat, acknowledging that he's aware I'm ignoring him.

"I see what the problem is…." My Grandma Rose takes over the conversation in my defense. After setting the glass down, I fidget with the flower centerpiece, continuing to avoid eye contact with anyone. "*Your* wife created a toxic environment! Sadie will never meet her impossible standards!"

My eyes wander upward in Diane's direction across the table next to Dad. Her head hangs low, gazing down into her lap where she's holding her hands. The corners of her lips sag, matching her downcast eyes. Diane slouches. The pang in my chest overwhelms me. Sympathetic sadness for Diane is difficult to avoid. It's *hard* to witness such a proud and strong person fold in on herself.

"If you think I'm at fault for your granddaughter's shortcomings in life, you're mistaken. As a parent, I'm supposed to help guide my daughter on the right path," Diane pours herself a mimosa from the pitcher that sits on the table. The calmness she exudes is off-putting, her matter-of-fact tone chilling. "If I weren't hard on her, she wouldn't be going to Johns Hopkins." Her eyes meet mine, even though she speaks to Grandma Rose. "She'd probably be pregnant in some trailer park…." she pauses as some sort of sick power move, turning her attention back to Grandma Rose. "She should be *thanking* me for the enormous role I've played in building her into the somewhat successful woman she is. It wasn't an easy road. *You're welcome!*" Diane concludes her statement with a sip of her mimosa and dabs her perfectly made-up face with the cloth napkin pulled from her lap.

Slowly, she places the napkin on the table in front of her and stands, her way of signifying the conversation is over. "All of this *lovely* conversation has made me lose my appetite. No use sitting at a table with no expectations of eating… Richard?" She beckons to my father, who always obliges her.

He sets his glass down on the table and stands. "I'll pull the car around." He places a hundred-dollar bill in the center of the table, which more than pays for the one pitcher of mimosas, and two waters that were ordered. Grandma Rose sighs and peeks at me through saddened eyes.

"Well… It's sort of a waste if we don't eat breakfast… right?" she says. I frantically bob my head, excited to be rid of the hostility.

We sit for a solid hour, talking about school and the wedding. She's eager to hear everything I have to say. Thoughts spew out uncontrollably. I'm not accustomed to having someone to talk to.

The waiter comes over with the rest of the tab. Glancing around the restaurant, I notice that we're the only two patrons left. Laughing sheepishly, I dig through my purse to pay the remainder of the bill, but before I can find my wallet in my messy purse, Grandma hands the man her credit card. She insists I save my money for gas or a good time with friends.

I giggle at that, because what friends? I give her a tight hug and kiss her on the cheek, which makes her blush. After we let go, she walks toward the entrance. She turns back to face me with a check in her hand, pausing briefly in front of the exit.

"Here… for the ticket. You'll know better next time, right? You can be late for me. Hell, we'll end up with better company, anyway." She grins and grabs my hand, forcing me to take the check.

"Grandma Rose, it's okay. I can—" Her scowling eyes stop me dead in my tracks.

She grunts as she says, "Now, you're not going to tell your grandmother what to do? You'll take this check and say, '*Thank you*'. Not another word." She's a stubborn woman with the best intentions. I force a smirk and grip the check firmly.

"I love you," I say, and she replies with a smile. A smug look spreads across her face, knowing she's won this minor battle.

"Of course you do, who wouldn't!" she replies with a laugh. "I love you, too, Miss Sadie Rose. You're too much like me, I guess that's why you have my name." She always makes that remark, showing how proud she is.

My smirk grows into a toothy grin. Unfortunately, the smile fades when I realize I'm going back to the house where Diane is inevitably waiting for me. The thought makes my stomach churn.

The drive home is filled with my thoughts circling around, attempting to prepare for this conversation. When I arrive home though, Diane isn't there. My father, however, is in his office. I stand in the doorway, silently waiting for him to acknowledge my presence. He peers over his glasses and back down at the document he's studying.

With a deep sigh, he places the paper down. I slink into the office and plop down into the chair across from his desk.

"What is it, Sweet Girl?" he asks, as if morning brunch never happened. I stare down at my hands, sensing the disappointment. Taking my silence as a sign of guilt, he starts the conversation.

"Sweet Girl, no one is perfect, even though your mother likes to act like she is."

I laugh slightly; he's trying to make me feel better about the whole situation. He hardly ever says anything against Diane, but this is his attempt to make me smile. "Everyone has gotten pulled over by the police. It's not a new concept. Do you need money to pay for the ticket?" He inquires, ready to jump in and solve my life problems.

"No, Grandma Rose gave me a check to pay for it. I told her not to, but you know how she is."

He grins at me, nodding. Quickly, he glances down at the paper. His hand juts to his clean-shaven face to rub his jaw. His glance turns into a squint until he puts his glasses back on and clears his throat. I stand up to leave, taking the hint.

"You know… your mother is very upset with what happened. It'd be nice if you'd talk to her," he suggests as I walk away.

I'm glad I'm facing away because if he saw my reaction, he'd be even more disappointed. I know he's aware of her criticism of me, but he has a deeper understanding of her inner workings. He loves her without fault, even though they don't spend much time together because of his work.

He misses none of her planned events. When they're together, he acts *mostly* interested in her frilly festivity planning. I don't understand how they work, but they do.

To get back into good graces with my father, I'll have to confront my mother. She's most likely out shopping, which is something she does to soothe her nerves. She probably won't be back until dinner, so I decide to go to my bed to lounge and consider how the conversation might go.

Apparently, I was exhausted, because when I wake up it's a completely new day. No one woke me for dinner.

When I go downstairs, I find myself home alone. Starving, I scavenge through the kitchen to find breakfast. After finishing a bagel with cream cheese and a handful of strawberries, I head back to my room to gather a plan for the day.

My priority is to pay for the ticket I received yesterday; no way can this linger over my head. Especially considering the time of year. Diane's festival, also known as our family's annual Fourth of July party, is coming up. I know pointless errands and frivolous tasks are in my future. I don't want this ticket to go forgotten, lost in the sea of Star-Spangled-Banner-Party Extravaganza.

Throwing my hair up in a messy bun and applying a touch of mascara doesn't take much time; neither does figuring out which one of my many summer dresses to wear. With it being so hot today, I choose a flowing coral dress with white floral patterns stretching across it.

After gathering my purse, and a bottle of water from the fridge, I leave. The drive to the courthouse is uneventful, leaving room for my mind to wander.

Upon entering the courthouse, a metal detector greets me. The florescent lights are bright and unsettling, like stepping into a medical exam office. Lines of individuals divide the large hallway; each waiting their turn to get to the window. I pass through everyone, begging for pardons as I sidestep through the lines that stretch from one side of the hall to the other. I walk for a few minutes, passing several lines before I make it to the traffic violations line. After asking at least three people where the line ended, I find my spot. About fifteen minutes into standing, with little to no movement, I hear a familiar voice from behind me.

He's talking to another officer. Without thinking, I look in his direction. His eyes catch mine. My cheeks burn, and I pivot my attention forward. My skin tingles up and down my spine. I fidget with the ticket in my hand anxiously, shifting my weight from left to right.

With his gaze on me, the burning sensation in my back grows. He stops his previous conversation and walks in my direction, getting in line directly behind me. I act like I don't know he is standing right behind me, primarily because I'm nervous and don't know what to say. He chuckles.

"Excuse me? Are you really going to hunt me down and not talk to me?" he asks with too much confidence. I roll my eyes and huff, annoyed he believes *I* was searching for *him*.

"I'm not here for *you;* I'm here for personal reasons." A frustrated tone taints my words. It doesn't seem to change his entrancing smile any, which annoys me even more.

Why is he so handsome and comfortable talking to me like this? How full of yourself do you have to be to think that someone you barely flirted with scoured around to find you?

"You do realize I'm a police officer, and this is a courthouse… right?" He smirks at me and glances down at the paper in my hand. His teeth disappear as his face drops, lips tightening into a straight line as he's realizing that I'm here for more than what he expected. "What happened? Are you alright?" He reaches for my hand holding the ticket. Reflexively, I yank my hand away. We hardly know each other, and he's inquiring about answers that he has no right to.

"It's none of your business." I'm attempting to sound less pleased at the idea of him being concerned for me, which is difficult because he's *so* intoxicating.

He smiles at my annoyed response. Between conversing with Garrett and awkwardly standing in silence with him behind me, I somehow make it to the front of the line. I approach the window where a young woman sits. She asks my name and the reason for my being here today.

Half-looking over my shoulder at the man who wants the same information, I respond, "My name is Sadie Rose Thomas, and I'm here to pay for a speeding ticket." Garrett's animated gaze beams into the back of my head, and heat rushes back to my cheeks.

"So… nineteen-year-old Sadie Rose Thomas was driving too fast, huh?" He steps up behind me, close enough to feel his breath along my left ear.

Attempting to ignore the chills rushing down my spine and stomach twisting into knots, I hand the young lady the ticket and the check from my grandmother. She grins bashfully at me, her eyes however remain locked on Garrett hovering over my shoulder, almost pressed against me. As if I didn't feel uncomfortable enough, I hear another familiar voice off in the distance.

"Sweet Girl?" my father calls out to me.

He's in court today; *of course he's here*! My skin flushes and head spins. I place my hand on the counter to stabilize myself and clear my foggy brain. Peering around the room, I notice no one is looking at the two of us. It's reassuring. Maybe I am misreading the interaction as more intimate than it is from lack of experience.

I turn to look at my father, and out of the corner of my eye, Garrett's confidence shrivels. Maybe I'm right about how intimate that was because Garrett's face loses color.

My father stops in front of us, his eyes darting between Garrett and me. "If I had known you were coming to the courthouse, I would've taken an early lunch." He stops, looking back and forth between us. "Hello, Officer Williams, I see you've met my daughter Sadie."

He nervously scrambles for words. "I... a...."

I step up and take over the conversation, though it probably doesn't make Garrett any more comfortable. "Yeah, we met. Ironically, he's trying to ask me on a date."

His eyes widen and mouth jolts open, gaping in awe. He glances at me, gaze shifting back to the officer he was conversing with before spotting me. With the other officer gone, he has no backup plan. At least, that's what it looks like.

Dad's face twists. Almost instantly, his jaw slacks, and eyes soften. I don't think he was prepared for it to happen right before his eyes.

"Oh, my apologies, Officer Williams...." he says, chuckling at the sheer awkwardness of the situation. "I didn't realize you had eyes for my daughter. I don't blame you... she's fantastic, though I might be a little biased, being her dad and all."

My discomfort peaks at the thought of my dad "pimping" me

out, advertising how great I am to potential suitors. "If you want… I mean if you're available… you could join us for dinner at our home tonight?" My eyes pop out of my head. With piercing *'what in the actual fuck'* eyes, I glare at my father. He quickly amends his suggestion. "Well, I mean, if that's something Sadie wants."

As if that makes it better! What am I supposed to say!?

I just nod in Garrett's direction. I am *so* mad that my father would even make that suggestion. A first date at a family dinner… with *my mother*.

"Thank you, Mr. Thomas, I couldn't imagine a better way to get to know your daughter." Of course, he's being polite. What other options does he have? He could say no and insult a lawyer that he works with, and the father of a girl he likes, or say yes and essentially get eaten as the first course at a family dinner… verbally, of course. I mean, his attraction to me doomed him from the start.

Chapter Eight
Walker Harris: Honesty gets you nowhere

SEVEN YEARS BACK

Booking at the station goes quickly, mainly because I'm so lost in thought.

My sister... my little baby sister... held down against her will. Exposed and abused. She must be so overwhelmed. I wish they would tell me if she's safe. No one should ever endure something like this, especially someone so young.

I'm so entangled in my mind; I get yelled at by officers instructing me to keep moving. I'm not trying to be noncompliant; I'm trying to wrap my mind around what happened.

"Turn," the officer taking the mug shot says, annoyed.

I'm not a violent person. At least, I didn't think I was. Glancing down, out of the corner of my eye, my stomach churns at the flash of deep red coating my fingers. I clench my eyes shut tight, creating colored orbs behind the lids. Nausea threatens to erupt from my body in forceful chunks. I fold over, clenching my stomach, which causes an uproar. The officer steps up to me when he realizes shouting isn't going to get me to stop hunching forward.

"Hey! Stand the fuck up!" He stalks over and aggressively pulls me upright.

I freeze, not wanting to cause any problems. They take the side-facing image and walk me downstairs to Inventory. I strip down, with an officer standing watch over me, feeling like an awkward kid new to the locker room. Only this time, the other people are staring at me… it's not my imagination. I peel away the clothes once soaked with blood, now stiff and crusted.

Goosebumps cover every inch of my body as I stand naked, placing my soiled clothes in the plastic evidence bag held open by the officer. Once he seals it, he hands me a khaki jumpsuit that's two sizes too large. I pull it over my head and shove my feet into a pair of slides that are too large. Swimming in the jumpsuit reminds me of how young I am, and the thought of hardly getting to experience life before being locked up rattles my brain.

Washing only the tips of my fingers to get my prints leaves me looking like I'm wearing red fingerless gloves. Fixing my sight on the bright florescent lights and white replaceable ceiling tiles, attempting to avoid seeing my blood-tinged skin, I turn inwardly to the darker corners of my brain.

Images from last night resurface to the forefront of my mind. Balancing between disgust in myself and disdain for Karl is a hard beam to walk. I lost control, seeing Clara in distress. Struggling in some hospital sits that pedophile… I honestly don't know if I feel bad for him. I feel horrible for my sister and Mom having to go through this… trauma. I *know* my mother will be in disbelief. She'll potentially blame herself.

The bars clank as the officer slams the door shut. "You'll get your phone call when I get back from the bathroom. A lawyer will be assigned to you for arraignment. Questions? No? *Good.*" The monotone words spew too quickly, not allowing me to respond. Not that I planned to.

Walking to the sink in the corner next to the toilet, I feel a throbbing ache in my hands. Peering down at the source of pain, the blood stirs my stomach once more. Rushing the few steps to the sink, I yank the knob to the smoldering hot. As the water runs red, I wince. The blood rinsing away reveals purple bruises beginning to form.

The officer returns from the bathroom, gripping his belt. Noticing I'm vigorously scrubbing my hands, a roaring chuckle echoes through the hollow cell.

"You can try to wash it away, boy. You did what you did, and you're gonna answer for it," the officer says in a low grumble, looking at me through the bottom of his thinly framed glasses with contempt.

The man is round, and his appearance is as stereotypical as you could possibly imagine. I pause to ponder his statement, looking down at the stained porcelain. He's right. Everyone will view me as a monster, as a person who has the gull to bludgeon another human being nearly to death. In the eyes of the law, there's no justification for that.

Feeling defeated, I turn off the water. *It's useless.* I collapse down onto the built-in metal-framed bed. Realization sinks in that I can *believe* he deserves it, but I'm not a judge, jury, or executioner.

I'm just as guilty as Karl.

Wiping away watery eyes from laughing at my fruitless efforts, he straightens his back. Chin upturned and shoulders rolled back, he reminds me of a bird spreading its wings to appear larger and more intimidating.

"You get one call." He unlocks the cell door after cuffing me through the bars. Escorting me to the phone with a shove, he walks me down the short, wide hallway.

Picking up the phone, I dial Mom's number. With each unanswered ring, the tense anticipation grows. Her voicemail message plays, and my eyes flash to the officer awaiting the call to end. I shrug at him, pulling the phone away from my ear as the beep from the voicemail sounds through the phone.

"Mom... is Clara okay? I'm at the police station. Just take care of her, I'm okay." Putting the phone back on the wall, the officer walks me back to the cell.

I continue tossing back and forth in my mind, attempting to justify my actions until morning. The buzzing of the station never truly settles down. Officers come in and out, chatting, with cups of coffee in hand. Janitorial staff walking about tidying and vacuuming the stained teal carpet. Ringing phones intermittently sound from different locations of the building, sporadic in timing, surprising me every time.

A female officer comes up to the desk across from the holding cells. *She's quite small for an officer.* Walking past my cell, she peers in briefly and looks back at her paper.

"This one's waiting for arraignment, but if ya' ask me, he don't deserve bail. He tried to kill a guy with his bare hands!" The cranky cop exclaims, forming fists and shaking them to emphasize his statement.

"That's for the judge to decide," she replies, shrugging and scribbling a note. They walk off as I roll over in the bed to face away from the cell door, my thoughts garbled. I bounce between Mom, my sister, and my guilt. I wonder if my sister told Mom everything. I've spent so much time bad-mouthing Karl, only for him to prove me right.

The female officer curiously approaches the holding cell, her aged eyes peering at me through the iron bars. She's older, maybe early fifties.

Softly she speaks, "Why'd you do it? I know in your police interview you said he deserved it and refused to go into detail." She pauses, waiting for me to respond.

I stay silent, sitting on the bunk on the other side of the cell. Accepting that I'm not going to talk, she continues, "It's on the report that you were attempting to kill this man. Is it true?"

Shifting her weight, I can sense her discomfort with murder in cold blood. I can tell that my age plays a role in how she views me.

Even though I'm a legal adult, this lady has softened, sympathetic eyes. She hesitates, waiting for my response before returning to her desk. As she turns to walk away, I feel compelled to explain what happened.

"I don't… I don't know what I was doing…." I start to say, standing up. "I just knew I had to stop him." It's not an abundance of information, but it's more than I've said to anyone else. She returns to the cell bars, confused.

I don't want to say it. It's almost like saying what happened will make it real. Tears form, threatening to fall. Pushing the palms of my hands into my eyes firmly, I suck in air, fast and hard, trying to stop the emotional response from progressing any further. Sighing, angry with myself for showing weakness, I walk to the door. Stepping back, she places enough space between her and the bars to protect herself.

"I walked into the house to find him ra…." My voice cracks. I take a rapid inhale, struggling to keep composure. "He was raping her." As I say it, I feel a weight fall off my shoulders. With that statement out in the open, my mind calms and my body feels heavy. With my mind finally quiet, not sleeping hits me like a ton of bricks.

"Why didn't you say that in your interview?!" Her eyes shift from soft to wide, her mouth opens in awe. Her eyes dart back to the common area of the station, searching for someone to share this information with. With no one there, her gaze switches back to me. I can see she's torn whether to get more information or run and get another officer. "That must have been really hard to see."

"I ripped him off… but he was talking… and trying to get to her *again*… I lost it." Talking, visualizing, and reliving it all together at once brings on a renewed sense of rage. I snuff the anger down, steadying my breath and closing my eyes. I turn away. With the information obtained, she leaves.

Walking over to bed, the force of exhaustion pulls me down. I need to sleep, even if it's just for a minute.

Shutting my eyes, I begin to dream about a simpler time. When I was young and playing at the Thomas's household on the Fourth of July. When things weren't difficult, and I still had Dad.

As my eyes open the next morning, daylight peeks through the small window. Abruptly, I jump out of my skin at the sight of the round man standing next to my cell, creepily watching me sleep. He doesn't even have the social decency to pretend he wasn't watching me. Slowly, he turns away as he makes intense eye contact. I shake my head in disbelief. *Why does this man hate me?* I mean, he acts like I beat *him* up and not Karl.

Having slept half the day and the entire night, I skipped any interactions with the night shift—outside of waking to the guard glaring at me. Luckily enough, his relief approaches the desk, where he plopped himself down seconds prior to her arrival.

It's the same kind, officer as yesterday. *This is good. I'll get to ask what happened with what I told her yesterday.* They do the handoff report and finish off the change of watch. He cocks his head to the left, muttering *'murderer'* as he walks away.

"He's *not* a murderer; the guy's still alive. Shut your mouth when you don't know what you're talking about." The kind female officer snaps back. He spins around to face her, eyes wide with disbelief, but without hesitation, his eyebrows cast down to display his anger.

"What the hell did you just say to me?" His chest puffs, arms crossed, shifting his stance to one side. She smirks.

"Cool it, Pete. We both know you've had it out for him since he got here... just because he looks like your son in prison doesn't make him guilty, too." Not quite yelling, she exclaims loud enough to stop two other officers as they walk in.

"Ya'... you... you don't know wha... what you're talking about! Wh—wh... who told you that!?" The round man, or I guess his name is Pete, stutters his words. Surprised and embarrassed, he looks at the other officers who stop to witness the disruption. He stomps away, avoiding eye contact with everyone he storms past.

Shortly after eating breakfast, the female officer makes her rounds.

"Excuse me, ma'am?" I ask, standing away from the door to ease any fears she might have. "Have you heard anything about my mom or sister?" The corner of her lip twitches upward briefly but quickly turns to a pitied frown. Her eyes sag into a saddened droop.

"I'm sorry, Walker. I haven't heard anything about them. No one has come to ask about you. I do know your arraignment is on Monday, though."

Something catches in my throat, and my stomach wretches into a twisted knot. I don't know what causes the sinking feeling: the fact that I'm going to be tried for attempted murder, or Mom's failure to check on me in two days since the incident. I hope it's because she is focusing on Clara. I let out a sigh as I step away from the door.

"Thank you, ma'am," I mutter, ensuring she knows I'm truly grateful for her kindness.

Nodding her head at me with pity creasing her face, she turns to walk away.

Even if Mom wants to pay my bail, I know she can't. Maybe I

should set up a payment plan with a lawyer that *isn't* a public defender. *If I encounter anymore people like Officer Pete, I'll spend the next twenty years to life in here... especially if the fucker dies!*

Pacing the cell, I allow my inner thoughts to spiral and take control of my emotions. Clenching my fists and jaw, my breathing becomes clipped. *I haven't even finished high school!* Thoughts of what my life will become swirl and build to a boil in my veins, fighting to break free.

I turn to the wall and push against it. Palms flat against the concrete, I push with all my force, like I can shove the wall over out of sheer will. Hoping to exert enough energy that my anger can level and lower to a simmer. It's useless to get angry. Nothing I do will change it.

After my breathing evens and muscles ache, I collapse onto the bed. The pulsing in my temples and neck pounds with residual anger and exertion. My hands push into my closed eyes as I exhale loudly. The sound of a throat clearing causes me to sit up abruptly. The female officer stands outside my cell, her teeth peeking through loosely pressed lips upturned in delight.

"You have a visitor!" she utters cheerfully. "Turn and face the wall opposite the door." I follow her instructions, and she opens the door and handcuffs me, preparing to transport me to the visiting room.

Walking in front of her feels strange considering I have no clue where I'm going. Upon entering the room, the bright florescent lights disorient me. The holding cell is dimly lit, even during the day. In addition to the lights, the opposite wall is full of large windows. Between us and the windows sits a plexiglass divider. My mother stands on the opposite side of the glass, dark circles under her red puffy eyes.

"Sit in the seat. We'll partially remove your handcuffs. You're not to stand without being told to do so." The officer unlocks one handcuff, and my hand flies for the phone.

Mom hesitates, worry and hurt in her eyes. After a minute of attempting to regain her composure, she sits down and picks up the phone from the other side of the glass.

Silence fills the phone, so I begin the conversation. "How's Clara? Is she okay?" It's the first thing I ask, even though it's clear Mom isn't okay. Not seeing my sister flips my stomach, and I feel a lump in my throat. She looks down at the table, completely ignoring my question. She has something to say, but it's difficult for her to form the words.

"Mom. Is Clara oh…" I begin to ask again, when my mother interjects in a soft but shaken tone.

"Why… Walker… why did you…." Her voice cracks: she can't finish the question.

I know what she's asking, but I'm confused why she doesn't have an answer. Did Clara not tell her? What about the officer? I told her, too. Wasn't it in the report? So many questions, but I'm on limited time. I sigh and look down at my bruised hands. She follows my eyes, wincing and quickly turning away.

"Mom?" I say calmly, attempting to bring her focus back to me. "Has Clara said anything about what happened?"

She shifts her attention back to me slowly. Her hand over her mouth, she swallows. Shaking her head, a few stray tears force their way through. I sit back in the seat, trying to sort out how to break the news to her. Why hasn't anyone told her?

In my silence, my mother takes over the conversation. "Karl's in ICU. I haven't left his side until now. Clara hasn't said a word," She pauses, rubbing the back of her hand across one eye. "They found her in her room. After taking you…." The crack in her words hints at the pain she's enduring. "Two officers attempted to question her… but she refuses to talk." Her face twists as she speaks, contorting in an unnatural grimace.

Her gaze flickers across my face, searching for answers as if they're written there. I lean forward, placing my cuffed hand, palm up on the table. I briefly forget the glass between us makes holding her hand impossible. Air rushes out from my pressed lips as I prepare to tell her something no parent ever wants to hear.

"I came home from work and—"

"I spoke to your work; they said they had to let you go. Did he say something? I'm sure you were already angry... I know how much you don't like Karl," she interrupts me.

She's already drawing conclusions. She doesn't know what he did. Does she think I beat this man because of a snide comment? Her questions certainly clarify what she thinks of me. I shake my head in disbelief. Although it may just be the dots she's connected with the information she's been given.

"Karl was...." I pause.

Is it even my place to reveal this? Obviously, Clara doesn't want her to know, but Mom has to know.

"Karl was hurting Clara." The lump in my throat pulls at my tongue, cutting my words short. Saying it out loud feels unbearable.

"Bullshit," she snips, refusing to accept the truth. Her head rocks with her mouth wide open, staring incredulously at me, she continues. "He wouldn't... he couldn't... she's like his daughter... that's not possible." Denial overtakes logic, and she stands up, her shock and questioning flip like a switch into irritation.

Her hands fly to the sides of her head. She turns, facing away from me, fighting an inner battle. She whips around and points at me. "Don't you say *shit* like that! He wouldn't do that! He loves us!" Rubbing her eyes again, she tries to stay strong, gaze trailing to the door she came in, a thought of fleeing the conversation seeps from her eyes. She forces herself back into the seat and closes her eyes. Letting out a heavy sigh, she tries to regain her patience. "He's a good man. He makes comments, but it's joking."

"Mom... *believe* me... he was...." My hesitation leaves a

perfect opportunity for her to interject again. She slams her hand down on the table forcefully, standing back up.

"I'm not listening to this! Clara would've said something! I know what you've told the cops, but you're just trying to cover your hide!" Her words are a hiss as she jabs at the air in my direction. "You *hate* him! It's too much! Enough lies!" Her shouting brings the female officer over.

I stand up, accepting that the visit's over. My mother slams the phone down and storms out the door. I watch, while being cuffed, as my mother leaves me behind. Of *course*, she has to leave me in jail, but she leaves her feelings for me behind as well. A hole rips through my chest, pain pinging off the inner-most parts of myself.

My mother doesn't believe me, and poor Clara is helpless.

If I'm stuck here, who's going to be there for Clara?

CHAPTER NINE
HOLLOWED SOUL, WEIGHT OF DESPAIR

SEVEN YEARS BACK

"I t's been weeks… no signs he's coming out of the coma, let alone if he'll ever be mentally baseline. It might be time to consider long-term care," the nurse whispers to the ICU doctor outside of the glass door. Overhearing the nurse while sitting at the bedside, Melony sobs.

She feels at fault for Karl, taking responsibility for her son's actions. When injured, Karl was placed in an induced coma. After trying several options, the specialists couldn't determine why he won't wake up. Melony has been by his side for weeks, while Clara spends most of her time in her room.

Her traumatic experience, and her mother's denial, cause Clara to wholly shut down and go mute. Not going to school, not caring for herself. She has sunk into a deep pit of despair, neglecting her hygiene and starving herself. The shell of her remains, but her consciousness burrows deep into the back of her mind with no signs of resurfacing. Melony is much too focused on Karl's medical state and following along from a distance with what is happening with Walker to notice that Clara is in grave need of intervention.

After numerous calls from the school with concerns about the number of absent days, you'd think that a mother would snap out of her denial. One of her teachers filed an anonymous complaint with Child Protective Services on Clara's behalf. A representative shows up at the house; luckily enough, it's while Melony is home showering and preparing to return to the hospital.

The house is in utter disarray, with trash strung about, making it clear that thorough cleanings aren't occurring. The stench of piled dirty plates, overflowing trash seeping onto the counters, and urine-soaked clothes unwashed in the open washer radiates throughout the home.

When Melony answers the door, the surprise wide-eyed gaze is difficult for the CPS worker to identify. Dark, swollen circles under her eyes make it difficult to widen and match her shock. The stress melts her face into drooping exhaustion.

"Hello?" Melony says, sounding shocked. The CPS worker peers past her, noticing the disheveled household. He glances down at his clipboard and makes a note. Melony gawks as she takes a half step back, her lips tighten and jaw tenses, feeling judged immediately. "Who are you?" she sneers at the note taking.

The CPS worker pulls his eyes from his clipboard. "My apologies, Ms. Harris. I'm Steven, from Child Protective Services…." Her eyebrows shift from downward disapproval to an upward angle. The tightness in her jaw slackens as her mouth gapes open. Shaking her head, attempting to collect herself, her body wavers back in a disoriented pattern. "May I come in?" He leans forward, asking politely, but it sounds more insistent than inquisitive. She nods, taking a sidestep to allow a small space for him to step past her.

If you ask Melony, she'd say this is an unnecessary visit, but she'll comply anyway to settle the school down. Clara is simply grieving her brother's sudden disappearance and her father-figure being in the hospital. Melony believes Clara needs only time to cope and understand what happened.

He stops in the living room, examining and letting out a held breath. Inhaling with disgust from the odor is difficult to avoid, yet he still attempts. "Ms. Harris, have you been living here?" he asks Melony in the calmest tone he can muster in this situation.

As Steven scans the room, he notices that the home is seemingly untouched. Dust accumulates on trash settled in certain spots. Dishes are visible from the living room, piled up on the countertops, bugs scatter across them, weaving in and out of the mold crusted food on the dishes.

Melony, already offended, scoffs at Steven. "Of *course* we've been living here! That's the *problem*! I've been working. I've been with Karl, who's in the hospital! Not to mention taking care of my daughter! I don't know if you can see it, but a lot's happened! *So* sorry if the house doesn't smell like I've been baking cookies and washing laundry all day!" Steven steps back, as Melony reassesses the irrational anger she's letting escape.

"Ma'am, I have no doubt your family has been through quite a bit. I've *thoroughly* read the file and excused absence notes you wrote. I apologize for offending you; I'm simply doing my job. May I meet Clara, please?" Steven asks.

He looks toward the hall, assuming that her room is that direction. Melony turns to follow Steven's eyes before turning back to him to respond, "Of course, her room is the last door on the right. She prefers to be alone. I was the same way when I was younger and upset about something." After being told that her house is essentially unlivable, Melony goes into the kitchen and begins cleaning.

An unanswered knock on Clara's door prompts the CPS worker to knock again. After not getting a response, he slowly enters the room. Clara sits in an office chair in front of her desk. She's facing the window over the desk, but the blinds aren't open. Steven walks over to Clara, who doesn't look up to acknowledge his presence.

"Hello, Clara. My name is Steven, and I'm here to see if you are doing okay." He pauses, awaiting some sort of response.

She stares at the window, body flaccid in the chair. After assessing her physical appearance, Steven notes Clara's matted hair. She's wearing loungewear that would probably be stiff if taken off. Her eyes are sunken, clearly emaciated and dehydrated. Based on her catatonic state, it's hard for Steven to believe Clara is caring for herself at all.

Steven's face crinkles as a pit opens up in his stomach. He attempts to talk to Clara more, but there is no verbal *or* nonverbal response. Speaking to her, he can see that she's still mentally present, a glimmer of hope peering back at him behind glazed eyes. Even with a glimmer of hope, her lack of physical care is much too prominent to let go on any further.

Steven leaves the room to return down the hall and finds Melony carrying a trash can around the house. Seeing Steven catches Melony off guard. She abruptly stops and sits the trash can down.

"Ms. Harris, do you believe that Clara is doing well?" Steven asks with concern coating his face.

"Well, of *course*, she's not doing well! What kind of question is that? Neither one of us is **doing well**! She's coping the best way she knows, and I'm here for her when she's ready to talk." Melony truly believes that Clara will reach for help, but she doesn't realize that Clara is already screaming for help. Clara is so deep in her trauma that no one can hear her tiny, drowned cries for help.

"Ma'am, I'm not here to upset you; please understand that I'm here to ensure Clara is in the best situation to allow her to flourish. I can't possibly understand what your family has gone through, but I'm here to help the only way I can." He hesitates, eyes trailing down to the clipboard he carries full of notes. "Does she talk at all? Or leave her room without your guidance?"

Tears begin to form in Melony's eyes. This question deeply hurts her, not because it's offensive but because she doesn't know how to make the problem disappear.

"No, she doesn't... but she will when she's ready... just... she needs time," Melony responds with minimal confidence in her statement. Like she's been repeating this several times a day, attempting to reassure herself everything will be okay.

"But... how long will you wait? She is emaciated and catatonic. It's clear that she's not keeping up with her hygiene, and I'm unsure if she's even sleeping. Clara's not okay... you need to understand that. I don't think she can stay here if that's something you can't see."

The thought of losing her daughter terrifies Melony. The growing tears morph into a sob. Steven can see that she isn't intentionally neglectful of her daughter, which makes the conversation with Melony harder. Steven knows he has to remove Clara from the home and potentially have her placed in a children's psychiatric ward for intensive therapy. That decision is reserved for the doctor, though he hasn't seen cases quite this bad *not* be admitted. Steven informs Melony that Clara needs to be examined by a doctor.

"Does she stand or move at all?" Steven asks, trying to determine if he needed to call an ambulance to transport her to the hospital.

"No. She won't get out of the chair. It's been days since I've gotten her to eat. She'll drink water, but only when I dump it in her mouth. I'm cleaning her up and trying to help her through this tough time."

Steven is appalled and can't believe that Melony has allowed her daughter to get to this point without attempting to seek outside help. Composing himself he lets out a forced exhale.

"I'll call an ambulance to take Clara to the hospital to be evaluated. She really needs both a medical and psychological evaluation," Steven says as he pulls out his phone, preparing to call.

"I'm a nurse! I can take care of my daughter!" she exclaims, attempting to change his mind. She grabs his hand that holds the phone and pleads with her eyes not to proceed.

Steven hesitates and peers up from his phone to Melony. He pulls his hand away forcefully. "Honestly, ma'am, the fact that you're a nurse and should be aware of your daughter's state doesn't help your case." Steven strides out of the house to speak to EMS in private on the front porch.

The ambulance arrives within minutes of the call being placed. The two EMT's enter the home cautiously with eerie judgmental glances between them. Rolling the stretcher into the room, they work together to determine the safest way to get Clara up.

"Hey, I'm Eddy. This is Rob. We're gonna get you onto this stretcher, can you blink if you understand?" Although she makes no sounds or major movements, her eyes flicker to Eddy. Stopping Rob from proceeding, Eddy locks eyes with Clara. "Can you hear me? Wait! I think she's listening to me! Clara, blink if you understand."

A long silence fills the air as both Rob and Eddy stare at Clara's eyes. Slowly she closes her eyes but doesn't open them again.

"I swear I saw her looking at me!" Eddy shouts as Rob chuckles.

"Sure ya' did, buddy." His chuckles dissolve as they load Clara up into the ambulance for a silent ride to the emergency room. Meeting them there, Melony rushes through the double automatic doors, with Steven straggling in behind her.

Due to the circumstances, they requested that she stay in the waiting room, but Steven made it clear to the receptionist that

Melony's neglect was unintentional. The neglect stems from the poor state of mind considering everything going on within the family dynamic.

By the time Melony is approved to see Clara, the physician has evaluated and diagnosed her with dehydration and malnutrition. An IV bag is running as Melony hurries into the room. Beeping from vital machines are drowned out by the sounds of bustling computer carts and medical staff swarming about the halls.

"My baby!" Melony croaks out as she snatches Clara's hands between her own. The doctor and nurse standing out in the hall speak loudly over a commotion in another room.

"I'm ordering total parenteral nutrition and a psych eval." The doctor shifts his weight as the nurse types the orders into the computer on wheels.

"I've never seen a case this… drastic," the nurse whispers to the doctor, hardly audible over the chaos of the hospital.

"Only one time, with a toddler that was abandoned. If they made it, so will she… even if she spends the rest of her life in a psych ward." He expresses it as a matter-of-fact statement, saying it so calmly and void of emotional empathy.

"Please, Clara, snap out of it! They're going to take you away! I'm trying, but you've got to meet me halfway!" The nurse walks in to find Melony desperately shaking Clara, hoping to snap her out of it.

Quickly coming to Melony's side, the nurse gently places her hands on Melony's shoulders. "Hey, Momma, let's step outside." Endearingly, she leads Melony out of the room. Melony's eyes rise to see a police officer walking alongside a moving hospital bed carrying a prisoner… it's Walker.

CHAPTER TEN
Sadie Thomas: Uncontrollably Falling

THREE YEARS BACK

As the clock grows closer to dinner time, my anxiety rises. I don't understand why this guy has me so flustered; he's just some guy.

I primp myself so that Diane won't draw attention to my looks. Not too much makeup but enough that she can tell I put in effort. I leave my hair down but straighten it, so the waves remain tame. I don't want to change out of my dress into something fancy because I feel like he'll notice that. Instead, I make small changes, like adding a bit of jewelry and changing my shoes. The goal is to make it seem like I didn't go above and beyond for him but also avoid Diane making dissatisfied comments.

I come down early, wanting to engage Diane before Garrett arrives. I want to get her usual remarks out of the way. Before I reach the bottom few steps, Diane walks into the foyer.

"Honestly, Sadie, how could you choose a *cop*." She says the word *'cop'* with such distaste that you'd think she took a bite out of a lemon. "I mean, come on... we're a family of status... of wealth. You don't need to be with someone who might as well work for charity." As she finishes her comment, the doorbell rings.

A little hasty to the door, I try to avoid Diane greeting him first after the oh-so-polite comment she made just moments ago. I open the door to Garrett, standing anxiously in brown khaki shorts and a light blue button-up shirt. The color compliments his dark hair and light graphite eyes.

I'm a little less self-conscious about my panicked primping when I notice, he trimmed and shaped his beard; in his hands are two carnation flowers. Leaning back and shifting his stance, he puts his free hand in his pocket, quickly replacing his tense demeanor with a boyish half-smirk.

"Why, hello, Ms. Thomas. I have a flower for you and one for the lady of the house." I take the flower from his hand, and Diane, who overhears him, peeks through the door.

"Oh, **now** I see why," Diane says hastily and storms away. Garrett glances at me, confused, and I shake my head as if I don't know what she's talking about.

And so, the night begins, the first comment already out there. Honestly, I thought I'd be the primary focus of her critiquing. I didn't expect her plan of attack to be degrading a guest in her home; she's always more proper than that.

My father strolls out of his office into the foyer, greeting Garrett. Diane's persona shifts. I find it odd, considering my father never slowed her down before.

"Hello, Officer Williams, welcome to our home. I hope you aren't allergic to steak and potatoes," my father says with a chuckle.

He reaches out his hand to shake Garrett's, who smiles and reciprocates the gesture, focus darting back to me with a cocky *'see I got this'* look. I grin and roll my eyes at the same time.

"Oh, you can call me Garrett. Thank you so much for inviting me to your home." He holds out the second carnation flower toward my father. "For the lady of the house," Garrett says, with an optimistic gleam on his face. My father's lip upturns, appreciating the attention to detail. He grasps the flower from Garrett and turns to Diane. She acts startled as if she weren't paying attention. Diane forces an insincere smile to the dainty flower.

She grabs the flower with two fingers and nods to Garrett. "Thank you for the **small** gesture." She saunters through the dining room into the kitchen. My father, looking annoyed, pivots away from Diane to Garrett.

"I apologize. My wife's not always the most… pleasant."

A smile spreads across my face. My father and I make eye contact and chuckle at his jokingly valid comment. I laugh harder in response to my father finding humor at Diane's expense.

"Well, *do* come in, Garrett. We invited you to have dinner, which won't be served on the front porch! Let's have a predinner drink in the den." Garrett enters the house as my father outstretches his arm down the hall past the stairs, gesturing to the den. I begin walking into the dining room, as usual, the predinner drink was for the men of the household, and the women gather in the living room to gossip.

When I enter the dining room, I cross behind Garrett's path. He slyly grabs my hand, insisting I follow him into the den with my father. Smirking back at me, he raises one eyebrow.

"Where do you think you're going? Isn't this our first date?" He smiles a little too proud of his own comment. I pause sheepishly and glimpse at my father, who notices Garrett stopped walking behind him. My father observes the two of us blatantly flirting.

"Sadie, you're welcome to join the gentlemen. After all, he's *your* suitor," my father uncomfortably retorts.

He's overcompensating, trying to appear nonchalant. I gleam with happiness; Dad's never asked me to join him in the den. I pull my hand from Garrett and follow my father into the den.

Dad sits in his usual chair closest to the fireplace. Upon our maid entering the den, Garrett stands as a sign of respect. My father looks at Lydia, our maid, smiling. Still standing, I shift uncomfortably in such unfamiliar territory. I'm in the den, *during* pre-dinner drinks, *and* with a guy that wants to date me.

"Sweet Girl, you don't have to stay if you're uncomfortable, but you're more than welcome to sit with us." My father's encouragement of my independence softens my tense stance.

I sit on the loveseat next to Garrett. I don't want to sit in the seat next to my father, because it might imply interrogation. Garrett scoots to the side, allowing room on the loveseat.

My father turns to Lydia, who stands off to the side awaiting drink requests. "Lydia, dear, I would love a scotch on the rocks, and I know my little Sadie would like some of the fresh lemonade you made this morning." He pauses and glances over at Garrett. "We've got just about anything you can think of. Is there anything you prefer to drink?"

Garrett's eyes flicker between my father and me. "I'd love a lemonade as well, ma'am, if it isn't too much trouble." Lydia beams and spins to scurry away, only to return moments later with the requested drinks.

During her absence, there's only silence. Garrett breaks it first. "I didn't realize you have a daughter close to my age, Mr. Thomas." It's an attempt to fill the awkward silence, only to make it worse. There's no way to turn that into a true conversation.

I gawk at him, acknowledging this. He shrugs his shoulders and sheepishly smiles. My father clears his throat and takes a dragged-out swig of his scotch. He sighs, as if the alcohol instantly calmed his nerves.

"Garrett, I'm aware of your reputation. We've worked at the

same courthouse for a good while." My father must be trying to relax Garrett, but it only seems to tense him up.

Curious, I tilt my head, eyes darting between them. What if he's not trying to calm him but warn *me*? Is Garrett a trouble-maker? He's got a reputation, enough of one that my father takes notice. My father rarely involves himself in social gossip outside of work topics. Jumping focus between a very tense Garrett and an inquisitive father, I start to draw conclusions.

"Okay, what don't I know?" I demand, breaking the silent looks. Garrett sighs, releasing his tense shoulders. He turns his gaze to me before staring at his hands in his lap, seeming embarrassed by what he has to confess. It couldn't possibly be that bad.

"I guess I built a bit of a reputation." Garrett pushes into the seat, rubbing the back of his neck. "They poke fun at me… like a little brother. I get caught in a lot of jokes… pranks." My eyes flee to Dad, who smiles quite a bit, like he's remembering a particular practical joke. Garrett follows my eyes to my father. "Well, I made a mistake by trying to return the favor to a pair of officers who kept pestering me. I waited in the courthouse bath-room with some fart spray; I thought they were coming in next. I coated the bathroom in the spray; one of them had a weak stomach… so I was sure they would puke, at least *that* was the goal. Unfortunately, I found out that I also have a weak stom-ach. I left the stall I was hiding in and instantly felt sick. Walking out of the stall, I projectile vomited… right onto the judge who was presiding over court that day."

My father aggressively rolls into laughter, his snorting inter-rupts Garrett's story. With raised eyebrows, I stare at my father, who is all too pleased.

"Oh, Garrett! I didn't know it was fart spray; everyone thinks that you took a massive dump and couldn't handle the smell of your own ass!" Doubling over in laughter, Dad gasps for air.

Garrett sighs, lowering his head until his eyes aren't visible. My father wipes tears from laughing so hard. Garrett stands up and walks across the room, facing away from us. His fingertips trace the frames of pictures on the wall, the professional family photos that Diane planned and positioned just right. It's an accurate representation of my childhood. Every picture is meticulously planned, prepared for, and serious.

Seeming to have calmed his embarrassment, Garrett turns back to us with a half-smile. "Yeah, fart spray. I was never any good at pranks. I was raised in a family that was very… proper, I guess you could say." As he says the word *proper*, he peers back at the family photos on the wall as if he experiences a sense of familiarity. "The constant brotherly antagonizing pushed me to try. It was the only time, and it didn't end well, *that's* for sure." He saunters back over to the seat next to me. He avoids eye contact with my father, who's no longer laughing, and meets mine instead. Shifting at the growing heat building in my cheeks, I force myself to focus on an award hanging on the wall.

"Poor kid, you've hardly lived that moment down! Judge Carter still talks about it to this day! He'll be at our Fourth of July party; you must explain to him what really happened when you come!" my father exclaims, all too excited.

My mouth gapes open involuntarily. Garrett is invited to the Fourth of July party, and dinner hasn't even started. Diane is going to be so mad. I know she just finished the final tally on seating charts and catering. *His invitation will go well at dinner.*

Garrett's cocky personality returns when he notices my mouth gaping open. "That's so nice of you to invite me, Mr. Thomas. It seems that Sadie may not be as thrilled with the invitation as I am." I turn away, tucking my hair behind my ear.

"I'm sorry, Garrett. I didn't mean to seem so shocked. I'm just surprised my father would be so bold to invite you after Diane confirmed the catering numbers and everything." I glare at my father, half expecting his face to turn white. His smile bends downward, and he straightens his back.

"I'm not afraid of your mother. She may plan the entire event and think she's in charge of everything, but *I'm* the man of the house. If she wants to have an issue with it, I can easily give Garrett *my* spot."

I roll my eyes, knowing Dad wants out of this party just as much as I do. We must be the *only* two people with no desire to partake in *'The Social Event of the Season'*.

"Dad, you can't use Garrett to get out of the party; good attempt, though." I halfheartedly clap for him to show my sarcastic enthusiasm.

My father grins at me and nods his head as if he were bowing on a stage. Just as he lifts his glass for another sip of his scotch, Lydia announces dinner is in the dining room. My father shoots up straight in his seat, slapping his knees as if to close the conversation.

"Welp! It's time to eat; I hope you're hungry!" My father and Garrett shuffle toward the French doors as I attempt to finish my lemonade. Diane doesn't appreciate liquids being carried from room to room without tops on them... not like she's the one cleaning up a spill, anyway.

Walking into the dining room, I see a shot glass half-full of water on the table, with the flower Garrett gave Diane cut and sitting in it. I can imagine her complaining about the measly single flower she had to prepare the tiny shot glass for. I don't think it's a coincidence that it's in front of the guest's table setting.

"Hello, you three! Did you guys enjoy your chat? Sadie joined you boys, I see; I hope the politics and business conversation wasn't too much for her. I imagine keeping up would be difficult." Diane smiles devilishly at me, knowing that insulting my intelligence is the one hit I rarely keep to myself.

I smirk, knowing she wants me to lash back and reveal a

subtle insecurity. It doesn't matter that I'm her daughter; *everyone* competes with Diane Thomas.

"Oh, I doubt it's difficult for Miss Thomas. Isn't she going to become a doctor? She must be smart." Did I mention that to him? I don't recall having that conversation with him.

He catches my eyes studying him with a perplexed look on my face, realizing that I didn't tell him that information. He cocks his head to the side, still glancing in my direction. "At least, that's what I heard at the wedding."

"She must've made quite the impression... considering you asked around about her." Diane cringes.

Garrett responds while making eye contact with me, happiness twinkling in his eyes. "Why yes, ma'am. She's beautiful and has such a powerful personality. After she spoke to me, I knew I had to see her again." He pauses to take a bite of food. "She didn't even give me her name, so I just asked one of the other bridesmaids." He grins at me again; it seems like he's just full of smiles, and I find myself smiling back involuntarily.

"Diane, stop berating Officer Williams. He's a good man." My father attempts to intervene. "Besides, I invited him to the Fourth of July Party." Following my father's statement is utter silence.

Diane's eye twitches. It's impossible to hide her complete disbelief that her husband would dare invite someone to *her* Fourth of July Party this close to the event, *especially* without discussing it with her first.

"Excuse me? I'm sorry. I think I heard you wrong. I just know that my loving husband wouldn't invite someone to a party I've spent a year planning and just turned in final numbers for this past week without discussing it with his wife first." Taking a deep breath, she stands up. "I apologize for my husband... he clearly didn't realize when he crossed a line. I'd be so happy if you joined us. I'll pray that one of our other guests on the list catches a cold... I suppose I can spare *my* seat.

Standing is great exercise anyway and I've been meaning to lose a pound or two." Now standing and clenching her napkin in her hand, Diane spirals.

"Diane, *seriously*! We have company! Weren't you raised with better manners than this!? He can have my plate and seat. I always spend the day running errands to help with this frivolous waste you call a party anyway!" my father jabs at Diane, disapproving of her lack of decency in front of a guest.

She huffs loudly, ensuring we're all aware of her distaste for the situation. "Don't *you* worry, Richard Eugene Thomas, you won't have to worry about a damn thing during that party! You never do! Down to the fucking clothes you wear!" She slams her hand down on the table, leaving the napkin behind.

Diane storms off toward the stairs, pausing momentarily to face the table. She straightens her back. Letting out a sigh of emotional readjustment, she says, "My apologies, I'm not feeling well. It's lovely to meet you." She continues her path up the stairs and slowly disappears. My father grunts with a sharp inhalation. He wipes the corners of his mouth as he pushes back his chair.

"Lydia, dear?" He calls out, not knowing she already entered the dining room. "Oh, my apologies, dear. We won't need dessert this evening, as Mrs. Thomas has retired for the night. If Sadie and Mr. Williams wish to have dessert, please assist them. I'll be retiring to my room as well." He rises from his seat and bows his head to Garret before heading for the stairs. Even angry, he's still cordial.

"Goodnight, Mr. Thomas, have a wonderful evening. I'll clean up everything tonight and return in the morning!" Lydia begins clearing the table of the half-eaten plates and dirty napkins. "Miss Sadie, would you or your friend like some dessert?" Lydia simpers, knowing that I'd say no, but might reconsider for Garrett's sake. I've never been fond of sweets, especially considering the mother I grew up with constantly watching my weight for me.

Garrett places his napkin atop his plate. His movement reminds me that I'm not alone at the table. I've grown accustomed to being the last one at the table. It's primarily due to a meltdown by Diane, followed by my groveling father walking up the stairs to apologize for something outrageously ridiculous.

I wait a moment longer to respond, looking to him for a hint. As he peers up from his plate to the silence around the room, his eyes catch mine. Face softening, he smirks yet again.

"Why do you smile at me so much?" I blurt. He chuckles as he fidgets briefly with the napkin.

Lydia nervously clears the room, leaving behind our plates. His eyes leave his fingertips, drifting up to my lips and then back to my eyes.

"You say whatever's on your mind, don't ya'? You do realize that some people could view that as rude, right?" he asks without breaking eye contact, one eyebrow pulling up. The corners of his lips twitching, awaiting my answer.

A burning sensation in my core grows and chills dance across my spine. I pull my eyes away as blood floods my face, burning with heat.

"I don't mean to… I'm sorry… I…" My legs rub together as I shift in my seat, uncomfortable. I raise the back of my hand to my reddened cheek, feeling the heat press against the skin.

Lifting his hand to mine, his fingertips trace the inside of my palm, gently caressing my hand before placing his fingers under my chin. With his thumb pressing into my chin just below my bottom lip, he pulls gently, guiding my gaze back to face him again.

"I didn't say I found it rude. I love that you let me into that mind of yours. I've been driving myself crazy wondering what the hell you're thinking." I yank back, feeling the burning in my core grow exponentially.

"Would you like to sit out on your front porch? We haven't gotten much chance to get to know each other. Besides, I saw a swinging bench," Garrett asks with a pleading look in his eyes.

The man that was so confident and cocky to me in the courthouse is nowhere to be seen.

She sees that I'm looking at her and meets my eyes. Lydia smiles an awful lot for someone who returned to clean off the table.

Giggling under her breath, she addresses me, "Miss Sadie, I believe he's talking to you… not *me*."

I'm not accustomed to this dating thing by any means. I feel so awkward… so… frumpy. It makes me feel so… so… inferior. *I hate feeling this way*. After being raised to believe anything less than perfection is weakness, I find it hard to believe I'm not making a mistake by staying in this situation—a situation where I feel lost and inadequate.

But when he smiles at me, that feeling melts away and makes my mind blank. It's intriguing how much a single person can affect you so unequivocally.

I nod and stand in the same motion. He follows me out onto the front porch and sits on the swing next to me. We talk for what seems like hours, about so many things, important topics as well as hilariously stupid ones. I don't think I've ever been asked such silly and pointless questions, but each one makes me laugh.

We stay outside until the air turns cool and my eyes grow heavy. He stands up when the conversation slows, realizing that it's two in the morning, and sighs, admitting he has to be at work at seven. I peer down at my freezing, clenched hands. We face each other, anticipation building. When Garrett leans in to kiss me, we knock heads and I stagger back, clenching my forehead. "Ouch!" I laugh, sitting back on the swing. He sits back down, reaching for my forehead.

"I'm so sorry! Let me see!" His hands grab the sides of my face.

He looks at my head, but I'm staring at his lips. They're slightly open as he examines my head. I realize I've been holding my breath and let out a small sigh. His eyes wander down to mine. I close my eyes and attempt to pull my head to the side. His hands prevent me from turning away, and he pulls my face slowly, pressing his lips to mine. The kiss feels short, but I know it's long for a first kiss. Smiling from ear to ear, he runs his thumb across my lips.

"Sorry, I couldn't possibly leave here without knowing what kissing you felt like. Miss Sadie, you've captured my attention." He puts one hand on my arm and draws me to him. I think he's going to kiss me again, but instead he kisses my forehead gently. "Thank you for letting me come tonight." He rises and strolls to his car.

My fingertips shoot to my lips, still buzzing from the kiss. I'm falling for this guy, and the feeling of uncontrollable impending chaos has my stomach in knots.

CHAPTER ELEVEN
WALKER HARRIS: OUT ON BAD BEHAVIOR

SIX YEARS BACK

The transfer process from the jailhouse to the prison is daunting. Because of my public defender being a truly wonderful and kind man, I take a plea deal and receive six years in prison, and one year of community service. I'm charged with assault and battery—a huge cutback from attempted manslaughter.

My six-year sentence is served at Blackburn Correctional Complex. As soon as I in-process, I'm assigned a cell and a cellmate. His name is Lenny, and he's a quiet guy. I try to start conversations with him, but it's all for naught. He keeps to himself, not just around me but everyone. He was already in the cell when I arrived, so my bed was chosen for me... next to the toilet. *It isn't ideal.* However, I'm just glad that my cellmate's not some hateful jerk or ax murderer. Blackburn is a medium security prison; I can't imagine they would put a serial killer here... *hopefully.*

I try to follow Lenny's example and keep to myself for the first few days, treading lightly, not wanting to upset the daily patterns of prison. I have no intention of drawing negative attention to myself. Lenny seems to stay out of trouble by keeping silent, so I mimic his demeanor. The only person I converse with, excluding the few interactions with guards, is him. Conversation is one sided, excluding the occasional chuckle that he can't seem to hold back. The guy seems kind, so I don't understand how he ended up in this place. He gives me direction, leading by example how to go about everything. He doesn't complain or seem bothered by my constant presence.

I'm out of sorts. Though, it appears to be like high school in some ways. The prison also divides itself into different social groups.

Blackburn keeps a pretty tight schedule, which doesn't allow for much downtime, but nights are unbearably silent. It's an agonizing amount of time for self-pondering until you inevitably fall asleep. Being a social individual and only talking to Lenny, who might as well be a wall, grows old quickly. The guy's nice, but I'm convinced he's mute.

I keep to myself outside of the cell, as much as a crowded prison allows. Somehow, I always seem to find myself near Ryan. Between being silent and having to listen to that egocentric, narcissistic jerk, I struggle deeply. Any normal human listening would be sick to their stomach and full of anger at his comments.

Unfortunately, I'm not surrounded by "*normal*" people. Most of those around me have done horrendous things. I find that most who did something more on the serious end are actually proud of it. Most blaming the victim for being in prison or *getting caught.*

This means that when Ryan goes off on a rant, no one really bats an eye. In these tangents, he mentions things like '*how quickly her skin turned red from his grip*' or how '*her dress was so flowy and easy to hike.*' The most blatant use of victim blaming is his favorite comment '*it's obvious she was asking for it.*'

When I hear the comments he thinks are bragging points, my body tenses up. My fists clench and unclench, and I have to grit my teeth to hide the distaste. Ryan starts to catch on that I'm not pleased by his presence and decides to push me. I notice him looking at me as he brings up these topics, with a sinister grin across his face.

Catching myself turning into a self-proclaimed martyr, I remind myself of the bludgeoned face and sore fists. The level of damage caused wasn't just self-defense… it was rage. I'm no less a monster than anyone else here, no matter how much I try to justify my actions. At the end of the day, I still beat another person nearly to death. But I mostly am displeased with the depravity of guilt.

I'm sitting in the mess hall eating lunch when Ryan sits next to me. He's uncomfortably close, and I slide down a spot. Without hesitation, he follows.

"Hey, you're that guy that beat the shit out of some dude… right?" I ignore him and turn my shoulder. I hope that he'll get the hint. He doesn't. "So, I heard the guy ended up in the ICU? That's pretty *sick*. Why haven't I seen ya' in the gym? Usually, the assaults end up with us." Ryan's focus shifts from my face to my arms.

Feeling judged on strength, I stretch to disrupt his stare. His straight face shifts into a demonic grin as his thoughts must have wandered elsewhere. His eyes flit to the upper corner, like a voice from inside his head speaks to him. Trying to take advantage of his distracted state, I stand, hoping to walk away from the conversation all together.

Ryan grips my shoulder and pushes me back down. "Look here, Walker… that's your name, right…? I'm a good guy to have on your side here. I suggest you take my generous attempts at conversation… be polite and return the favor." He removes his hand from my shoulder as I sit for a second looking him in the eyes.

Was that a threat or a suggestion to help me make it in prison? His tone is so mellow and face so cheerful, I can't imagine it being a threat. Whether it's a threat or suggestion doesn't matter, I have no desire to associate myself with such a morally dark individual.

"I'm not here to make friends, nor am I proud of anything that resulted in my being here. Please let me keep to myself." I feel my response was more than civilized, but it seems to strike a nerve in Ryan. I think he's the type of guy who gets mad about everything that doesn't necessarily go his way.

Ryan stands abruptly; fists balled in anger. "Oh, so you're too good for us here, huh? You must be one of those smart guys who know the bigger picture!? Ain't none of us too good to be here, or else we wouldn't be here!" A gravel sound garbles his words. His knuckles turn white with the clenching. Shouting at me brings on a scene, which pretty much destroys my hopes of flying under the radar.

"I didn't say I'm 'too good' for anyone. I'm saying that I'm not exactly proud of what I did to end up here, no matter the reasons. That seems to be something we don't have in common. I don't want to brag about my wrongdoings." With a matter-of-fact edge to my voice, I attempt to stand and walk away once again.

"You think I'm all proud I got caught and thrown in here?! Now who's the stupid one?" Ryan's face falters to hide his hurt, scrunching in a flash. He still musters up enough faux confidence to utter a sarcastic snicker. "I didn't do anything wrong! That bitch had it coming!"

I cringe and can't help but revert my thoughts to my sister and what she had to endure. *The sights that I saw.* The anger I felt then floods back in so rapidly. I lean close enough to Ryan so he can hear me whisper to him. Clearing my throat buys me a moment to settle the steaming boil within my blood that threatens to combust.

"No one deserves what you did, and no one ever will... except maybe you...." I rebut in a grizzly tone, biting my tongue as I say it.

With the movement of inmates leaving and coming, the sound of clanking metal trays against the cold metal lunchroom tables, and the constant hum of talking, I was surprised he could catch the last comment at all. I could've barely muttered the words, or screamed them, and it wouldn't have mattered. Ryan is already hanging on every word. At this point he's looking for a reason to clean my clock. What I didn't foresee was the team of meatheads that rally around him, not even aware of the conversation, that assist in the brutal beating they assume I've earned.

I get punched once by Ryan, which knocks me to the ground. Before I can get up, three other guys beat me. I put my arms up around my head, attempting to protect myself from the fists raining down on me. I hear whistles off in the distance as the guards approach to break up the fight. Maybe fight isn't the word, as I'm on the ground, hardly even protecting myself, let alone fighting back.

When there's a pause in the punches, I remove my arms and look through the blood dripping into my swollen eyes. I see the bottom of a shoe coming down toward my face faster than I can flinch. The force of it renders me unconscious. The darkness envelopes me before I can process the pain.

I wake to the sound of distant beeping and phones ringing, my face throbbing. My hand jerks up to touch it as I wince in pain, groaning. My hand meets resistance, and the clinking of the handcuff against the metal frame of the hospital bed reminds me that I'm a prisoner.

Forcing my swollen eyes open, I glance around the hospital room through slits. It's dark, except for the IV pump, which clicks every couple of seconds. As my eyes fall on my handcuffed wrist, I see a police officer step up to the bed. He hadn't said anything yet, probably letting me come to.

"Am I in the hospital?" I ask, acknowledging his presence. He huffs as he walks back to a seat in the corner of the room.

"Yeah, some guys gave you a pretty good beatin'. The hell you do?" The police officer isn't looking at me as he speaks. He's busy flipping through a paperback book. He's curious, but not enough to get invested in a genuine conversation.

"I told a rapist that no one deserves to get raped, except him." I say in a nonchalant manner. A twinge of pain throbs in the back of my head, causing the cool temperament to melt into agony. I try again to reach my head, forgetting I had handcuffs on. My comment makes the officer put down his book and look at me.

"Hm." He pauses as he assesses me. "Here... you need pain meds." He moves to press the call button, treating me like a human being. That's not something I've experienced since I first got picked up. As he presses the call light, a nurse walks into the room.

"Look who's awake! How ya' feeling?" The nurse is quite peppy, for it being so late at night. I wince at the loud cheerfulness. She may just be pleasant, but I'm not accustomed to that these days, so it seems excessive.

"Like I got hit by a bus...." I moan slowly, squeezing my swollen eyes together. She softly giggles at my retort.

"Well, you definitely got hit." She laughs a bit harder. "But I don't think any of 'em were named bus." She pauses, waiting for the joke to land. The officer gasps.

"Oh, Lynn! That's hilarious!" He wipes tears of laughter away from his face, slapping his knee in exaggeration. She smiles at him and shrugs her shoulders before shifting her focus to me, examining my face with a light and gentle touch. I pull away as she lightly presses on different parts and shines the light in my eyes.

"Good news… you still have sensation! Any issues seeing?" Lynn asks as she types on the rolling computer. I don't respond for a second, which causes her to peer toward me. "You have very reactive pupils. I'm asking if you have blurred vision… or any other issues?" she clarifies her question.

"I can see, it's just hard to open my eyes," I respond, hoping she has some sort of remedy.

"Good! That'll go down in time. Your assessment and CT look great! You'll probably get discharged tomorrow." She smiles widely at me, as if that's good news.

Back to prison, with hardly enough eyesight to protect myself from the group that did this. A knock at the door interrupts the nurse, and an older lady peeks her head in.

"Lynn, the… umm…." The older lady looks at me and then to the police officer. It seems the police officer knows what the lady is trying to say and stands to walk to her.

"Ma'am, if you're referring to the individual that was here a bit ago, I'll handle it," he says, and she nods, disappearing from the doorway. Lynn returns to her computer, looking nervous. This makes me curious.

"So, I need to get some vitals. I could get ya' some Tylenol if you'd like?"

I nod too fast, making the pain throb more intensely, and the dizziness takes me for a spin. Within two minutes, she and her computer are out the door. Shortly after that, the police officer walks over to me and speaks in a hush.

"Listen here. As a prisoner, you're not allowed to have visitors. The hospital is very aware of that. I've heard about your case. What you walked into that got you in this mess. Now, I'm not saying what you did is right. As a father of two girls....” He pauses, shifting his weight to his heels. “One's about your sister's age... If I walked in on... I mean... If I saw what you saw.... Let's just say I'd probably have to do just as much time... if not more.” I stare into my palms, remembering the night and having some much unneeded flashbacks. He sees me zoning out. Even through the swelling and bruising on my face.

“Look, the point is your mother's here and has been sneaking this way several times throughout the evening. She's here with your sister, who's in some rough shape... Anyway... She's here trying to figure out if you're okay. Legally, I'm not allowed to say a thing. However, I could nod to imply you're okay.” I smile at the officer's kind gesture.

I bob my head. “Please? thanks.” It's good to know that my mother still cares for me.

He nods and grabs his vest, walking over to the door and opening it wide, which allows me to see my mother standing in the doorway. She's visibly exhausted. I can see that from across the room. Her hair is a mess, and she's still wearing scrubs. I'm assuming they aren't even from today. She has mascara caked under her puffy, red eyes. Either she hasn't washed her face, or she's been crying.

“Please... I know he's eighteen...but he's still my son....” She wraps her arms around herself. “What happened? He start another fight?”

Well... she's not entirely wrong. My smart mouth started this one-sided exchange.

She takes a deep breath as the police officer allows her to get out what she has to say. “Is anyone else hurt? Oh, God... did he hurt *another* person! I can't do this! I wish he knew the heartache he's causing me!”

She's sleep deprived and stressed. It still stings when she points out that I'm at fault for all her troubles. If that's the case, then why is she coming to check on me?

The officer puts up his hand to stop her from spiraling further. Once she takes another deep breath, after a few exaggerated exhales that show just how distraught she is, she levels.

"Ma'am, I can't give information regarding the inmate. I can't confirm that he was attacked, nor can I confirm or deny that he's going to be okay," the officer responds as he aggressively nods.

He goes above and beyond to give her information but manages to follow the rules. Mom begins hysterically crying. Deep down, I think she would've started crying whether I was doing good or not. *Too much stress.*

She attempts to compose herself and responds calmly, "Thank you, sir, for **not** telling me anything about this inmate. I truly appreciate it. Now, I must go to the ICU...." She raises her voice, making sure I can hear her. "I'm going to check on Karl, who's slowly doing better, while they evaluate Clara for malnutrition and psych treatment!" She backs away from the door, slowly leaving my sight.

CHAPTER TWELVE
CLARA HARRIS: TIME HEALS... KINDA

FIVE YEARS BACK

Blink. Breathe in. Blink. Breathe out. Swallow.

I can do these things without thinking, but without thoughts, these words rattle in my head.

My arms are heavy... too heavy. My eyes flicker around at my surroundings. I've been in this hospital bed for what feels like an eternity, but every time I glance around the room, it's like I've never seen it. Like I can't remember. Everything is being pushed away to a void in my brain that I can't see or feel, disappearing behind the space that was once me.

Breathe in. Blink. Breathe out.

The pain of not eating clutches my stomach, gripping growls echo in the empty minimalistic psychiatric room.

They're coming, I can hear the footsteps thudding in the hall. Two people, one much smaller than the other. *The nurse and the nurse's assistant.* The pills they're bringing me have brought back my ability to move, but not my ability to fully *remember*.

Flashes of what feels like a nightmare come and go.

Breathe out. Breathe in.

A knock causes me to flinch, which brings more aches to my frail muscles, still weak from not eating for so long. I push myself to move. If they come in and I'm too stiff, I'll get more medication. I want to come out of this fog. If I get swallowed back into the darkest parts of myself, they'll put me out again, and it will be impossible to feel connected. I already struggle every second of every day. Trying so hard to feel… to connect to my emotions… to bring back my thoughts. My biggest problem used to be fitting in with others. Now, I just want to feel like I belong to myself again.

"Hello! Good morning, how did you sleep?" Silence fills the air between the nurse and me as the nurse's assistant enters the room.

Smile. Smile! Pull muscles in face up! Must show progress! My inner thoughts scream at me as the muscles in my face burn, begging for me to stop. My eyes meet the nurse's, neck stiff as I turn my head slowly to face her. Everything moves in slow motion, which is more than the frozen existence of yesterday. My lips crease into a forced smile. The nurse's genuine smile flattens in discomfort.

"Well… you're trying to smile! That's an improvement!" The nurse's assistant had brought in a lift to help me get out of bed. My legs are still unpredictable, but I'm working on moving my toes and ankles. Progress feels more like struggling against a mountain that I can't see the top of. I can see the beginning and the end, but as I live it, the end seems to be infinitely in the distance.

Releasing the straining muscles in my face, allowing the smile to fall, feels like sitting after running a marathon.

"You have company coming in for breakfast… let's get you into the chair." The nurse and nursing assistant work together to use the lift, transferring me to the high back supportive wheelchair.

They strap me in for safety, but feeling the restraints

tightens my throat. My tongue dries as stomach acid rises in the back of my mouth. My breathing hastens. I clench my eyes shut, trying to shake the dread before it turns into a panic attack, and I wake up tomorrow from the injection they'll give me.

Breathe in. Pause. Breathe out. Pause.

Calm the storm. Breathe in.

Calm the sea. Breathe out.

The water crashes, but the cliff stands strong. Breathe in.

I'm the cliff. Breathe out.

The problems will wash over me and wash away. Breathe in.

I'll stand strong. Breath out.

As I exhale, they wheel me into the common area where we typically eat and have group therapy. Mom stands as they push the wheelchair near her chair.

"She smiled at us today," the nurse's assistant notifies Mom of the progress I'm making. Mom's grin grows into a full smile. She does it effortlessly, making me jealous that she can move her muscles without trying.

PTSD inducing catatonic depression. Fancy words for physically frozen from fear and sadness, at least, that's my take on it. Part of me is glad I can't fully remember what happened.

As they give me the medications, and I go to therapy, hearing other people's situations trigger a flood of images. Partial moments of a nightmare that seems like it's happening to someone else.

"I knew you could do this! You're amazing," Mom says, sounding endearing, but the sincerity doesn't reach her eyes.

She's emotionally destroyed and drowning. The stress radiates off her like a thick perfume. Everyone can sense it, but no one will say anything. She returns to the seat by the window, glancing out at the garden briefly before moving her focus back to me. "Well, I wanted to let you know that Karl...." Flashes of *his* face and dread wash over me, like the storm I battled moments ago.

Slow breath in. Slow breath out.

Look outside. Visualize the ocean. The waves breaking as they hit my ankles, washing over my feet. The sand squishing between my toes.

My clenching eyes worry her, and she leans in, grasping my thin shoulder. I force my eyes open wide. She sighs, relief edging her breathing to normal. "Good gracious… I know you don't like talking about… him… it won't be a problem any longer… he's… he left."

Tensing throughout my body brings about a soreness in muscles I forgot existed. "He doesn't want to be a part of our family… well, Walker's family…." Her hesitation to continue fades into silence as she looks to the window again.

Dabbing the corners of her eyes with her sleeve, she heaves a broken breath in and out. Mom hasn't been working. She's taken family medical leave from work, and pulled money from my brother and I's savings account. Having lost custodial rights, she's doing everything she can to petition the court. Not that I would be home with her in the condition that I'm in, but I've come a long way.

"Anyway, I told you about Debbie… that lady I work with whose husband is a guard at the prison… she had some updates that I thought I'd tell you." The psychiatrists insisted to Mom that talking about Walker regularly as a form of desensitization would help with the healing process.

It was bogus because I looked forward to hearing about Walker. He's the only person who knows what truly happened to me… even myself included. "Well, that Ryan guy… from the fight… he got transferred to another prison." Grabbing a bottle of water, she removed the cap and took a swig, reminding me of how dry my mouth is.

Conveniently, the nurse's aide brings over a tray of food and places it in front of me. Mom pulls the tray to her and begins mashing and cutting pieces into chewable bites. The clanking metal on ceramic is deafening in the almost empty common area. The first bite tastes bitter in my mouth, making me wish Mom started with a sip of water. She is feeding me and helping to take care of me, so I can't complain, even if I want to.

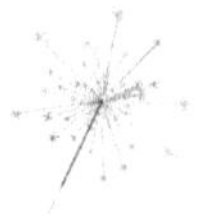

THREE YEARS BACK

"Clara. Do you agree with what Melony said?" The psychiatrist repeats himself to me, realizing that I was zoning out. Before I can gather myself to respond, he turns his focus to Mom. "With PTSD, this may occur frequently. I recommend you to thoroughly read the printout I gave you." He shifts his gaze back to me, and smiles half-heartedly.

After a long two years of living here, and Mom battling for custody, I'm being discharged.

Mom grips my hand; the excitement and relief bring tears to her eyes.

I can't talk still... *won't*. I'm not able to truly discern the difference. I'm not sure if sound would even come out if I tried. I remember... regularly. It haunts me in my sleep and when I'm not busy, which is a constant here. The only good thing about having a true mental breakdown is that when you do remember what happened, it doesn't feel like it happened to you. It's more like your memories are a cruel, sick movie of something that happened to someone else. Psychiatry calls it dissociation... I call it mercy.

The discharge process is lengthy. They do everything but put a bow on me and tuck me into the car, like Mom is going home with a new puppy. Walking still feels awkward and unsteady, and walking out of the facility is even more uncomfortable.

We make it to the car and drive back to the house that I once called my home. On the way, Mom lists all the renovations and redecorating she's done to make sure that everything looks completely different. She doesn't want to *trigger me.*

"Honey, did you hear me? I painted the living room a gray tone instead of the tan… it actually brightened up the place." Noticing I'm not interested in her remodel, she adjusts the conversation. "So… you'll continue with online school for now… and you'll have therapy daily until we can get you talking again. Things are going to be better, I promise."

This is what she does: she rains down optimism, leaving no room for anyone to have any other emotions. I nod and look out the window as we approach the house. Flashes of red and blue lights coat the house in a memory, and I swallow, compartmentalizing to the darker, hidden parts of my mind.

Entering the house, the anxiety doesn't take over like I expect. With new furniture, walls, floors, and décor, it looks unrecognizable. Mom, carrying my belongings, bustles into the house and sets everything down on the glass top coffee table. I walk into the living room space, staring at the wall above the television are pictures of Walker and I when we were much younger. My fingertips trace my brother's face, having not seen him in so long.

Mom walks up behind me. "Oh, I'm so sorry! I forgot to take those pictures down. The doctor said I should avoid anything that might trigger you in the first couple days and not even ten seconds in…." She places herself between me and the picture and removes it from the wall.

I grab the end of the picture, clutching tightly. "Clara… do you want it? It's not too upsetting?"

I shake my head violently, hoping that it doesn't reveal too many emotions and change her hesitation. She releases the picture frame into my grasp. I return it to the wall.

Mom opens the blinds, and the sound brings about memories of Walker and *him* fighting after… what happened. I spin around to see *him* standing in the living room, hands clenching his belt. A blood-curdling scream bellows, bouncing off the freshly painted walls and new hardwood floors.

Mom rushes to close the few steps between us. *He* disappears into thin air, threatening my sanity. As Mom touches my forearm, chills race up my spine. Tears stain my cheeks as my stomach twists and tightens into a viselike grip. My throat strangles the scream with a rigid, tense grip that threatens my breathing.

I race to my room, which is exactly as I remember it. Darting for the desk, I squeeze myself underneath. Bringing my knees to my chest, I wrap my arms around them. My teeth grit as I rock back and forth. My heartbeat thuds in my ears and thumps in the back of my throat.

Breathe in. Breathe out.
Breathe in. Breathe out.
Be strong. Like the cliff.
The waves will break, and I'll remain.

Chapter Thirteen
Walker Harris: Old habits die hard

ONE YEAR BACK

The chain-link fence rattles as Lenny plops himself down next to me on the hot cement, picking up a book from the pile.

Studying is my primary focus these days. Being locked up, your options for passing the time are limited. I got my GED and now I'm working on my bachelor's in business. I might as well do something useful with my time.

I continue to read as he flips through the book like a monkey discovering something new. The smell of old textbooks catches the breeze. I grab the book from him before I no longer have a copy of microeconomics.

"I'm almost done studying, then we can chat," I hesitate briefly, glancing in his direction before I bust up chuckling at my own joke. He nudges me with his elbow, which is the most communicating he does. "Why don't you talk? We've been cellmates for a few years now, what gives?" Lenny shrugs as he picks up another college textbook to flip through, avoiding my question.

"He lost his tongue running his mouth." Liam, one of Ryan's previous lackeys in the group, who's now running the gang, leans against the gate. He fidgets with an unlit cigarette between his teeth.

Squinting up at him through the sunlight, I give him my attention. His stocky build is still no match for the sun. He squats down to my level, too close for comfort, and opens his mouth wide, pointing at his own tongue. "Lenny used to talk a lot of shit, so his last roommate cut it out. Dude got transferred to Kentucky State." My eyes shoot to Lenny in shock. He shrugs again, attempting to come off calm, but his eyebrows collapse inwards. Scrunching his eyes, his hand moves to his lips. I assume he's recollecting, based on the pain contorting his face.

"That can't be true...." Disbelief raises my eyebrows as I turn back and forth between the two of them.

Liam stands back up, stretching his back while he rubs his hand along the side of his neck tattoo. He walks off, rejoining the group that is gathered off to the side. Turning to Lenny, holding out my book for me to take, my eyes soften with pity. He slowly opens his mouth to reveal that he doesn't have a tongue. I cringe without pulling my eyes away. Closing his mouth, he stands up, peering around as he stretches and adjusts the bottom of his jumper. He moves close to the doors that leads back into the prison.

Lenny was me.

I've always joked in sensitive times to help cope with the uncomfortable situations. If I would've ended up with another cellmate, I could've been in the same boat as him. I owe him for helping me navigate this culture shock. A shiver takes hold of me, like my body wants to shake away the thoughts of losing my tongue. I sigh as I resume studying for my last semester.

PRESENT

It's only been about three months since I've gotten out, and I'm still struggling to adjust to life on the outside. An inclusion program called Dismas Charities helped me get an apartment as well as a job.

While in prison, I graduated with a bachelor's in business administration, but being an ex-felon makes work difficult to come by. I got a job working on a ranch just five miles north of my apartment. My sentencing requires that I perform 260 hours of community service within a year of being released. Lucky for me, The Hope Center for Men is diagonal from Park Plaza, across the street from my apartment complex.

Monday through Friday, I walk five miles to and from work, leaving before the sun comes up to get there on time. Having a job that starts and ends early in the day makes getting in my required community service hours easier.

Daniel, the supervisor at The Hope Center for Men, is pleasant. He treats me no differently than any other volunteer there. He knows why I'm there and speaks to my parole officer frequently on my behalf, but he pretends I'm the same as the rest. With work and community service, I haven't found myself having much human interaction outside of Daniel. While in prison, I kept to myself mostly, so it isn't difficult.

The lack of definitive structure is what's made the past couple of months difficult. Also, knowing I can see my family is hard. The only court ordered restraint that I have is on Karl, who from what I know, left town.

I haven't spoken to my mom or sister in a long time. I always used to envision how that conversation would go. Now that I'm out, it's hard for me to think of what to say. I don't think my mother is eager to see me, so that has also slowed down my return. I feel shitty about leaving Clara and not coming back.

If she wanted to see me, I'm sure she would've. I'd probably trigger her after what she went through. It's better I don't see her… at least, that's what I tell myself to help me sleep at night.

I'm lost in thought as I walk to The Hope Center from work. It's hot today, making me pace myself in strides. I approach the front door of The Hope Center as Daniel steps outside.

"Hello, good to see you! It's been busy here. How's your day been?" Daniel is always friendly and genuine when asking about others. No matter how busy or overwhelmed he is, he always finds a way to slow down for others.

Even though I'm hot and tired, I can't help but muster up a smile for him. "I've had a pretty good day so far…." As I begin to tell him, a red car pulls up into the parking lot and parks at the front of the building. A thin blonde woman wearing a floral white sundress steps out of the car. Daniel's attention turns to her, and he moves for the trunk, motioning for me to follow.

"Sadie! Good to see ya'! I'm excited to hear about you graduating undergrad! Sad that this'll be your last year volunteering!" Daniel shouts as he approaches the woman.

"I know, exciting! Sorry, I won't be around much after this year! Can you give me a hand? I've got a few boxes." I'm standing off to the side of the woman who's preparing the boxes to be unloaded. Her green eyes flicker up, and she's startled by how close I am.

"Ah!" I reflexively step back.

"Oh! This is Walker, he'll be volunteering with us for about a year. He's been with us for a few months and has been very helpful," Daniel says as he reaches for a box to hand to me.

"You're fine, just startled me." Her eyes flutter from me to Daniel, who's smiling a knowing grin.

I smile at her politely, but I think I just make her feel uncomfortable since she's doesn't return the favor. I quickly grab the box from Daniel and pivot to take it in. When I come back to get more, they're approaching the front door. I hold it open for them. As the woman sits the box down on the front desk, Daniel's phone rings.

"Sadie, hold back a sec. I need to talk to you. Don't run off! This'll only take a second! Maybe you and Walker can get to know each other," Daniel says as he shuffles off down the long hall to his office.

I walk over to her, but I feel her avoiding my eye contact. The smell of body odor fumes fills the lobby area from the common room through the double doors. I scrunch my nose and shift my focus to the woman. I take a few steps toward her, the echoing of my shoes on the ceramic tile floors enunciating the silence between us.

"How are you, ma'am?" I ask her, trying to make polite conversation.

She glances toward me, pulling her focus from the pane glass windows at the entry. Then, her emerald eyes dart back to the window. I feel like we must know each other, but I can't quite place how. Then it dawns on me. She resembles Mrs. Thomas. A blonde version of her. "Ohhhh…. I know… I recognize you… Little Sadie, right? Small world. How you been?" I try to make pleasant small talk with the girl I barely know, but she's more spirited than I remember.

"I'm fine. Surprised you remember me considering you never wanted me around when we were younger," she replies with condescending hostility, catching me off guard. I remember her being so fragile and quiet. Obviously, she's grown up quite a bit, into a beautiful woman who's clearly able to defend herself.

Striving to smooth out the conversation, I apologize. "I'm sorry for excluding you… I was just a stupid boy and didn't want much to do with girls then. Not much of an excuse, but I promise I've grown up a bit." I smirk at her cute, angry face.

I'm struggling to avoid flirting with her. She's pretty and witty, and I haven't had many interactions with women since being out. The apology catches her off guard, and her eyes soften, as if she's been waiting her whole life to hear an apology from me. But when I smirk, her face tightens. She rolls her eyes, seemingly unamused with my boyish charm, proceeding down the hall to Daniel's room. I follow behind her. "Sorry for offending you…" I pause, waiting for her to respond. She doesn't, so I continue. "We're probably going to be working together… uh… maybe it'd be a good idea if… we could… bury the hatchet?"

She turns to me slowly. A lack of enthusiasm edges into her voice. Her face calms as her head kinks to the side slightly. "I don't have a hatchet… do you have a grudge that you'd like to resolve?" Her response brings a smile to my face. She either dislikes me or likes me quite a bit, but I can't discern which. As we look at each other silently, I see her self-confidence waiver.

Her eyebrows furrow and eyes dart down to the floor.

"I don't have any issues with you… if that's what you mean." I shift my weight, feet aching from walking so much. Her eyes trail up to meet mine. I smile, uncomfortable with the situation. This makes her unhappy *again*.

"Well, I'm glad we don't have issues with each other." She crosses her arms, shifting her weight to one side.

"I'm *so happy* we're on *good terms*," I say sarcastically, intending to irritate her further. She's highly volatile, probably because I didn't remember who she was. Her eyes slit as she opens her mouth to rebuke. Daniel interrupts her before she speaks.

"Sadie… I'm glad you didn't leave. I was hoping to talk to

you about your availability this summer." Daniel's eyes float between us. "Though… if you two were discussing something important, I—"

"No, we're done with whatever *this* is," she snaps, her blazing green eyes meet mine. I haven't had much to look forward to lately, but her coming to volunteer here has piqued my interest.

Chapter Fourteen
Sadie Thomas: Let the childish games begin

ONE YEAR BACK

I dig through my bag for my phone. Once I find it in the mess, I text Garrett while I walk out of the campus library.

Another late study session where I couldn't get everything done that I wanted to.

> Hey, can't come home this weekend. Didn't get my paper done. Sorry.

Send. Hitting the side button to bring up the lock screen and I place it into my backpack pocket, hardly making it to the bottom step before my phone rings.

"Hello?" I answer, acting like I don't know who's calling or why.

"Babe… this is the third raincheck in a row. Come home and write your paper here," he pleads, sounding genuinely sad. I hesitate, considering, but know that the library has many more resources, and I'd be losing work time on the long drive home.

"I can't afford to lose study time to driving."

"I drove there last time. We agreed to take turns. You keep

canceling." His tone is calm, but his words are accusatory. I sigh, knowing he's right, but it comes off more disappointed than defeated. "Seriously? Is my love annoying you?" I roll my eyes at his guilt tactic.

"That's ridiculous...." I say, but truly he isn't far off.

We've been together since my first summer break from college. In the beginning, his love was intoxicating, and I used to look forward to the phone calls. As months turn into years, the constant need to be in two places at once feels... smothering. Like I have to breathe shallow in conversation, or he might leave.

He says he loves me, but every time we talk, his needs take center stage. I *need to see you more.* I *need you to call more.* I *need you to be around more. I... I... I... more... more... more.* The common theme is my needs don't matter, and he wants more from me.

"Is it? You've been annoyed every time we talk."

Taking everything in me not to huff, I stop walking. Pinching the bridge of my nose, I hold my breath to process my response.

"I'm just stressed. I'm so close to graduating. It's just overwhelming me. I'm sorry." But I'm not sorry, I just want this almost-argument to be over.

"So... you're not coming?" He phrases it like a question, but he pitches his words like a statement.

"No." I attempt to sound sad, but I edge into annoyed. He huffs in disappointment.

"I took off work because you were coming... I want to see you so badly. I miss you." As the conversation turns lecture, I proceed to walk to my dorm.

He drones on about his limited PTO days and how he traded shifts with someone so he could have this time off. I jangle my keys as I shift my bag on my shoulder to unlock the door. Before I can fully open the door, a force pulls it open from the side.

I stumble into my room, crashing into a shadowy figure. The familiar smell of vanilla and tobacco fills my nose, and my body melts into his, knowing exactly who embraces me.

"You really thought I'd expect you to come home with everything you have going on?" He places his hand on the small of my back, pressing me further into him.

His lips gently caress my forehead; a warm breath tickles my skin. The weight of stress surrenders to calm, even breaths. My shoulders drop as a sigh of relief heaves outwards. Long distance plays tricks on my mind, making me dislike him... or at least that's what I hope is true. I slip into my safe space, surrounded by him, wondering if I love him, or if it's just the first time I'm loved by someone else for being myself.

PRESENT

Flipping my blinker on, I brake as I near the turn. I plan to meet Garret for an early dinner, but I have to drop off some donated items to the men's shelter that I volunteer at every summer. Garrett and I are discussing his moving closer to my school, where we'll get an apartment together.

I passed my entrance exam, and I've been accepted into the medical program at Johns Hopkins. We've discussed getting a place together in the past, but this summer, I plan to make it official. I pull into the near empty parking lot, putting the car in park.

Leaning over into the passenger seat to grab my purse, movement catches my attention. Involuntarily, my eyes jut in that direction.

It's hard to believe that he's so different, yet somehow, the *same*. Walker Harris stands outside the entry of The Hope Center talking to Daniel, the supervisor. Instantly, my childhood feelings of inadequacy and seclusion rush in, and anxiety builds, putting a lump in my throat.

I haven't seen him since I was young, and yet, I still have waves of anxiety wash over me. *We're both older... much older. He won't recognize me.* I know that won't be true. Of course he'll recognize me. I'm a clone of my mother, just like he's a clone of his father.

I shake my head, trying to dismiss the internal running dialogue. Forcing one foot in front of the other, I move to the trunk, avoiding looking at him. With my head in the trunk, I hear Daniel calling to me.

"Sadie! Good to see ya'! I'm excited to hear about you graduating undergrad! Sad that this'll be your last year volunteering'!" Daniel's voice grows louder as he walks toward me.

"I know, exciting! Sorry, I won't be around much after this year! Can you give me a hand? I've got a few boxes." I lift my head to see Walker following behind Daniel, who watches me pull the boxes forward in my trunk. When I turn, I'm startled by how close he is. "Ah!"

"Oh! This is Walker, he'll be volunteering with us for about a year. He's been with us for a few months and has been helpful," Daniel says as he reaches for a box to hand it off. Walker smiles at me. Not the smile I'm accustomed to seeing from him. Not the boyish grin, but a polite and quaint, distant-looking smirk. He quickly grabs the box and turns to take it inside.

I peer down at the box that Daniel pulls from my hands. "You're fine, just startled me." My eyes drag from staring at Walker to Daniel. He follows my line of sight, seeing that I'm watching him intently. Daniel smiles a knowing grin.

"Well, I haven't really told Walker about you, but it seems you guys will do just fine getting acquainted?" Daniel says, holding back giggles. I smile politely at him and bump my arm into him.

"Excuse you, I'm a happily taken woman. Besides… I know Walker. That's why I'm surprised. We kind of grew up together." I grab the last box.

Shutting the car trunk, I stride to the front door. Walker hurries out to hold the door open for us. As I sit the box down on the front entry desk, Daniel's phone rings.

"Sadie, hold back a sec. I need to talk to you. Don't run off! This'll only take a second! Maybe you and Walker can get to know each other." Walker glances between Daniel and me. Daniel answers the phone, scurrying off down the long hall.

Walker moves closer to me, his eyes meeting mine hesitantly. "How are you, ma'am?" He asks politely. His voice is so deep, resonating in the quiet room.

It's strange seeing Walker and hearing such an *adult* voice. Realization hits him. "Ohhhh… I know! I recognize you… little Sadie, right? Small world. How you been?" He's pleasant, which catches me off guard. He isn't the same little bratty boy that I remember, but it's hard not to remember him in that light.

"I'm fine. Surprised you remember me considering you never wanted me around when we were younger," I reply with too much hostility behind my voice.

He takes a step back. Seeing him so pleasant in conversation makes me angry. It's like all those years of treating me poorly never happened; like it's all in my head. Rage boils beneath my skin, fueled with an anxious energy that makes me combustible. The rational part of me knows he simply outgrew his immaturity. My brain tells me to stop feeling *feelings*… but there's the little girl that's buried deep inside, screaming with pent up resentment and hatred for being bullied.

"I'm sorry for excluding you… I was just a stupid boy and didn't want much to do with girls then. Not much of an excuse, but I promise I've grown up a bit." He smirks at me, minimizing the apology I was originally open to.

I actually thought he was different, but he's just a wolf in sheep's clothing. I roll my eyes at his smirks and move over to the long hall that Daniel scurried down. I stop just short of Daniel's office. He's still on the phone.

Walker follows me down the hall, looking to trick me into believing he's changed. I understand we're sort of stuck together in volunteering here and the desire to act civil. It feels like he's mocking what he put me through. The teasing, the exclusion, and of *course*, the awful comments that made me feel unwanted. I already struggled with those feelings within my family; I didn't need another person adding reason to feel that way.

"Sorry for offending you." He pauses, waiting for me to turn to him before he continues. "We're probably going to be working together... uh... maybe it'd be a good idea if... we could... bury the hatchet?"

There it is... the reason he's apologizing isn't that he genuinely feels sorry. It's because he doesn't want waves at his volunteer job. He doesn't want me to make him uncomfortable. This is about him. I'm tired of everyone around me only being concerned about how something affects them... no matter the cost to me. I compose myself, straightening and softening my face against its will. I paint a fake smile on, attempting to force a customer service grin to appear genuine.

"I don't have a hatchet... do you have a grudge that you'd like to resolve?" I ask nonchalantly, attempting to bury the hostility and swallow the feelings of hurt and anxiety that still circulate. I turn away from him after the brief silence.

"I don't have any issues with you... if that's what you mean," he says, sounding confused. He shifts his weight impatiently, visibly uncomfortable.

My retort caught him off guard, which makes me feel prideful. Then he smiles at me, and the pride leeches away. My smile falls, annoyed at the lack of gratification from this reunion.. In my mind, he would tell me how sorry he was and how much he wanted to be with me. I would look him in the eyes and tell him *not a chance in hell*. After that, he would feel the pain that I felt as a child…the icy sting of rejection. This isn't living up to the vision I had built up in my head.

"Well, I'm glad we don't have issues with each other." I cross my arms and shift my weight to one hip, meeting his eyes as I say it. His head cocks to one side with the corner of his lip twitching upwards, a sparkle of happiness glimmering in his cerulean eyes.

"I'm *so happy* we're on *good terms*," he says, smile stretching wide. The sarcasm wasn't subtle like before; this sentence seeped with it.

My frustration rises back to explosive as his sarcastic, witty retorts bruise my self-esteem. I grit my teeth, exhaling through a clenched jaw. My fists ball, attempting to hold back the emotions building. My mouth rushes open to respond, but Daniel opens his office door to see both of us standing in the hallway.

"Sadie… I'm glad you didn't leave. I was hoping to talk to you about your availability this summer." Daniel's eyes dart between the two of us; my hostility in contrast to his cheerful, sarcastic smile. "Though… if you two were discussing something important, I—"

"No, we're done with whatever *this* is," I interrupt abrasively.

Both Daniel and Walker snicker quietly at my discomfort. Daniel takes a step back, allowing me inside his office. I sigh a breath of reprieve at being able to escape the confrontation that is *Walker Harris*.

CHAPTER FIFTEEN
SADIE THOMAS: PARKED PLANS

Garrett walks into The Hope Center before Daniel finishes discussing the summer's plans with me. Off in the distance, I can hear Garrett talking to Walker but it's not clear enough to distinguish what they're saying. I will admit, with Walker just recently acting sarcastically flirty with me, I'm uncomfortable with the two of them conversing.

Daniel's telling me about a few job fairs he plans to host, and some food donation locations that we'll need to have pickups done—things that I usually coordinate with him to lighten his responsibilities. You can tell that Daniel appreciates summers, because he has some extra hands to help around the center, which allows him to be home with his family more.

As Daniel rattles off the dates, I take note of them in my phone calendar. We set up a schedule for me to come in during the morning to help open, take in the donations left outside and ready the cafeteria for the first food rush. Once the first food rush is done, I'm free until the evening rush, which allows me some time to study or run errands. I shake Daniel's hand as we stand to leave his office. "I look forward to helping out this summer." I smile at him, and he nods.

"I'm so glad you chose to come back! Between you and Walker, I wonder if I'll have anything for me to do." He chuckles, acting like he doesn't keep the place together and running smoothly. As he attempts to follow me out of his office, the landline rings. He turns to look at the phone, and then back to me. "I'm sorry, I'd walk you out, but...." He glances back at the phone. I smile, acknowledging his intention and bow my head in acceptance.

I show myself out. Garrett and Walker stand at the end of the hall in the entryway next to the front desk. Both shift their focus to me at the sound of the office door closing.

Garrett's face lights up as he runs to me, ecstatic to embrace me in a warm and loving hug. "Oh, jeez... I didn't realize how much I missed you till I felt you in my arms." He inhales softly; his face pressed to the top of my head. "You tired?" The distance that had grown over the past semester melts away, making it feel like we're never apart. He squeezes tighter, sensing my whole body relax. My safest place—where I'm not required to be something great. He loves me either way.

"I was tired... until I saw you." I can hear my smile in my voice. He tries to move away, but I grip him a bit tighter for a second or two longer.

He giggles softly into my ear as I pull away. "I'm so glad you're back," he mutters under a huffed sigh. He tucks a strand of my hair behind my ear. "Ready to go get food? Or do you have more to do? I can help... took the evening off." He smiles at me as he offers.

"No, I'll be back tomorrow. Let's go eat, I'm starving! Skipped lunch and snacked on the road." I say as I grab his hand and pull him toward the door. Garrett pulls back a bit to pause and turn to Walker.

"It's nice to see you again... under better circumstances. It's good to see you're doing well." Walker nods politely.

This piques my interest; *Garrett and Walker know each other.*

We walk to my car, because he brought his patrol car to the center. He opens the passenger door for me before proceeding to the driver's side. I want to ask how they know each other... but I also don't want to talk about Walker. We have so many other things to catch up on, and Walker will be last. I'll bury that question for another day.

A few hours pass, and the re-connecting comes naturally. We're back to joking about random things that don't truly matter and the ability to create conversation out of thin air seems effortless once again.

We spent the past year almost exclusively apart, but it no longer has any weight. The way Garrett looks at me with such longing in his slate-gray eyes causes my stomach to flip. His heavy eyes force me to buckle, like I did when we first met. But now... this is *different*; there's weight to the silence. A pressure that's ready to break. He sighs as he puts the car in park outside The Hope Center. It's quiet for the first time, the sound of the engine humming emphasizes the silence. An unspoken conversation builds tension in the air.

The yearning for him is hard to explain. I can't find words to describe it, especially having never experienced what I'm wanting. A tingling sensation vibrates beneath my skin, spreading throughout my body.

Sure, we've attempted in the past—always running into roadblocks, inhibiting us from successfully achieving that level of intimacy. It doesn't help that I'm a virgin and have been very hesitant. We've had time alone, but it rarely lasts long.

It's unfortunate, really. I mean truly, how many virgin college graduates do you know? My guess is probably zero.

I peer up from my nervously twiddling thumbs to find Garrett staring at me for who knows how long. He sighs once again and pulls his eyes toward the steering wheel. I open my mouth to talk but can't form words. Tonight... it was so perfect. I can't imagine following it up with *Hey, wanna go back to my place to finally do the deed?*

He appears nervous—being with him for so long, I can sense it. What could he possibly be nervous about? I certainly won't be his first experience with a woman. Maybe it's because his feelings are strong; at least, I think they are.

"I missed you so much... I'm happy you're finally back." Garrett breaks the silence with an audibly sharp and forced exhale.

I grin at him sheepishly, gulping as my stomach flips and heart pounds in my throat. Turning away nervously to look out the window, I shift in the seat. He grabs my hand quickly, catching my attention. I clench my hand reflexively and hesitantly rotate back to him. My eyes drag up his arm to meet his stare.

The silence cuts into me, the depravity of sound adding to the insurmountable tension. I don't know how to end the ache; the desperation for him is *excruciating*. A strong, lustful hunger pools in his graphite eyes. My throat tightens, and cheeks flush.

"Garrett...." I pause, trying to catch my breath after holding it in the heat of the moment. The air between us thickens, not just with lust, but with the weight of unspoken words. I can't help but feel both nervous and excited; *is this the moment we'll finally cross the line?*

He takes the opportunity to lean into me hastily and press his mouth to mine. His lips part as his tongue slips out. He traces my bottom lip with the tip of his tongue, my lips part slightly. We fuse together, and he embraces the back of my head. Gripping a large cluster of my hair, he interlaces his fingers in the strands. My arms wrap around his neck tightly, pressing my peaked breasts into him.

The intensity grows as we're intertwined in the front seat of my car. His free hand slips up my thigh, climbing steadily between my legs. I'm ready for him, so there's little need for preparation.

I pull away slightly to moan gently in an exhale on his lips. His hand gripping my hair pulls back to expose my neck. I don't resist as he kisses the crook of my neck, leading down to the top of my breast that's exposed in the sweetheart neckline of my sundress. The gasp I release intensifies and the kisses migrate lower, his hand climbing higher. His fingers reach the crease of my leg, where my underwear lay soaked from excitement.

He groans deeply at my wetness for him. His kissing grows more frantic as his fingers trace my flesh through the thin layer of fabric. My breath heaves as my hands move to wrap my fingers in his curly, charcoal hair. His face now pressed to my chest, beard scratching my skin as he kisses between my breasts.

One finger moves to the edge of my underwear, moving it to one side. Time moves so slow… like he's dragging out the minute to exaggerate the pleasure he's anticipating. Either that… or… he's taunting me.

At this point, we're both in the passenger seat. My head presses against the passenger window, and he kneels over me, one knee positioned between my sprawled legs with the other pushing against the dash. The other is stretching toward the back, with my calf resting on top the driver's. He unbuckles his pants, releasing the pressure his zipper places on his growing bulge. As he slips his fingers beneath, my phone rings. His kissing pauses as he raises his eyes to mine. Frozen, awaiting my response.

My eyes meet his, my ragged breathing steadying out.

"Ignore it," I say.

With my hands on the back of his head, I push him back to

where he once was. My dress is shifted down, with my breasts almost completely exposed. I release the back of his head and shimmy the top of my sundress down under my breasts, revealing my perky nipples.

Stunned for a moment, he slowly lowers his head back down and takes a nipple into his mouth, tracing around the tip with his tongue. I arch my back into him as he bites down playfully and pulls back on my nipple, only to take the other up into his mouth. His hand that once held my hair now clutches the small of my back, the fingers of his other hand returning to my now exposed flesh.

I let out a loud gasp as he plunges one finger inside of me with no warning. I look down to him. With my nipple in his mouth, he smirks mischievously up at me. He drags his finger back only to return it.

My head sinks back uncontrollably at the pleasure he's releasing within me. He drops my nipple and begins kissing toward my mouth. Hot breath falls over my lips when my phone rings again.

We both stop, silently panting, listening to my phone roll over to voicemail again. We're about to resume when his phone begins to ring.

I huff and pull away, almost knocking him into the dash unintentionally. The sexual frustration peaks to an all-time high. He grudgingly pulls away with a sulk. Grabbing his phone out of the driver-side door, he brings it to his face, the light emitting enough glow that I can see the frustration smeared across his face.

"It's Diane. She's texted and left a voicemail." I find it funny that Garrett calls her by her first name, like I do.

I huff again and retrieve my phone from the middle console of the car. Sure enough, she's left several voicemails on my phone and texted more than a dozen times. I can't imagine what she needs at this time of the night, but I'm certain that it's not important enough to interrupt this.

"Ugh, I'll call her. She won't stop till I do." I pull her up in the contacts of my phone with one hand as I readjust my sundress to cover my breasts and fix my undergarments back into place. Diane answers on the first ring, as if she was staring at the phone awaiting my call.

"Where are you!? I've called so many times! I even called Garrett trying to get ahold of you…." The heavy breathing and panic seeps into her voice shifts my annoyance into hyper-awareness. She pauses just long enough to settle her breathing and force composure into her voice. "Something's happened. You need to be home. *Now*. I'll explain more when you get here. Please, hurry home." *Click*. She hangs up without allowing me to ask a single question.

CHAPTER SIXTEEN
CLARA HARRIS: FEELS LIKE YESTERDAY

**Trigger Warning: Chapter contains severe depressive
descriptions and suicidal ideations
PRESENT**

umb. I stand in my room, utterly alone with my thoughts. No matter how hard I try, I can't *feel.* Seven years have come and gone, yet I still feel his sweaty breath on my face. *I'm so tainted.*

Anytime I start to sense emotions come to the surface... memories flood, like pictures flashing behind my eyes. I begin to break down the wall I have so diligently built, hoping to move on in life... and the unresolved experiences of that day rush back. It's easier, truly, at this point to avoid feeling anything at all.

After seven years, no one cares about the little girl who witnessed her brother nearly murder some guy her mom was dating. If they knew why, they wouldn't care either. What's the point in talking when no one cares to listen?

I've never said out loud what *he* did to me—the cataclysm that occurred. The guilt of not confessing *his* crimes against me hangs over my head. The guilt of silence is heavier than anything I can carry on my shoulders. What should have been said, what was never said–it suffocates me in ways that no one else can understand.

It's not only my life that's been drastically affected by my silence… but my brothers. Walker has always been there for me, all my life. He's so much more than a big brother. Walker accepted so many roles with no complaint, and he was always the person to turn to when something went wrong. He was the first person I wanted to tell when something went right. I talk about him in past tense because my mother mourned and moved on ages ago, even though he's still very alive. I'm not allowed to mention him. If I do, she brings *him* up, immediately triggering memories that are better left unsettled and buried deep.

Here it is… the middle of June, and we're still attending school. Snow days pushed back the last day of school. Unfortunately, I also have to attend summer school this year, thanks to a not-so-kind English teacher. *Someone needs to knock her off her high horse.* Summer school doesn't start for a few weeks though, so at least I get to have a brief break from being secluded in a sea of *peers.*

"It's time to get up for school! The bus will be here any minute!" Mom shouts from down the hall in the kitchen, letting me know that she just got in from work.

She has cut back hours at the hospital, so she'd be home more; breaking through the walls that I eloquently hide behind. Sometimes… I'm able to pretend I'm okay. I can pretend well enough that Mom will comment on how "perfect" things are turning out. If she only knew the inner struggle that I battle every day.

I'm tired of hurting myself to feel something, anything at this point. It's better than nothing. Hidden beneath my pants so that no one will ever see, unless… unless *it* happens again. If it happens again, they will see… see that no matter what they do… no matter how much they try… no one can hurt me anymore. I will never be vulnerable again.

"Clara, I said it's time to…." Mom says as she barges into my room. "Oh! You're awake."

I attempt to look startled and annoyed by her abrupt entrance into my room. That's how a regular teenager who feels their emotions would respond… *right?*

"You gotta be shitting me! You can't just barge in! Privacy! This is *MY* space. Remember what Dr. Hirschire said?" I ask rhetorically.

She's beyond knowledgeable about what my psychiatrist says about everything. *He* left her, Walker got sent to prison, and I was admitted to the loony bin. With all this trauma, Mom makes her entire personality about my healing and mental state. If it were a possibility to force a person back to normal, I'd be giggling with all the other gushy-eyed fifteen-year-old girls in my school.

Mom takes a step back, visibly giving me the space I requested. "I'm sorry. Just as I think things are back to normal… I'm yanked back to reality." She fidgets with the doorknob, standing just outside my room. "I know I'm supposed to give you space. I understand. It's a *trigger*. I don't want to bring back anything."

I roll my eyes without any regard for Mom seeing it. I don't see how she doesn't see it. Not to mention… saying *trigger* and not wanting to *bring back anything*… it'll definitely bring something back. Luckily enough for her, I'm already pondering these thoughts. Suffocating them isn't difficult to do.

I force a smile to reassure her. She doesn't deserve to dwell in the past, where I exist. I'm frozen in time, mentally running away from something that's long since passed. It's exhausting, and I don't want to push my mother into that cycle.

If she knew what *he* did, she'd inevitably blame herself. She tries so incredibly hard to better her life, she doesn't need me weighing on her head. Although it's her job to protect me, she didn't know better. I want to fully push her away, because the weight of everything I can't say is suffocating in this false normal.

Walker was always the one who protected me. I can still remember the way he would carry me to my bed if I fell asleep and tuck me in safely. His arms would cradle me gently. That immense security seems like a distant dream now, something that was ripped from me. Walker tried to protect me… he did as much as he could.

I gulp with my inner thoughts walking that fine line of *'too much'*. I catch Mom glancing at me, and I smirk at her in a light-hearted way, an attempt to reassure her further. I spend most of my time convincing others that I'm not the shattered little girl I remain, forever frozen at ten.

She stops pretending to fold the clothes that sit on top of my dresser haphazardly and puts the shirt down. She shifts to me, seeming to consider touching me for a brief second. I flinch in anticipation of the touch, which stops her in her tracks. She reluctantly pulls her hand back.

"I'm sorry for lashing out. I shouldn't… I was just thinking about Walker and lost in thought. You startled me… you didn't scare me." The sound of his name makes her wince. She always functions better when she's pretending that he's dead. Her reaction starts me on the forbidden conversation. "You know he's still out there. He should be out by now."

She interrupts me, "You don't need to worry about that, he's not coming back. He's not allowed within 100 feet of Karl. He probably thinks that he's still around. I'd be hard pressed to believe he even wants to return. Don't worry about him, love," she says in a *'this conversation is over'* type voice and walks out of the room. I try to shrug off the tense conversation and prepare for a long day at school.

After a long tedious morning of mundane end-of-year topics that our classes prepared to occupy us. Most of our class gather in the cafeteria at the front of school for lunch. Some of us are mindlessly moving toward the smell of pizza like zombies. The rest are over-enthusiastically messing around.

Out of the corner of my eye, behind the glass windows that blocks off the main office from the noisy crowds of high school teenagers, stands Walker. He's laughing as he converses with the office secretary. I freeze in place, staring at him. I'm almost *certain* that it's not actually Walker, and I have lost the last bit of my mind. I struggle between disbelief and longing. *Is he real or a figment of my fractured mind?*

I cautiously take three steps toward the office door, just in case he truly isn't real. I swing the door open, catching the attention of everyone in the room, including Walker. We stand, staring at each other, studying one another. He takes a tiny step forward, stopping himself before finalizing the step. He's wanting to give me space and time to consider whether I want to scream at him or endear him.

I rush forward, hugging him around the waist, tears begin to flow as I sob into my long-lost big brother. *The man who saved me from the monster.* The only person who truly knew me and what all I endured. As I heave all emotions and longing to be myself into hugging him, he clasps his arms around me. Hugging me back he whispers in my ear, "I will never leave you again, Clara. I promise you're safe with me as long as I breathe." The sincerity in his voice makes my heart clench in my chest.

I don't know what to say. The words are stuck in my throat, but somehow "I missed you" is the only thing I can get out. My voice shakes with a violent tremble, tears flowing uncontrollably.

For the first time in who knows how long, I feel something.

CHAPTER SEVENTEEN
SADIE THOMAS: NOT SO FALSE ALARMS

"Babe… Diane sounds frantic. Something's really wrong. We should go… even though…." He traces the top of my thigh with his fingertips, entranced. If that were the case, why is he pushing so hard for us to rush home? He shakes his head, trying to pull himself out of it.

"It's Diane… she's probably panicking over something that went wrong with the Fourth of July party. She always freaks over nothing. We can take our time." I lean in to kiss him, hoping to light the fire again.

He puts his hand out to stop me from coming in, shaking his head firmly. He's decided on his own that we're leaving now.

All I can think about the entire way home is how much of an inconvenience Diane is tonight. She's done this sort of thing so many times in the past. Her party planning always has some sort of catastrophe that we all have to drop what we're doing, or *who* in this case, and come to the rescue.

As we arrive at the house, the sound of my mother shouting echoes through the front door. I glance to Garrett in a panic. Opening the door to a dark house contrasts the fluster of Diane shuffling throughout the house, phone in hand.

A heavy, cold shift in the air makes my skin tingle as I enter. Diane frantically races around with random personal effects of my father in her arms. She's shouting about some event that'll have to be postponed for now. She keeps saying '*Richard's in the hospital*' so nonchalantly. *She always does this.* Focusing on the smaller problems and dissociating from the bigger ones.

Hearing that Dad's in the hospital makes my stomach lurch into my throat. When we were in the car, I dismissed the call as another one of Diane's overblown emergencies—something about the wrong-colored napkins or seating arrangement snafu.

The guilt of wanting to continue and ignore her washes over me like cold, violent ocean waves. My throat collapses, and my mouth turns dry. I realize that this isn't just another family drama; *this is real.* When she says the word *hospital,* my muscles go rigid. The flushing creeps to my cheeks and down my neck into my chest. I almost collapse, taking one stumbling step to stabilize myself. Garrett wraps one arm around my lower back.

My mother, in between breaths of rage, catches a glance of us in the foyer. "Oh, thank God! You're *finally* here! I thought you would've gotten here sooner!" She was mid-sentence when she hangs up the phone, shifting her focus to us. "Garrett, go look in Richard's office for the living will. You know how disorganized he is… I'm sure it's buried somewhere." Her off-distance stare draws our attention to how disheveled she looks… unhinged even.

Diane's hands tremble slightly, clutching the bag of clothes. Her jaw clenches, forcing the shakes away. She stands straighter upon feeling the quiet gaze on her, running her hands over her dress while taking a deep breath. Her hands move to her hair to check the status of her usually meticulous style. Taking another slow deep breath, she sighs.

She turns her attention to the two of us, still standing there observing her mismatched emotions and appearance. She's hyper-fixating on tasks to ease the anxiety that she's burying.

"What are you two standing around for? Your father is in surgery as we speak." Diane's masking nervousness behind a veneer of impatience.

"Surgery?" My voice hitches at the end. The word *surgery* grabs my throat and punches me in the gut. I've never been abused with a single word like this before.

My body freezes, the world blurring around me. Diane sees the confusion on my face and comes to the realization that I'm in the dark about what's happening. I wait in the silence for her to explain. She huffs, annoyed that she's wasting time to catch me up.

"Well… if you were home with the family instead of out with your *friend,* then *maybe* you'd know." With her sharp words, she cuts through my disorientated state.

It's difficult to have a conversation with Diane on a normal day and nearly impossible in her current state. She sighs again. "Richard felt lightheaded most of the afternoon. He said something about feeling short of breath… but I didn't think much of it considering we played doubles with Charlene and her *rotund* husband, Marcus. What she sees in that man I will never know…." Diane retraces her day. She's less informing us and more trying to calculate where everything went wrong. What cues she should've picked up on.

"Mom," I quietly state, annoyed but attempting to steer her back to the reason for the conversation. Pausing to find where she's heading, she shifts in her high heels.

"They took him to surgery. The doctor believes there's some sort of blockage that needs opened," she states it so plainly, like she rehearsed it. "I'm trying to gather some of his belongings to make him more comfortable. I've been here too long already. I'm sure he's recovering now…." She scurries off to get a bag for his clothes.

I stand there for a moment, watching Diane leave in a swirl of annoyance and desperation. Garrett's eyes burn into me, his expression unreadable. I can't shake the feeling that something is off, but I don't have time to dwell on it; I have to help. His eyes sympathetically study me.

"I'm going to go find the will." Garrett starts down the hall to the office, grabbing my hand. He stops, turning back to face me. I hesitate a moment to try to gather myself.

My father is the one parent I'm close to. I can't lose him like this. He has so much to be around for still. I shudder, shoving the thoughts from my mind. He's alive and being taken care of right now. That's what I need to focus on.

"I know exactly where it is. You should help my mom. She seems... *unsettled*. I don't handle her well when we're both emotional." I release his hand and begin down the hall to my father's safe.

He's always been a prepared analytical man. He had me memorize where these things were and how to get to them. I remember what he told me, all those years ago.

Sweet Girl, your mother is so emotional. You're like me. We're strong and think before we feel. It's important... if something happens to me... It's important someone I trust can handle financial and legal affairs.

I never thought about the day I would have to collect this, nor did I expect it to be so soon.

Entering his office, the one place that was so definitively his, now seems unfamiliar and frigid. The dark leather chair behind his desk, where he spends most of his free time working or helping me learn to manage life's complexities, is now an empty symbol of what I stand to lose. The heaviness stifles my breath, as I choke back tears and approach the safe.

My mother said that the surgery should be done by now, but wouldn't they call to let her know the outcome? Is it taking longer than expected? Did something go wrong? I open the heavy safe door, revealing folders of papers and envelopes of cash. I retrieve the will from the designated folder and hasten out of my father's office. Feeling the depravity of his presence within his haven pings a sharp pain in my chest.

As I enter the hall, I see Garrett hugging Diane. It looks like he's comforting her, inaudibly speaking to her endearingly. As I stroll up, Diane spots me and straightens. She pushes Garrett away, acting caught in a compromising position. In contempt she gives a snarky jab. "I don't need reassurance from *someone* whose income is paid from *my* taxes. Don't touch me again." She exits out the front door, bag in hand, and drives off.

Garrett shrugs at me. "I was just trying to make her feel better. I didn't know how to help her. She's a mess." There's something off in his quickened explanation, like he's anxious. Maybe it's just the situation. I nod, not wanting to delve into this further; I need to get to Dad.

Garrett's eyes peer down to my hands. My eyes follow and flick back up to his. With a sigh, I walk to the door. "Let's go, I want to see him… I need to know he's okay."

Garrett lets me out at the door and parks the car. I don't wait for him as I follow the receptionist to the recovery rooms of the emergency department. The smell of astringent stings my nose as I inhale. The fluorescent lights and loud bustling hospital are a stark difference from the dark, silent car.

The beeping machine tells me that Dad made it through the surgery and is okay. A smile spreads on my face, without even seeing him yet. I don't know what I expected. My grin drops when I step into his room. He's such a powerful and strong figure in my mind. Seeing his pallor face with darkened circles rimming his eyes and wearing a hospital gown in a bed weakens him.

Although he's alive, he's nowhere to be seen. Not the man that I've been raised by. My eyebrows fall, caving in as I acknowledge that he's truly not invincible. I'm so focused on my father that I don't notice the doctor standing at the bedside talking to Diane.

"His LAD was 100% occluded. In the cath lab during the procedure, we placed three stents to open the artery. Everything went well, but with the significant hit his heart took, its best he stays overnight." He releases the top paper, letting it fall back to the clipboard. He shifts in his stance, placing the clipboard under his arm. "All things considered, he's doing really well. We'll start him on blood thinners and get him set up to talk to our heart clinic and discuss lifestyle changes." Diane begins to sob at the good news. She flips her head from the doctor to Dad.

"You can't leave me like this! I *need* you." Her voice cracks as she sucks in a stabbing breath and pulls a tissue out of her purse to dab at her eyes. She enunciates each word as she insists that Dad stays.

I've never seen her this vulnerable. The weight of the fear, uncertainty, and confusion I've been carrying for the past few hours slips away. My knees buckle, hands trembling, and for the first time since arriving at the house, I can breathe again.

CHAPTER EIGHTEEN
WALKER HARRIS: I MISSED YOU

Walking to the shelter from work during the summer is probably my least favorite part of the day. The summer heat is edging in. At midday, the sun is unavoidable. Ranchers like to start their day before the sun comes up to beat the heat.

Living in Kentucky, home of the famous Kentucky Derby, horse ranches are common and constantly looking for help. I'm saving for a car, but trying to have enough will power *not* to buy one until it starts to cool down. Until then, walking is my main mode of transportation.

As I prepare to cross the paved road a little less than two miles away from the shelter, Sadie's car comes to a stop.

She rolls her window down. "Good *God* Walker, you look pathetic. Get in if you want a ride."

I smirk at her. She's been excessively rude to me, covering up the fact that I'm growing on her. She sees I'm smiling and rolls her eyes. As I reach for the handle, she lets her foot off the brake and the car jolts forward a few feet. My hand slips from the door handle and she laughs, "I'm just kidding! *Goodness*! I won't do it again… promise." She puts the car in park and her hands up to show she's innocent.

I open the door, kicking my work boots on the side of the car to get excess dirt off, before I slide in. "Well Miss Thomas, I do believe you're supposed to be at the shelter already. Why you running so late?" I half-smirk at her as she huffs and rolls her eyes again.

"I went to the shelter already. Daniel sent me to pick up donations. I've got one more stop… I saw you looking so bored… so I figured you can help." She shoots me an exaggerated smile and puts the car into drive.

I chuckle under my breath and her smile lingers longer than usual, eyes softening. I wonder if she knows how much I cherish these moments with her.

"So… you just want to spend more time with me? Jeez… if you want a date just ask." I laugh again, running my fingers through my hair.

I need a haircut; it's too hot to have it touch the back of my neck. She sneers at me, not finding my humor funny today.

"Trust me, Mr. Harris, that's not something of concern." She nudges me playfully in the arm when I pretend to cry at her response. "Oh, shut it!" She laughs as I rub my arm, acting like it hurt.

I don't know if it's the heat of June or simply her company, but I'm disoriented. I normally run from any sign of relationships, but she's different. Maybe it's because she's in a steady relationship, making her unattainable, but talking comes easy.

Seems odd, considering *how* we talk.

"You think I want to end up like all your jailhouse lovers?!" she jokes, faking a gag. I laugh and shove her playfully.

"I told you that in confidence!" I joke back, knowing damn well I didn't have a *jailhouse lover*.

The memories of being in prison flood in along with the uncomfortable silence, swallowed by the humming of the engine. I force a grin through the discomfort of the memory. I don't want to talk about my time in prison. She found out overhearing Daniel and I talk about community service hours.

"We're going to your old high school," she says.

This pulls my attention from prison to my sister. I nod. My sister's old enough to be in high school. I'm not allowed to be near Karl… but Clara's school isn't off-limits.

I haven't heard anything from either of them. I wonder if they want to move on from me. I promised Clara I'd always be there, but with each year apart, the weight of that promise feels heavy. Each day feels like a betrayal, a distance between us that I can never erase. *It's been too long.* Abandoning her was never the plan, but what do I say when a shattered promise of forever stands between us?

Sadie glances at me from the corner of her eye. "Hey…you okay?" She asks with no hostility coating her words, which isn't normal. "Hey if it's about the joke… I was kidding."

"No, it's fine… I realized something, is all."

I don't want her feeling like she can't joke with me. We're friends now, and I don't take relationships lightly. *Relationships reveal weaknesses.*

We pull into the school parking lot, and my chest tightens. I'm not sure that she's in there… but she *could* be. I miss her and need to know if she's recovered. Surely, she's recovered by now —it's been five years.

The thought that I haven't seen her in years and might run into her is hard to process. Sadie notices that my silence again. She doesn't say anything but studies me.

I shrug my shoulders with an exhale. Opening the car door, I put one foot outside and glance over at Sadie, who's still watching me. "Are ya' ready to go and get this done or do you want an invitation?" I state with a halfhearted smirk.

Her focus darts between my solemn eyes and half-smile. I

think she notices that my grin isn't spreading across my entire face.

"If you want to stay in the car... I'm sure I can muscle the damn boxes on my own; I'm strong enough. Just don't want to show off my guns if I don't have to," she replies as she flexes her arm. She quickly kisses her biceps and then winks at me with a tongue click. Her fake cocky rebuttal makes my smile reach every crease in my face. I can't help but laugh at her ridiculous behavior.

"Come on, Schwarzenegger, let's get these boxes," she snickers, pulling the sunglasses off the top of her head that was holding back her long, wavy hair. Letting her face fall serious, she straightens.

"I'll be back," she says in the deepest voice she could muster, which isn't anywhere near low enough to mimic a man. Her natural voice is so tiny for the personality she has.

I laugh as I exit the car, shaking my head. She's swiftly behind me as we approach the school. She presses the button attached to the speaker outside the front doors.

"I'm Sadie, a volunteer from The Hope Center. I spoke to someone earlier about us coming to pick up the donation boxes." She smiles and waves in front of the camera that's situated next to the speaker button.

The door clicks. She quickly grabs the handle and pulls; mouthing *thank you* into the camera. The lobby is directly across from the front doors, making checking into the office upon arriving incredibly easy and accessible. We walk through the large entryway next to the cafeteria toward front lobby, surrounded by all-glass walls. A savory aroma envelops me, memories of the square-cut pizza the school served making my mouth water. No one's around, which tells me the lunch bell hasn't rung yet. The familiarity all around me takes me back in time.

Sadie enters the office before me, but I'm able to see that the lady at the front desk is the same woman who worked here when I was in high school.

She recognizes me, stiffening in her seat. "Oh, Walker...." Her hesitation drips with discomfort.

Sadie, always so quick to pick up on the mood of the room, interjects to repair the exchange.

"Oh good! You know one another, that's terrific! Walker volunteers at the shelter and has been an invaluable asset to our team. He's here to help me get the donations today! Where would those be exactly?" Her smile doesn't break as she shifts the conversation to business so seamlessly.

The lady behind the desk clears her throat and glances to papers in front of her.

"Yes... of course." Both Sadie and I peer at the boxes she points to and back toward the secretary holding out the log for Sadie. "I apologize for my... *behavior*. I remember you frequenting this office in your high school days... you were always polite," she apologizes as she peeks up at me.

I smile politely to ease her discomfort and relax my stance to ease tension. "You were always so nice to me when I came here for my weekly visits," I reply, chuckling.

She responds with a laugh and tells Sadie a story about some of my visits to the principal's office, making us all laugh at the childish actions featured in my high school years.

The air shifts around us, something I can't quite place. The office glass door flings open with urgency, and before I'm able to turn, an uneasy flop of my stomach slows my movement.

Laughter from Sadie and the secretary fades, replaced by the thrumming of my heartbeat echoing in my ears. I haven't seen my sister in years, but part of me knows.... This is it. Rotating to the sound, I can sense *who* is standing there.

We stare at each other for a moment. I take a half step toward her, wanting to reach for her... to feel *if she is real*. I've waited so long for this moment. I stop, unsure how she will receive me. Before I'm able to make that decision for her, she rushes to me, wrapping her arms around my waist and sobbing. Her shoulders slouch, and she caves into me as I embrace her.

She's tall enough that her hair tickles my neck and chin. Her small sobs turn into bellowing as she releases what seems to be five years' worth of pent-up emotions. I hold her tighter, as if I can squeeze away the years we've lost. She's still my little sister, but there's a depth to her now—an ache that I can't undo. She's grown, and so am I. Yet, in this moment, I feel like the young boy holding his tiny sister to protect her from the thunder. Just like thunder, this storm is unavoidable. But we can weather it together.

Her despair creeps into my skin and sinks into my bones. A lump catches in my throat, a hurt from deep down. I lean down to allow my lips to align with her ear.

"I'll never leave you again, Clara. I promise you're safe with me as long as I breathe." She squeezes a bit harder around my waist.

She's been needing me, and I haven't been there for her.

"I missed you," she whispers shakily and pulls away enough to look up at me. Even through the tears in her eyes, she smiles, her hopes seemingly restored.

CHAPTER NINETEEN
KARL REED: TRIFLING THROUGH TRINKET

Her room smells different from the last time I was here. A newfound sense of cool fresh air lingers in the room, mixing with the warmth of vanilla. Scanning the room for disruptions, I stroll to her desk, noting the drawer is left ajar. I pilfer through, looking for something out of the ordinary, when I stumble across her journal. *A black plain composition notebook.* I skim through the contents, filled with mentions of her struggles with emotional detachment.

Truly never understood the longing for emotions. They seem irrational and lacking in substantial gain. There's no *power* in feeling sad. There's no *gratification* in feeling love. The complexity of human emotion is a wasted effort designed by the elite to encourage the lower class to settle for generic happiness instead of pursuing more.

I stop on a page that stands out. A practice suicide note. The ones she's written in the past all have no hope engrained into the pages. No reason stopping her from feeling such titillating disdain for life.

This particular letter was addressed to someone in place of the generic address. *This is an apology to Walker.* A waste of ink.

If you off yourself, how can you reap the reward of an apology? The irony in the controversial perspective evokes a clipped chuff in humor acknowledgement.

Walker,

You are the beaming light that seeped into my utter darkness. The broken pieces of myself were forced jaggedly and haphazardly back together after you came back into my life, smiling and full of hope. If it were only you in my life, it would've been worth living. But it's not only you. I'm sorry.

-Clara

I scoff at the last sentence written. It reminds me of my childhood. Saying *sorry* would be the difference between eating dinner or going to bed without supper. How unrealistic to set up a child to associate eating with concern for other people's emotions. Why am *I* responsible for how you react? Why are your feelings something *I* have to preserve? I have nothing to gain from *your* happiness.

I rip the page from the notebook and crumble it up, letting it fall to the floor. I place the notebook back into the drawer, returning everything exactly how I found it. Walking over to the closet, I glance at my vibrating phone.

A voicemail from Susan. *Again.* She's relentless. Her constant reaching for connection. Much worse than the psychiatric nurse that worked at the hospital Clara was at. It's pitiful, really. I took up a relationship with her to gain access to Clara's school. Susan, being the lonely older lady with confidence issues; I couldn't have asked for a better in.

I text her a smiling emoji and tell her that I can't talk. Which is true. Snooping my ex-girlfriend's house while no one's home isn't exactly socially acceptable but doing it while talking to my current girlfriend is just tacky.

The creaking of old hinges on the bi-fold oak doors to her closet resonates through the room. Residual smells of her waft through the room, surrounding me. Inhaling deeply, I recollect that night. The audible rapid beating of her heart. The innocence that so easily caved to temptation. The cat-and-mouse game… the game we're still playing.

I grab a tank top from the hamper on the floor. A mix of the vanilla stench she coated the room in and her true scent. I shove the shirt into my cargo short pocket for later. The morning shines through the now open mauve curtains, casting light throughout the small bedroom. Her bed, unmade, still shows a clear outline of her slight frame. Her body is bigger than before but still inviting. I run my hand along the crumpled sheets, tracing her outline with my coarse fingertips while I contemplate her soft, youthful skin.

I'm so enamored with thoughts of her that the sound of a car pulling into the drive doesn't draw my attention until it's too late. I hiss under my breath, frustrated at my lack of attention. Melony usually takes longer at the grocery store; she must've forgotten something.

I turn my head to the window, listening for the footsteps in the house to determine my exit strategy. The clopping of steps reverberates down the hall. She's in the kitchen, looking for something from the sound of opening and closing drawers. She huffs as she searches. I wait for the slam of a drawer to open the window, and another to close the window behind me.

This isn't the first time I've visited *my* Trinket's room, but Melony walking in isn't anticipated. Awkward… I can imagine most people would feel that way with the thoughts of being confronted with their ex.

Life was easier when we were in a relationship. I didn't have to work or care about how or when I'd get alcohol or drugs, she was overly willing to ply me with whatever I needed. Pathetic little thing, seeking any form of reassurance at any cost to herself. I miss the simplicity that I created. She's so broken, I hardly had to mask.

Her son created issues; but Melony was so wrapped up in me that Walker was a nuisance, not a hinderance. *Except that one day.* I grit my teeth, seething with frustration at the humiliation he brought onto me. Images of me in the hospital, laying there like a weak, sad sack of shit, blur my thoughts as I dip between houses to the outlet road behind the neighborhood where my car sits.

He'll pay for destroying the image I built… the reputation I created. He'll regret challenging me.

Placing the brown paper bags filled with bottles in the floorboard of the passenger seat in my car, I turn my focus to my usual afternoon activities—dulling my inner voice and inhibitions. My phone vibrates for the fifth time today. Susan. *Again.* I mean to ignore her, but fumble with it and accidentally answer it.

"Hello?" Susan asks in a meek voice, wearing her insecurities in the tremble of her tone. It's like a purr to my ears, soothing my annoyance.

"Hello there, my dear. What can I help you with?" I force forward the endearing voice I mimic from that romantic comedy movie I watched ages ago. I switch the phone to speaker, while I drive.

"Oh… I… ah… I wondered if… maybe… if you're free… I go on lunch in a bit… and…."

My eyes roll at the lack of confidence. I thrive by feeding off their insecurities, but sometimes they make it…. *too easy*. Not *my* Trinket though, she's the perfect little mouse. Innocent and ignorant but quickly flutters just out of my grasp… for now.

"Would you like to go for a picnic lunch?" I ask after noting that I spent the last of my extra finances on the bottles clanking as they roll around on the floorboard. She giggles sheepishly. Audibly gulping the nerves down, she swallows loudly.

"I would love that, but I was just going to ask if you wanted to sit with me here in the lunchroom?" I ponder for a moment the potential of Clara seeing me and grin.

"Of course! I'll be there soon." I hang up without awaiting her response. As I drive to the high school, my inner voice runs away with my thoughts.

She's happy. He can make her feel things.

They'll talk. Tell everyone. You'll get caught. They'll lock you up. A caged animal.

He's watching you. She knows you're watching. She's not scared.

She's not yours anymore. He's taking her.

Gripping the steering wheel with white knuckles, I grit my teeth. Muscles in my jaw tense as I hiss.

Walker is taking her away from me. My innocent little Trinket. He humiliates and deprives me of the power I held in that house. Now, he's pulling apart everything I built. The fear and self-doubt she's plagued with—the numb existence that clouds her. I've worked so hard to create the perfect *tiny and timid* mouse for me to hunt.

I need to re-establish my dominance. He caught me off guard, but I won't be distracted next time.

I pull into the parking lot, coasting into a front guest parking spot. Flipping the gearshift into park, I grab my wallet out of the center console and shimmy it into my side pocket. I feel her shirt that I swiped and pause. Running my fingers along the fabric, I relax my jaw, reminding myself of the point of this *relationship.* I pull the shirt from my pocket to place it in a zipper plastic bag, needing to maintain the integrity of her scent. As I squeeze the air from the bag, movement out of the corner of my eye catches my attention. I peer up briefly, reacting to the motion.

Walker and his bauble walking to a red car. Walker carries two cardboard boxes in his arms, while his tramp opens the trunk. I *knew* Walker was seeing Clara. I haven't been able to determine where and when. He visits her at the school, but *why?*

I study their vehicle, looking for any logos that would give me the answer without digging. No stickers. I sigh, realizing that I'll have to watch him. He's up to something, sneaking around as if no one will catch him. Walker's close to discovering my presence, and I can't afford it. I must strike first. My eyes dart between the school and their car, sweat building on the back of my neck. I yank my phone from my pocket and text Susan.

Work emergency, rain check?

I watch through my rearview mirror as Walker gets into the passenger seat. I prepare to follow them, placing my seatbelt back on and putting my wallet in the center console. Reverse lights in the mirror alert me that it's time to start counting. *One... two... three* They drive slowly to the end of the parking lot, coming to a stop at the sign. *Five... six... seven...* The left blinker flashes momentarily, and they turn. *Nine... ten.*

Time to find out his plans and what he wants most... so I can crush it.

Chapter Twenty
Health Fair, See ya' there

"Miss Harris, return to where you should be. This is a school, and although family reunions are wonderful, this isn't the time nor place." The secretary stands and walks around the countertop, preparing to separate the two of them if needed.

Walker kisses Clara's forehead and releases his hold. Stepping back, he faces some resistance from Clara who attempts to cling to the embrace.

"Don't worry… we'll see each other again. Maybe you can come to The Hope Center shelter sometime, we can catch up," Walker says to Clara, a smile on his face at the thought of him getting to spend time with his sister after so many years apart.

Clara nods as a small grin flashes across her face. She swivels away and walks out the office doors. As she exits, she turns back to glance at Walker. Her smile fades into a forced, fake smirk. Distance clouds her eyes, as if she's resuming the dissociative state she assumes in the sea of rowdy teenagers. Her emotions drift away in the current of the hallway.

"I'm amazed you got a smile out of her. Poor thing never speaks much less smiles." The secretary clears her throat, which turns into a coarse cough directed into her elbow. "Oh, my! Excuse me!" she exclaims, stepping over to the boxes. "Here's the donations. Let us know if you need help." She glances to Sadie, who's finishing up the sign-in sheet.

"Thank you again!" Sadie exclaims as Walker closes one box and places it atop the other before he picks up both.

As he waits for Sadie to open the door, he peers in the direction that Clara disappeared but finds no trace of her. Silence surrounds the walk back to the car. Sadie knows Clara is part of Walker's family. However, Clara was much too young to recognize Sadie.

Unlocking the car as they approach and opening the trunk, Sadie peers at Walker. "Well, that was… *eventful.*"

She waits for his response that never comes. He sits the boxes down in the trunk and closes the hatch. Returning her gaze, Walker shrugs his shoulders silently and proceeds to the passenger seat. Sadie sighs, feeling left out of the loop. After getting into the driver's seat and closing the door, she turns to look at Walker once again. The silence is deafening, creating tension.

"How come you haven't seen her since you got out?"

Walker knows what she's asking would bring on a deeper conversation than they've shared. He told himself he wouldn't go back, knowing *who* is there. He doesn't want to bring up memories and pain for Clara either, but she deserves more from him than giving up.

Walker opens his mouth briefly, hesitating to speak. He glances over before he presses his lips tightly back together and stares out the passenger door window. "Let's get back to the shelter, Daniel's probably swamped." His voice is too calm.

Walker is building a wall, and Sadie's not happy about it. She understands the struggle with letting your guard down, having spent most relationships with a well-built concrete wall around her emotions. Empathy outweighs curiosity pushing her to drive back to the shelter.

Walker lets out a small sigh and rotates back toward Sadie, preparing to let a piece of him peek through the surface level relationship they have built over the past few weeks. "I don't have a car… Besides, I'm not supposed to go near someone who lives with them… I assume they live there still."

The silence builds up again. Sadie wants to pry, but in her experience, if someone shows a piece of themselves… digging can cause them to shut down. Instead of prying, Sadie nods her head in understanding and stays silent.

Without him continuing, the thick emotions lingering in the air unsettle her. The wind blowing around the car creates a white noise. Walker's fingertips grip the seat; eyes fixed on the passing yellow lines on the paved road. He'd do anything to avoid looking at Sadie, whose glance stalls over him. Sensing his discomfort, Sadie shifts the mood of the conversation.

"Man, not having a car must suck… at least you're getting great leg muscles. Wouldn't want to be top heavy," Sadie replies to Walker with a joking grin.

It eases the tension, but the events of the day and mystery behind the interaction still leave Sadie confused and curious.

The school isn't very far from the shelter, making the drive short. Daniel is standing outside the facility speaking to a strange gentleman who's wearing a suit. They're laughing, undoubtedly about something Daniel said. Sadie parks the car in her usual spot and pops the trunk, preparing to bring in the donations.

"Oh great! My two favorite people! I'll catch them up to

speed on the plans we've made! Thank you again for thinking of the shelter for this opportunity. Wonderful meeting you!" Daniel exclaims as he shakes the man's hand and smiles excessively.

Daniel's excitement is palpable. The years of effort becoming fruitful shimmering in his eyes. He waves as the other gentleman drives off in his BMW.

His attention flips to Walker and Sadie, and he exclaims almost breathless, "This is huge!" His hands shake in excitement.

Walker and Sadie glimpse at each other and back to Daniel. "You won't believe it! The health fair the local hospital hosts at the Legacy Hall downtown... we're going to have a booth!" Daniel's excitement pours out as he involuntarily rises on his toes. "Can you guys believe it! I've been trying for years to get the shelter into that health fair! It's a great place to get more volunteers and local business donations! It'll be so good for the shelter!" He's talking so quickly he can hardly contain himself. "It's going to change everything. It's our chance to really make an impact!"

Sadie matches his enthusiasm. "That's amazing! We'll have to order some stuff to hand out! I can make some pamphlets... how exciting!"

Sadie grabs the lighter of the two donation boxes and heads for the shelter. Daniel rushes ahead of her to open the door. Walker follows suit, picking up the remaining box and closes the trunk.

"When is it? I might need a ride if it's far," Walker asks, wondering if they'll want him there.

"It's this month. The twenty-sixth from five in the evening to nine-thirty at night. I can give you a lift. However, I have to go back to the shelter. Someone has to stay back to open it for the dinner rush and run it for the evening...." He trails off, looking off to the distance as he contemplates the logistics of the night to come. "But I trust you guys to run the booth. Do you think you can give Walker a ride back to the shelter after the event? We need to bring back any leftover supplies anyway," Daniel asks Sadie, exacerbated.

Sadie gazes over to Walker and then back to Daniel. "Sure. No big deal."

She starts in on the box as Walker begins filling in the details of the health fair onto the calendar. Only two weeks left. There's so much for the three of them to accomplish in such a short time.

CHAPTER TWENTY-ONE
SADIE THOMAS: DRUNKEN DUMBASSES

Preparing for the health fair has been extremely stressful over the past week, but Walker's been helpful. We finish setting up the booth with enough time to rehearse my spiel. From now until it's over, everything should be smooth sailing. I designed, printed, and folded all the pamphlets, and I'm so proud of them. I decided to hand them out myself and let Walker oversee running the booth. Everything's going well until a few drunken dumb-asses stumble into the health fair.

"Holy shit! That dress is fucking amazing... I bet it'd look even better on my bedroom floor," one slurs, spitting as he shouts at me. They all snicker, uncoordinatedly wobbling around with a sinister, drunken smirk painted on their faces.

"Wow... that line's so good, too bad I'm not desperate. Get lost." Redirecting my attention to Walker, who's listening in, his body tense and jawline taut.

"Oh, is *shrimpy* your boyfriend?" He sways to the side to point at Walker, nearly falling over. "Looks more like a *girlfriend* to me. Besides, I can tell you're a fucking easy ass slut by how much leg you show...." He steps forward; his fingertips brim the bottom hem of my dress. "I just want to see how high you'd hike it for a real man."

Walker suddenly appears at my side and shoves him off me. His movement is so jarring, I wince. Anger radiates off him, a wild look in his eyes and a smile on his face. "And where's she supposed to find one of those… among your pathetic group? Don't ya' know what *no* means? I got put in prison for showing someone what it meant… I'm an excellent teacher, wanna find out?" His voice rattles with anger, disjointed from his smile—unhinged at best.

"Jeez dude, fucking chill. I was joking. The bitch needs to learn to take a joke. We're leaving, calm down." The rest of his group is already walking away, and the guy has to jog off to catch up.

Walker takes a few shaky breaths while I stare at him, waiting patiently for him to settle. His fists tremor and knuckles are white from clenching. I touch the back of his hand hesitantly, anticipating him to lash out. Instead, his face softens at my touch. I *knew* he went to jail for assault… but clearly, he had a purpose.

"I didn't know…." I try to talk to him about it, but he looks down at the pamphlets he crumpled in his hand. He smiles lightly, blowing out a huffing breath that helps to further relax his shoulders.

"I'm sorry… guys can be jerks. I know we joke around a lot, but I have grown to view you like… a friend. I know you can handle yourself, I just feel protective of people I care about." He looks over to the booth and back to me. "You can take my spot at the booth if you want. Gather your nerves and take a break from standing out in the open. I can hand out pamphlets for a while."

I nod, not knowing what to say. The image of Walker as an inmate, and that kid who bullied me growing up, teeters in and out of view. After seeing how defensive he became over me and learning what happened, it's hard to avoid seeing him in a different light.

After his bullying me all those years ago, it's interesting thinking of Walker as a friend. That's what we've become... maybe even more. I tell him about my mundane day-to-day problems. We spend a lot of time together, joking and talking about nothing and everything at the same time.

By the time I reach the booth, I'm confronted with lots of eyes looking for the freebies we offer. I immediately smile and go right into telling them about all the different events and the amenities we have, as well as what the rehabilitation the shelter offers as well. I can't help but look over at Walker every spare second I get. *It's difficult not to.* The revelation that we're friends, and the new information I learned, make him the center of my focus.

He's talking with a group of elderly women and handing them each a pamphlet. His smile is so charismatic and natural it reminds me of that young boy who always managed to make my anger at him melt away. I'm watching him a little too closely. It's distracting. I hardly notice someone else had approached the booth. They startle me by clearing their throat. I jump before laughing nervously when I see who it is.

"Garrett! You startled me... I'm waiting for those older ladies to come my way after Walker shows them over," I say, giggling a little too anxiously. My cheeks flush with heat, and I swallow, noticing my throat growing excessively dry.

Garrett's eyes follow my line of sight and return to me. His smile lessens after hearing the nerves pitching my words. "I just came to check on how things are going. I'm on my lunch break and patrolling out this way. Thought I'd take advantage of it and come show support." He pauses and glances again at Walker.

I bend down to get the bag of pamphlets out of the box under the table and reorganize the bowls of freebies on the table, avoiding eye contact with Garrett.

While looking at Walker, he asks, "So… how's it going? Last time you texted, you said you were handing out pamphlets… that's why you couldn't talk much." His eyes float back to me as he awaits an explanation.

"Some drunken jerks were messing with me and…." When I look up from the bowl of keychain freebies I'm refilling, Garrett's face switches from straight and relaxed to tense and downturned.

"Where are they?! I'll escort them out for public intoxication." His voice deepens with anger as he spins around to survey the space. Walker approaches the table.

"Hey, Garrett. They took off, man. Don't worry, Sadie handled them like a champ. They didn't stand a chance," he says to Garrett, while looking at me.

When Garrett's eyes fall to me, Walker winks at me playfully and mouths, *you're welcome*. "Anyway, I came to get more pamphlets. These little old ladies drained me dry, saying they'd hand them out at their church."

I hand him another stack of pamphlets, and he smiles while saluting me. As he walks away, he points at me with a click of his tongue. "You're the best."

I drag my eyes away from Walker giggling, and my smile quickly drops when I'm met by Garrett's straight face. He doesn't seem amused by Walker's playfulness. He shakes his shoulders out in a stretch, almost like he's trying to shrug the feelings of distaste he has out of his body.

"Well… like I said… it's my lunch, so I can't stay long. I'm glad you managed to handle those drunks… but next time just call. A group of guys can do a lot of awful things with even worse intentions. Just… be safe."

Little does he know how totally safe I am thanks to my *friend*. I grin at him and lean over the table to kiss him on the cheek, which makes him smile.

"What time does your shift end? Wanna hang? I'm here till nine forty-five," I say with too much hope in my voice.

We've had a hard time spending time together. He's always working, or I'm volunteering. He gives me a sad smile, which I know means no. After all the times that no was the answer, you wouldn't think it would hurt. It still stings… every time.

"Sorry, babe. I work till midnight. Rain check?"

I nod, disappointed but understanding. He leans over the table this time and kisses me on the lips.

"I love you. Someday our schedules will line up perfectly, and we'll live together. Everything will work out. I got to go, but please keep me updated on how things are going here and call if you need me." He strolls off into the crowd of people, walking around and bobbing between booths.

Chapter Twenty-Two

Karl Reed: Happy Coincidence

Swirling the sip of scotch in my glass, I watch the warmcolored liquid slosh side to side. The music booming from old speakers shakes the glass on the wall, a garbled hip-hop song breaking with static when the bass vibrates. I tap the mahogany bar counter, signaling to the bartender that I'd like another. He glances up at me and back down to the drink he's working on.

"Here." Steve, the bartender, slides a glass of water to me. I furrow my brows, bringing the side of the glass up to my eyes.

"This isn't Scotch," I huff.

He chuckles and moves to the next customer, beckoning his attention.

"I decide when I'm done!" I say, loud enough to quiet the clusters of conversations intermingling throughout the hole in the wall bar.

Steve turns to me, noting my disdain for his cutting me off. He puts the glass he was preparing down and walks over to where I sit.

"Karl. I'm not trying to control you. I have a limit for all my guests to ensure safety. The bar gets a bit rowdy if I pour endlessly." The calmness in his voice reminds me that I need to mask my personality… I'm not at home. I nod slowly, mimicking his movements of fluid composure.

He smiles at me and walks back over to the drink he left behind. I sip the water, calculating the potential outcomes had I physically challenged the bartender in my inebriated state. I chug back the water and slam the glass down on the counter, feeling the glass vibrating from the force tingles in my hand. I check my phone for the time, knowing that Walker and his *trifle* are working at the health fair just blocks away.

A few young, intoxicated men stumble into the bar. They collectively tease one guy in the group about getting shot down. Two of them part ways to the bar, and the other goes off to the bathroom.

"Dude… you can… can't even… get your dick wet at a fucking *health fair*." A man with glasses and an overgrown black fade jokes as he hiccups and slurs through his statement. The long-haired guy shoves the fade guy in a burst of anger, which catches the barkeeper's attention.

"Hey! Take it outside!" he shouts and points to the door.

Both men put their hands up and sit next to me. They order two beers and sit, discussing their evening. My attention falls away from their conversation until one of them says something about the shelter that Walker works at.

"That bitch from that Hope Center place… she's hot but damn… she's feisty." Without looking at them, I listen in. The long-haired one was the one who spoke about Walker's plaything. "But I'd love to fuck that attitude out of her… if she'd let me."

An idea dawns on me. A smile pulls my muscles in an unfamiliar pattern. Usually, I force them to appear… normal.

"Who says she wasn't challenging you to do that?" I stir the metaphorical pot, planting the seed of the idea.

Both men gawk at me, not connecting the dots. "What was that old man?"

I chuckle at the misplaced aggression. These guys are looking for trouble tonight, and I'm going to point them in the right direction. I lean forward over the bar while the bartender has his back turned. Reaching down into the small black sink, I grab a half drunken beer bottle. Glancing out of the corner of my eye at the two young guys still puzzled by my statement, I take a swig.

"You talking about that girl with blonde hair? Mousey with green eyes? Works at the homeless shelter?" They both nod in synchronization with each other, as if they timed it out. "She's into it. She wants the thrill of the fight. Her man likes to watch. I got with her once. Dirty fucks, but she's a freak. Even likes the roleplaying." I play it up, hoping that one of them takes the bait. The long-haired one is more likely to go for it, having his ego already bruised with something to prove.

"You laid her? Damn old man… that's… wow." The guy with the fade rubs the back of his neck, shaking his head in disbelief. I shrug, signifying that it's not a big deal, and take another sip. I place the glass bottle down on the table. The long-haired man pinches his chin in contemplation. "So… you mean to tell me… it was a test?"

"He just said that! You dea—" His friend attempts to respond before the guy with long hair interrupts.

"Shut the fuck up! She wanted me, and I just didn't play the game?!" He grows louder, but his friend with the fade hushes him to prevent a scene. I turn my phone over on the bar, showing the time.

"Well, the night's not over yet… the health fair shouldn't be done for another half hour. You could always… go back and do better this time. Be more… forceful. That'll make her really wet." I raise my eyebrows, copying their pleased look. The long-haired man chugs the remainder of his beer and pounds it down exhaling sharply.

"The nights not over. I still got a chance. Catch ya' later, Phil." He strides confidently out the entrance.

I unlock my phone to the contacts application. One name in particular stands out to me. *Melony Harris.* I try to form a plan… my next move. There's only one way out of this. I need to permanently silence Walker, but I need to gain access to Clara before I do that….

How else will I skip town with *my* Trinket?

Chapter Twenty-Three

Sadie Thomas: Aggressively Almost

Trigger Warning: Chapter contains graphic depictions of violence and suggested sexual assault

The turnout of people is amazing. Much better than recent years that we attended but weren't a part of. We even ran out of some of our free handouts. The pens and key rings are gone, and only notepads and magnets are left.

Walker and I begin packing up the table as the night comes to an end. Only a few people are walking around.

"I'll take these two boxes out to my car, and you start tearing down tables." Walker hesitantly gazes at the two boxes on the floor and back at me. I reassure him with sarcasm. "If you try to take these boxes and have me fumble with those heavy folding tables, I'll kick your ass."

He smirks, nodding and picking up the boxes. I start getting flustered, but then he hands them to me. "Damn straight," I smile.

Walking outside into the semi-empty parking lot, the cool summer air chills my skin. Most of the cars left in the lot are owned by other people who worked at the health fair. The darkness of the parking lot is broken by scattered streetlights, illuminating just enough to see the shapes of cars.

As I approach my car, I hear footsteps behind me. "Jeez, Walker... take a hint. I got it covered!" I huff as I set the boxes down next to the trunk and spin around.

A shadowy figure I can hardly make out stares at me silently. "Oh! Not Walker. Sorry, I thought you were someone else," I apologize, squinting as I attempt to make out the dark figure.

My heart still races from the startle. His jagged white teeth shine through the darkness. The sinful smile beaming in the night sends a shiver down my spine. The drunken jerk must've been abandoned by his posse. I stiffen, feeling less confident in a dimly lit parking lot with nobody else around to witness.

"Hey, Mouthy, my name ain't Walker... but if you want something to scream, you can call me whatever you want." He approaches me with a slow, confident stride.

The space between us lessens too swiftly for me to process what's happening. Off in the distance, the door to the hall flings open, letting out a glimmer of yellow light. I parked far enough away from the building, making it impossible to see who opened the door.

My eyes flicker back to the stranger. I puff my chest and inflate my confidence to tell this man off. If I can't get him to leave me alone, I'll have to fight for my life. I can't do that if I'm stiff and scared. Wishing I was fighting for *only* my life, I grit my teeth forcing a hiss into my voice.

"I told you earlier. I'm not interested, leave me alone," I say with a twinge of shakiness in my voice, forcing myself to sound confident.

He moves closer, and I take a step back, feeling the cold, metal trunk of my car pressing into my back. He encloses me up against my vehicle and, in a panic, I shove him. I attempt to shoulder check him and manage to get mostly through. He grabs my upper arm with an aggressive grip.

"Where you going, slut?" His eyes are vacant, almost as if he's not present in his body. His face looks predatory, animalistic. Like I'm the little bunny the fox is about to devour.

I attempt to rip my arm free and scream as I pull, but his hand doesn't release. I shake at the sound he releases from his tightly pressed lips. It's not quite a laugh, maybe a groan in satisfaction mixed with a slight chuckle. I hit him repetitively, and his chuckle grows into a roaring laugh until I land a punch, leaving a tint of blood glinting in the streetlight. He licks his now bloody lip, laughing ceased and winces briefly.

"You fucking bitch!" He strikes me, dropping me to the pavement. Grabbing my arm again, he yanks me back to my feet. He fist raises to strike me again. "I'm gonna show you the time of your life, and *that's* how you thank me!?"

I close my eyes tightly together, facing away from him. As quickly as he snatched me off the ground, his hand releases. A loud thud echoes in the parking lot, followed by sharp gasps coming from behind me. I straighten from my hunched over stance, spinning to the commotion.

Walker stands over the man with his hand on the stranger's head. He forces him onto the car, pressing his head against the trunk.

"The fuck did you *think* was about to happen? Did you seriously think you'd hurt her? Her boyfriend's a fucking cop, and I'm an ex-con. You'll be lucky to walk away alive!" I struggle to process what Walker is saying with my thudding heartbeat racing.

Walker digs in the guys' back pocket and pulls out his wallet. "Now I know where you live. Imma let you go. Don't pull shit. We have your info if she wants to press charges." Walker loosens his grip on him just enough to let the stranger stand upright. As the stranger turns, Walker quickly grabs the front of his shirt and pulls him close enough to hear the threat. "I'll gladly go back to jail for her... you understand?!" he growls under his breath and releases the stranger.

Without hesitation, the stranger takes off running down the parking lot and ducks between the cars to the next lane. Walker, still vibrating with adrenaline, releases a ragged breath. He looks down at the driver's license and back up in the direction the stranger took off. Closing his eyes, he takes a few jagged, drawn-out breaths. The shaking settles as he turns to me, holding my arm in pain.

His attention, the way he's holding himself completely changes. He's so vicious and intimidating one second, and the next he's concerned and caring. I don't know how to handle it; how to read him.

"I knew I shouldn't have let you go to your car alone. I should've known better, I'm so sorry. It's all my fault." The hurt on his face is easy to read, he blames himself for that jerk.

I was almost… well, I could've… I could've been killed. But that's the best outcome of what was about to happen. He saved me.

"Thank you," I say as I fall to my knees. The adrenaline catches up to me, and my legs are so weak.

Walker comes down to the ground with me, panic enveloping his face. "Sadie?! Are you okay? What's wrong? Did he hurt you?!" He's studying me up and down for any signs of injury.

He glances over at my small purse on the ground near the tire. He reaches for it and pulls out my phone to call Garrett.

I'm so overwhelmed with what could've been, I can't think straight. My eyes well with tears, and I repetitively say in a hushed, raspy voice, 'Thank you' and 'I'm okay.' Walker cups my face, but I'm staring *through* him, not at him. He comes close, almost like he's about this kiss me.

"Don't worry, I've got you. I'll stay with you." His voice low and raspy, whispering his words.

In the silence of the still summer night, crickets chirp off in the distance, wind whirling around pushing my stray hair against my cheeks. His arm slides under my knees and behind my shoulders. Lifting with ease, he picks me up off the ground and carries me through the elongated parking lot and into the building.

I'm propped against the wall of the hall that held the health fair, and someone brings me a small cup of water. A crowd of people gather around me, asking questions in muttered tones that blur together in a hum. Walker holds up his hands, asking for space. It doesn't take much coaxing to dissipate from the small crowd. Walker crouches down to me.

"I'm sorry this happened to you. Garrett's on his way. Don't worry, he's coming." Walker reassures me, but Garrett isn't who I want in this moment.

Pulling my focus to Walker, observing me with concern, pressing his face tightly downwards, a pitiful gleam in his eyes. I reach up to touch his cheek, attempting to ground myself. Cupping his cheek, his lips twitched upwards, not quite reaching his eyes.

"I got here as fast as I could! What did he do to you?!" I peer up to Garrett rushing into the hall, two EMS workers hot on his heels.

He slows to a stop when he sees my hand cupping Walker's cheek. Uncertainty cocks his head to the side. I drop my hand to the floor and roll my head to the side, away from them both. I don't want to recollect the thoughts, but I'm sure it'll happen a few times tonight.

"Other than some slight bruising on my arm... nothing." I started to settle down right before Garrett arrived, but the thoughts have permanently altered my brain chemistry.

Being asked what happened only makes me think of what could've happened. I wasn't strong enough to fight him. I would've never been strong enough to stop him. I shake my head, pushing my thoughts away.

Walker, still kneeling by me, catches my attention. "He saved me. It'd be a lot worse if Walker wasn't there."

Walker pulls his eyes away from my bruising upper arm to my eyes and gives a sad half smile for a moment longer than usual. Garrett clears his throat, crowding behind him uncomfortably close. Walker stands, making room for Garrett to get closer. Garrett hesitates, trying to decide if he should rush in, or let the EMTs help me.

Garrett's attention turns to Walker, voice shaking with adrenaline and concern. However, seeing the deep concern on Walker's face forces a shift in Garrett's eyebrows from worrisome scrunch to straight. "Thanks for keeping *my* girl safe. I don't know what I'd do if I lost her." Garrett peeks back to see the EMS workers standing near, waiting to get an assessment.

Walker shrugs, never breaking his focus on me. "I kept *Sadie* safe." His tone is passive with the correction.

Garrett huffs a single laugh, "Yeah, like I said, *my* girl. Thanks." Walker side-steps to the door to follow me to the ambulance.

"Nothing to thank. She needed me, and I was there. *Always* will be." Walker never pulls his eyes away, watching over me.

The hesitation in his voice screams matter of fact with a hint of passive aggressive confrontation. I turn to observe the silent aggression between the two of them, but I'm met with Walker's eyes intensely watching me.

He's looking after me, like I'll combust. He isn't being aggressive or possessive but distracted by worrying about my well-being. Garrett, on the other hand, is pretty wrapped up in the silent challenge.

As I step outside the building and into the back of the ambulance to be further examined, I find Walker staring at me, and

Garrett looking between us. One is focusing on my mental and physical state after what happened… and it definitely isn't the man I'm in a relationship with.

Chapter Twenty-Four

Walker Harris: Too close, too personal

After Sadie is examined, Garrett hands me the keys to her car. "You have a license?" I nod to him, knowing it's a slight dig at fact that Sadie drives us everywhere. He nods. "Okay, good. Can you drive her car back to the shelter?"

I nod again. Even in this situation, it's difficult to talk to Garrett, being law enforcement.

I hand him the man's wallet, placing it in his hand that's holding out the keys to the car. "What's this? You stole the guy's wallet?" One of his eyebrows lifts in suspicion. The left side of his face twitches upward, in a faint smirk.

I meet his eyes slowly, the tense air forcing me to take a shallow breath. After a quiet moment of confusingly intense eye contact, my focus trails down to the wallet. Shrugging my shoulders, I push my hands into my pant pockets. "No. He dropped it... while assaulting her. I picked it up. He was running so fast, didn't get a chance to give it to him." Through the discomfort of straight-faced silence, a small smile tugs lose the corners of my lips. I struggle to bury it.

Garrett smirks and nods, acknowledging that it's not the truth. His facial expression reassures me that he understands and approves. He folds the wallet back up and places it in his patrol car. Sadie's sitting in the passenger seat.

He ducks out of the patrol car to peer back at me. "I'm going to take her to the station. I'll give Sadie's dad a call... have him meet you at the shelter."

I put my thumbs up awkwardly. *Dumbass.* I internally scream at myself for the embarrassment. Sighing at my humiliation, I grab the keys that Garrett's dangling and turn on my heels as they peel out of the parking lot behind me. Turning on the engine, it sputters for a moment before turning over.

I try my best to shut off my emotions. In prison, I could hyper-fixate on a random, trivial topic and my emotions would fall away. I know it's an unhealthy coping mechanism... at least, that's what anger management therapy taught me.

I find myself falling into a slippery slope of emotions. Having compassion for others is difficult. Having deeper feelings for someone doesn't just complicate things, it devastates them. Especially when it's unreciprocated.

She's in a relationship. We are... *friends.* I can't let myself ruin her perfect life. She's going to be a doctor, married to law enforcement... he'll probably end up a detective. They'll continue to live their perfect life, having little trust fund babies and throw lavish parties.

With Clara, my love is genetically programmed. The compassion I feel makes sense. Familial love is simple. She's my little sister and, as her older brother, I'm predisposed to love and protect her.

My feelings toward Sadie are uncontrollable... dangerous. The extra complexity of attraction complicates things. I *have* to swallow those feelings. I thought it was only physical attraction.

I creep through the parking lot, drifting around the remaining ambulance and police vehicles that haven't yet left the scene. I pull out onto the main road.

Finding her next to her car, fighting with that drunk piece of shit... the immediate defensiveness... forcing myself to refrain from going back to prison.

I'm in love with her. There's no other explanation.

She's compassionate... funny... and... absolutely gorgeous. She's perfectly good for someone better than me.

I turn the heat up; the cool night air bringing on a shiver. I shake my head, concluding that I can't trust myself to keep my powerful feelings from destroying her life. The pressure takes grip of my chest, and I struggle with the weight of my thoughts.

The red glow of the turn signal dimly flashes on the curb as I turn the car into the shelter parking lot.

We'll part ways soon anyway when she leaves to go to medical school. It's what's best for her... and for me. I'd hate to spend the rest of my life worrying about how I pulled Sadie down to my level.

A Mercedes Benz G class, sits running in the parking lot. The gleam of the headlights casts a soft light. I park in Sadie's usual spot. Rotating the key, I shut off the engine. A slight hum from fluids shifting in the vehicle cuts the quiet of the night.

Seeing Sadie's dad brings on memories I didn't realize I had. Memories of the last time I saw him. My dad's funeral. The ping of loss resurfaces. I gulp; swallowing back pain I don't have time to process. As I exit the car, surprise engulfs his face.

"Walker? Is it really? Wow... you're the spitting image of your father!" He strolls over toward me, seeing his old partner, but in a different font.

The tears well, but he chokes them back. I outstretch my hand to shake, but he pushes it out of the way and pulls me into a tight hug. "When Garrett said a volunteer from the shelter was bringing Sadie's car here... I wasn't imagining you!"

My skin twinges with discomfort at Garrett not even mentioning my name. Guilt beads up beneath the surface. For Garrett to reduce me to *a* volunteer, my presence must be threatening.

Richard holds me tightly for a moment longer than a typical hug. He was once a father-figure to me. It feels like a lifetime ago. Losing my father created a hole that was never filled.

The firm hug forces my shoulders to relax, letting my guard cave briefly. His mood shifts when he recollects the reason for the reunion, shifting back in his stance. Folding his arms over, he grips his elbows tensely.

"What happened to Sadie? Garrett wouldn't give information over the phone." The disapproval for how Garrett is handling the situation colors Richard's words.

Garrett doesn't seem like a guy who handles conflict well. Ironic, considering he's a cop.

"Sadie was walking some boxes to her car, and a guy approached her with… bad intentions. I… removed… him." I shift my weight, rubbing the outside of my left arm with my right hand. Having a record, I need to be careful how I word things. "She's safe. They're on their way to the police station."

I could've been arrested for assault and robbery. Luckily, the cop that I handed the wallet to happened to be grateful for what I did.

I pull the keys from my pocket, hold them out for Sadie's father. He gazes down to the ground, pondering what happened, like he's doing the math on the logistics of what occurred. Ignoring the outstretched keys, he grabs me for another embrace.

"You saved her," he says, his voice shaky and breathy with relief. "I don't know how we could ever thank you. Your *father* would be so proud." A crack in his words reveals a sincere hurt.

Pulling away from this uncomfortable level of nicety isn't an easy task. "Thank you, sir." I give him an awkward, forced smile, attempting to show my gratitude for his kindness.

He lets go, still holding onto my arm endearingly. This much physical contact has my skin crawling. Over the years, in prison, you grow accustomed to avoiding all forms of touch.

"I have an idea! Next weekend, there is the annual Fourth of July party! You must come! I won't hear of you saying no!" As quickly as the invitation is given, Sadie's mother flings the car door open aggressively.

"Richard! Ugh...." She stomps over to where we stand and shifts her weight to one leg. Popping one hip out and putting her hands on her hips. "I swear you have air in your head instead of a brain!" Diane words are clipped in anger, perturbed at the invitation. She clicks her tongue and lets a hiss escape through her teeth as Richard responds.

"Oh, hush Diane! He can have *my* seat if that's *your* issue." He peers at her and back to me with a slight annoyed chuckle under his exhale. "*Women*, I swear!" he whispers toward me, not quite low enough.

Diane hears, rolling her eyes and crossing her arms. "Anyway... I'll expect you there! Remember, I know where you volunteer!" Sadie's dad slaps my arm, smiling as he jokingly threatens.

I pause, eyes flickering between the annoyed look on Diane's face and that hopeful look of Richard's. I remember the parties well, which discourages me from agreeing to go. I would absolutely be socially out of place. Richard tilts his head, encouraging a quicker response.

"I'll be there. Thanks for the invitation, sir," I respond, with little choice to respond any other way.

CHAPTER TWENTY-FIVE
SADIE THOMAS: DISSOCIATIVE DREAMS

I've struggled immensely the past few days with reoccurring thoughts of the health fair. I had to call Daniel to let him know I couldn't volunteer on Monday. He understood, knowing what happened; Walker must've filled him in.

That guy's vacant darkened eyes peering through me is burned into my brain. The smirk of a predator encircling his prey. Shivers run down my spine, and a pit forms in my stomach. My head shakes, pushing the thought out of my mind. I keep telling myself it could've been worse, but it doesn't stop the feeling that something inside me is cracked—permanently altering my brain chemistry, a shattered fragment that I can't glue back together. I want to move forward and pretend it never happened... it didn't happen. The fear keeps circling back in my mind, spiraling in and out of focus.

"Babe?" Garrett leans into my rolled down car window. "I was shouting... you've been sitting here for a few minutes. Everything alright?" His eyebrows furrow, gaze lingering on me longer than usual.

His eyes soften, revealing the exhaustion weighing down his face—the heavy toll of wanting to protect me but not knowing how. Garrett's insecurities about Walker mix with his guilt for not knowing how to talk to me, and he defaults to handling me like a fragile porcelain doll.

My lips crease at the corners forcibly, hoping to change the subject entirely. He's been more than supportive over the past few days. So many women are put in similar situations, but with a not so happy ending. Too often, there's no knight in shining armor to rescue the damsel in distress. I feel guilty for being so affected.

"I didn't sleep much last night. I'll be fine." Peeking down into the passenger seat, I reach for my crossbody purse. He's in his uniform, which tells me he's returning to work today. "What time do you start patrol?" I ask, grabbing his arm playfully, raising my eyebrows suggestively.

His eyes dance at the playful gesture I make, knowing he can't act on it. "In an hour. If you need me… don't hesitate… call me, and I'll let dispatch, and the sergeant know." He changes the subject back to my fragile state, his voice dripping with worry.

I love him, but it's tiring… already. I don't want to constantly be reminded of this. It'll never go away if he keeps coddling me.

He pulls up to the front of the shelter to drop me off. I position my purse over my shoulder after unbuckling my seatbelt.

"No, *really*. I'm fine. Stop coddling me." *Treat me normal.* I want to say that to him, but he means well… so I keep it to myself.

Leaning in, I kiss him lightly on the cheek. I get out and slam the door shut behind me, turning back to wave at him as I rush up to the shelter entry. Pausing briefly, I take a harsh breath, willing myself to focus. The weight on my chest doesn't lessen, but I bury the pressure of discomfort deep down as I step through the threshold. I force a smile, preparing to ignore the thoughts pounding against the walls I've built.

Walker stands behind the main counter, rustling through papers that he has no clue how to organize. "Oh, thank God!

Look who finally decided to show up!?" Slow clapping sounds from the back of the building. I swear Walker's smart ass is rubbing off onto sweet Daniel. *I've heard the kindest hearts are the easiest to corrupt.* "If I didn't know any better, I'd assume that you were too good for us simple folk now."

I can't help but laugh at the blatant, sarcastic humor, but it feels like a thin veil over the thoughts swirling in my mind. I push them away for a moment, just enough to enjoy this small escape. This sense of normalcy is exactly what I've been yearning for.

I curtsy like a princess to her well-respected dignitaries. "I *am* better than *you,* Walker. For example… I know where those papers go that you've been shifting side to side." I snatch the papers out of his hands.

Walker squints his eyes tightly, faking being offended. "Daniel just lets you stand around pretending to work nowadays?" Chuckles echo down the hall from the other end of the building.

"Get back to work, you freeloaders! I don't pay you to stand around!" Daniel shouts from his office. He can hardly bellow the sentence without bursting into a fit of laughter.

"You don't pay us at all!" Both Walker and I shout back at the same time. We both look at each other in astonishment. Snickering erupts throughout the entire building.

The laughter slows as I flip through the stack of papers in my hands. Walker's smile fades away when he sees a slight tremor in my hands as I try to organize the pile. He steps closer, lowering his voice to a whisper.

"If you ever need to talk about it… you know I'm here." His eyes don't carry the same pity that Garrett's held. He isn't looking at me as if I could be broken. Admiration sparkles in his deep blue eyes.

My body relaxes as my gaze locks on his, a smile scrunching my nose and creasing my eyes. He shakes his head, as if he's enamored looking at me, and pulls his hand back. Playfully, he punches my arm. "Clearly, you're tough as nails."

If only I *were* tough as nails. I'm glad I come off as that, but deep down, I'm still queasy. I harshly swallow, pushing the thoughts away again. *It's over. It's over.* I swallow. *I'm safe.*

We divide up to do our daily duties, getting the shelter up and running. Every so often we run into each other, making jokes and sarcastic comments. For some reason, being with Walker is comfortable and effortless, like drinking water. Like breathing fresh air.

As the days roll by, nearing the weekend of my family's Fourth of July party, I begin to feel normal. Walker and I spend most days joking with each other about nonsense. If something were to truly be wrong, Walker is the first to stand behind me in support. How can someone who's been around for only a few months become such an irreplaceable part of my life?

Friday finally arrives, brewing tension as Saturday hangs over my head. Tomorrow, I'll have to dress up and parade around like a trophy. But I can't shine as brightly as Diane. It's something I've perfected over the years. It makes me feel like an underpaid and overqualified actress.

I spend the day creating potential conversations in my head… preparing to say exactly the right things to avoid *her* contempt. I can already hear Diane's voice, perfect and poise, talking circles around me. Even with my mood improved, I anticipate being quiet. Someone who smiles and nods, pretending to fit the image she wants me to be. It's easier to comply. I can't help feeling like a shadow in my own life.

I spend the day quieter than usual as I contemplate. But what could *he* be thinking about? I'm buried so deep in thought, I hardly notice that Walker's also been silent.

"Hey, you know you don't have to come if you don't want to. To be honest, if I could get out of it, I would." I offer an out to Walker in the off chance he's trying to mentally prepare himself for the party as well.

"No, I'm fine. I'll be there." He smirks half-heartedly, coming out of his thoughts. "Besides…your mom made a point to tell me that summer formal attire is not a graphic tank top and colorful board shorts. It's funny she thinks I can't figure that out for myself. I'm considering wearing Crocs just to see her face glitch out." His perfect white teeth peek through his partially opened lips, with that same mischievous boyish grin he's always able to do effortlessly. His smile manages to reach his beautiful dark blue eyes.

I'd forgotten how handsome he is… until now.

CHAPTER TWENTY-SIX
CLARA HARRIS: NIGHTMARE TURNS REALITY

Trigger Warning: Chapter contains severe depressive descriptions and suicidal ideations

I used to think that good and evil balanced each other out on a cosmic level. That life somehow gives you back the things that are taken from you. Slowly, piece for piece, and that's what helps to heal you.

But as I stand there watching my mother embrace *him*… the very man who stole my peace… who shattered my innocence… I realize how naïve that belief was. How false hope lingers in the darkest hours only to ensure you don't release your grip on life completely.

The time of waking up excited to go about my day slipped away abruptly and has never truly returned. Over time, the days that were once so long became more bearable. The flashbacks slowly transformed from constant background noise to requiring triggers.

This is the best I can be.

I struggle with whether to open up since things have improved. I know that if I did share what happened, I'd have to go to court. Everything would be discussed at length and vividly, reliving that day over and over. I understand how selfish that is, considering Walker was sentenced more harshly because of my silence.

The fear consumes me. Not knowing when, or if, he'd come back crippled me. Seeing Walker changed things. He was supposed to be my universal balance. Maybe life does have retribution. The universe owed me for my innocence... so my big brother came back to me.

At least, I was starting to think that way, until *he* knocked on our front door.

My mother, half paying attention to the TV in the living room, turns down the volume with the remote. "Hold on! One second! I'm coming!" she shouts as she shuffles her feet.

Sitting in my room working on summer schoolwork, I hear her gasp loudly after opening the door. I assumed Walker came back. I should've known better. Yet, foolishly, I run to the living room. Actually excited, my heart leaps and skips a beat. I mistakenly believed happiness was falling into my lap again.

I can hear my mother's voice, eager and high-pitched, echo down the halls. "You're back! I missed you!" My mother squeals as she rushes into *him* for a hug, wrapping her arms around *his* neck.

He returns the hug, but his eyes lock onto mine. Seeing the fear and my ragged breaths, he winks at me, and my insides shrivel. My pulse thuds in my neck, echoing into my ears. The air in the house thickens, suffocating, as if it's pressing in on me.

I don't know how to breathe... how to exist in the same space as *him*. Stomach acid lurches up my throat. I place my clammy hand on the wall beside me, keeping myself from collapsing.

"Isn't this great! We can be a family again!"

I attempt to force a smile, but a disheveled breath escapes in its place. As I turn to go to my room, my mother mutters an apology. Disoriented, I stumble down the hall. Entering my room, I lock the door behind me and barricade myself in. Even with my door barricaded, I still struggle to sleep.

As the sun comes up, footsteps rustle about, down the hall and into the kitchen. I scramble to get changed and prepare myself to leave the house.

My mother knocks on the door to wake me. "Claire-Bear… sweetie, it's time to wake up! Last day of summer school!" Sounding chipper, she hums as she strolls to the kitchen.

I know they spent the night together from the sounds that haunt my mind. After going to my room last night, I peeped outside to find his beat-up car full of boxes. He knew she'd take him back.

I have to escape… before he hurts me *again*. Before he forces himself onto me *again*. I can't endure this *again*.

I skip showering. I don't want to put myself in closed quarters; to risk myself being vulnerable is a mistake. He preyed on me once and is confident enough to come back. Like nothing happened. I wait until the bus pulls up to our house before leaving my room. Once I see it stop, I sprint through the house, out the front door.

"Clara?" My last period teacher approaches me in my seat; her brows furrowed with worry. No one else in the class remains in the classroom. Staring down at the vandalized tabletop in front of me, I realize that I lost track of time. "Honey, I'm concerned for you. Normally you can at least, look to the front of the class… occasionally take notes. Is something troubling you today?"

Shaking my head, I lift myself from the seat and stalk out of the room.

Throughout the day, I spent my time trying to compose a plan. I can't go back home. I'll go to the shelter and ask Walker if I can stay with him until I figure things out. I don't want to burden him again, but who else can I turn to? Walker's safety and freedom matter… but what choice do I have? I need him. I need somewhere safe to go.

As I cross the threshold of the classroom, I can hear my last period teacher shout after me, "Good luck next year in your classes!"

I walk to the bus stop from the school and take the three-thirty bus to the shelter that Walker does community service at. I jog from the bus stop to the shelter; afraid *he's* out there watching me. Sweat beads on my brow and drips down my neck as I open the door.

Sadie and Walker are laughing together. The way they look at each other differs from the last time I saw them. *Something's different*. Walker glances over Sadie's shoulder at the sound of my heavy breathing. His face drops with concern when he sees me.

"Clara…." He pauses, setting papers down on the counter. He steps around Sadie and comes over to me. Standing face to face, he looks me up and down. "Is everything okay? Why are you here?" I had full intention of being strong and having a civil, mature conversation, but looking into Walker's eyes makes me buckle.

My voice pitches and tears swell. *"He's* back!" I shrill out in broken words. Tears drop down my cheeks as I fall into his chest. His muscles and jawline stricken, turning rigid.

"When?" he snarls out in a low, controlled growl. He sounds almost animalistic. The anger blackens his eyes.

He surely would kill him if he had the opportunity. Fear of

the smoldering rage on Walker's face forces me to look away. I meet Sadie's eyes, who also seemed leerily worried.

"Is everything okay? Who's back?" Sadie reaches over the edge of the counter and places a hand on Walker's shoulder. Sympathy mixed with worry etches her voice.

I feel him relax, only for a brief second, to her touch. He shakes his head, trying to shrug away the feeling of her and the thought of *Him* co-existing in the same space in his head.

Ignoring Sadie, he returns his full attention to me as I attempt to recompose myself. "Clara, what did he do? Where is he?" More questions arise as his protective nature inches to the surface.

"He moved back in last night. He hasn't done anything… yet. Can I come live with you?"

There it is… the question that I didn't want to ask. It flies out of my mouth with ease. Turning to Walker has always been easy. His presence has brought back that piece of me, the scared little sister who looks to her brother as a savior.

Walker gazes down to me, his eyes dark with a storm of emotions. He wants to protect me, but the price of that protection is great. I can see in his clenched jaw, the tightening of his fists. He doesn't want to risk going back to prison, and I can't blame him.

"You can stay with me until we can figure out a better solution. I sure as shit don't want you staying there with *him*." I hug him tighter, thanking him deeply. He releases a deep breath and pulls back to face the hallway leading to Daniel's office. "I don't want you to sit around my apartment either, though… I'm going to ask Daniel if you can help here at the shelter."

Sadie sighs, understanding that she is being intentionally left out of the loop. I turn my focus to Sadie, realizing she's genuinely concerned.

She seems close to Walker, so I give her more information than I've given anyone else. "A guy my mom used to date… he…

uh… he was hurting me, and Walker caught him and hurt him back. That's why Walker went to… you know."

Sadie's eyes soften. Her shoulders slough, showing the weight of her concern. It's the most I've spoken out loud on the subject, which makes my skin crawl. Feeling panic rising in my chest, I stretch and move in my stance. Trying to shake the sensation away usually temporarily works. Sadie nods her head sympathetically and doesn't ask any questions.

"Thank you for sharing that with me… it must've been so difficult. You're safe with Walker and me. If you can't stay with Walker, you can stay with my dysfunctional family." The corner of her mouth upturned in a slight smirk, she seems like an incredible person.

Sadie wasn't just offering me a place to stay, but a piece of peace… something I haven't had in a long time.

"Can I ask you a favor?" I sheepishly ask, knowing I'm already calling in a favor from someone I've only met a few times. She waits silently for me to ask. "Do you think… if you don't mind… you could take me to my mother's house… to pack… and take me back to Walker's? He can't go near… *him*…. and I don't want to go alone."

"Of course I can. I wouldn't mind at all. We can go right after I get done volunteering." She smiles, a full smile this time. Her green eyes sparkling with genuine kindness. I assess her fair skin and beautiful blonde hair. She's gorgeous, radiating from the inside out.

No wonder Walker is so obviously in love.

CHAPTER TWENTY-SEVEN

NEW BEGINNINGS

Trigger Warning: Chapter contains graphic depictions of violence and domestic abuse

It's the Friday evening prior to the Fourth of July party.

Sadie sits in Clara's room as she gathers her belongings into any bags she can scrape together. Boxes and bags lay skewed about the faded cream-colored carpet. Sadie sits on Clara's loosely made twin bed flipping through funny videos on her phone.

"Did you hear about the new sports complex the city's building on the other side of town? Diane's been bitching about it at dinner every night. It's going to *ruin high society*." Sadie tells Clara while her eyes stay trained on her phone. Clara packs a plushy purple blanket into an empty Amazon box she found in the recycling and chuckles slightly.

"Did she really say *high society*?" Clara asks, surprised that someone would have so much audacity. Pausing as she holds her composition notebook filled with her very private writing, she traces a thumb over the cover.

Sadie sighs, rolling over onto her stomach on the bed and

pulling Clara's attention back into focus. Sadie glances upward into the noticeable silence. She finds Clara staring at her, awaiting a response.

Sadie sits up and raises her nose to the air, imitating her mother in a dramatized voice, "Can you *Bah-lieve* the *audacity* of the city for building a *SPORT* building on *OUR* side of town! Next will be *dive bars* and *homeless camps*." She exaggerates Diane's typical posture and movements.

Both girls laugh at the imitation. While giggling, Clara arranges her bags and boxes, preparing to tote them out of the house to Sadie's car. "Your mom must be quite a character. Mine's a saint. Her only problem is picking the wrong people to love." The room falls quiet.

Melony, on the other side of the door, whimpers softly to herself. She can sense what's coming. The air in the hall feels heavy as Melony attempts to hold back tears. Sadie shifts to sit at the edge of the bed, acknowledging the change in conversation. Clara begins picking up bags and slings them over her shoulder. Sadie hops off the bed to join her.

Melony stands on the other side of Clara's bedroom door, preparing to knock.

Clara's smile falls as she opens the door, guilt plastered across her face. "Mom."

Melony's eyes roll down from Clara to the bags and box in her arms. The ping of loss shutters through Melony's body. Confusion and hurt twist on her face in a sour sting.

"Whe... where are you going?" Melony's eyes flicker to Sadie, curiosity crossing her face. She's wondering where she knows Sadie from. Melony can't quite place a name to the face but knows that she recognizes her.

"I can't stay here." Before Clara can utter why, agony creeps across Melony's face as she takes a wounded step back. Shaking her head in denial, refusing to accept what Clara's saying.

"I can't let you leave…. Clara… I can't lose you, too!" Her

voice quivers with a mix of desperation and disbelief. A hint of shame tinges her words.

Suspicions arise, guilt that she should've known *what* happened all those years ago. Clara didn't say, but the timing of her leaving… the pain in her face… Melony didn't have to ask. She shakes her head violently, denial taking over to preserve her heart from guilted grief that's trying to eat away at her. Clara's hands tremble, the contents of the box rattling with the movement. Seeing the distress her mother is feeling swells Clara's throat. "I need to protect myself, Mom." Clara forces the words under a sharp exhale.

Melony's denial shifts to Walker. She can't accept the truth that she brought home the person Clara speaks of. She's her mother… the person who should've been there to protect her. Melony gulps against the resistance of her tight, dry throat.

'Walker has to be who she's talking about. I can't be the reason… I can't be the one who caused all her pain.' Melony battles her inner thoughts, forcing denial to take deep root in her mind.

"He can't hurt you! He can't come back now! He'll go back to jail! You *ARE* safe."

Clara's anger boils. With eyebrows furrowed and teeth clenched together tensely, she pushes through her mother. Clara can't believe that her mom truly believes that she's referring to Walker.

'How clueless can she be?', she thinks to herself. Sadie shrugs apologetically as she sidesteps past Melony.

"Clara! Wait for me!" Sadie's voice cuts through Clara's thoughts, but she can barely register it. The outside world feels distant, like everyone else is in a different universe. Sadie chases after Clara to catch up. "You okay?" Sadie places the pop-up cube full of bathroom essentials under her arm. Reaching out, her hand hovers over Clara's shoulder, unsure how to comfort her newfound friend. They both continue to move to the sedan out front. "Clara?" Sadie attempts to get her attention again.

She doesn't respond as she leans forward to place her belongings in Sadie's trunk. She uses her body weight to close the trunk. Before the trunk fully shuts Sadie hurriedly throws one of Clara's duffle bag in.

Clara sulks over to the passenger seat, a garbled cloud of frustration and pain hanging over her. Struggling, she internalizes all the hurt from her mom and the anger she harbors on behalf of her brother.

"Are you alright?" Sadie asks as she gets into the driver's seat, closing the door behind her. She nods, but it doesn't feel truthful.

"Yeah… I'm *fine,*" she whispers, but the words ring hollow, bouncing off the walls of her mind.

The sound of her mother's sobs bellow in the background, burning into her mind as a core memory she wishes she could forget. She'll bury it when she feels again… right next to all the other memories that haunt her.

Clara numbly fixes her eyes on the neighbor's house across the street. A young adult woman works in the well-kept vibrant flower garden. The lady's two young children play in a small plastic pool. Two young boys, laughing and splashing each other without a care in the world. Clara feels the adrenaline leave her body with the relaxation of her muscles and loosening of her jaw. A small exhale draws Sadie's eyes off the road to the passenger seat.

"What was that all about?" Sadie asks calmly, hoping her question doesn't bring back the tension from a few moments prior.

"My mom thinks it's because of Walker. I don't know how she can't see it." She peers down, not wanting to meet Sadie's eyes. Quiet consumes the car as Sadie recognizes Clara won't open up past that.

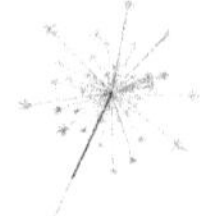

Collapsing onto the couch crying, Melony gasps, eating the air around her sobs. The loss of both her children and her late husband rolling together and drowning her. She lies on the couch and gives way to the hurt that pulses through her in waves. The weight of grief suffocating her, pushing her firmly into the flimsy tan couch cushion. Rubbing her face vigorously, like she can peel away the tear-stained skin, she sits up abruptly. *'Make the pain go away,'* she thinks as she propels herself toward the kitchen.

Melony never drinks... but she does keep alcohol in the house for special occasions. Pulling a stepstool to the front of the fridge, she scales to the upper cabinets. As she pulls the vodka down, Karl walks into the kitchen through the side door. A smile pulls his face up, seeing her hold the glass bottle.

"Are we having a good time tonight love? I hope you don't mind that I started without you." Karl pulls Melony into him, smelling like he bathed in beer. He gives her a wet sloppy kiss on the cheek, forcing her to wipe her face.

"You reek. Did someone spill their drink on you?" she asks, placing her hand on his chest to push distance between the two of them.

Karl stands up straight at her distaste and huffs as he snatches the bottle from her hand. In two stumbling steps, he moves to the cabinet where the glassware is. Grabbing two glasses, he pours two drinks. Without making eye contact, he takes his glass past Melony into the living room.

Melony adds two extra shots to her glass and follows behind Karl to the living room. "Where's my little girl? Already in bed?"

Karl asking about Clara triggers Melony. She places her hand on her forehead, shielding her eyes and swallowing back tears as she winces at the pain of thinking about her causes. Karl sits up, sobering to the sound of her sniffles. "Where is she? Is she okay?" He stands, approaching Melony to console her.

"She's fine." A shallow hitching breath interrupts her sentence. "She decided she doesn't want to stay here. She went to stay with a friend of hers."

Karl pulls his hand back. Noting Clara slipped through his fingers again, his frustration grows. He came back to Melony to keep tabs on Clara. To take her back as *his*. To ensure she doesn't blab. The last thing he wanted was for her to start getting confident enough to leave.

This is Walker's fault. He's changed her. Karl thought to himself, trying to shift his frustration from Melony to Walker.

With his jaw clenched and body tensing Karl hisses. "How could you let her leave?!" He steps away from her, attempting to keep his mask firm and not let rash decisions run rampant... but he had a bit too much to drink and feels himself slipping. "What kind of mother let's her little girl go stay at a stranger's house?!" Karl presses his palms to his eyelids, forcing himself to try to level with his inner thoughts.

She's gone. Telling the world. You're a joke. Nothing to fear. Walker doesn't. Clara doesn't. Melony laughs at you when you turn your back. They all know. You're weak. A pathetic excuse for a man.

No one's scared.

She's. Not. Yours.

His inner voice provokes him to lose control. Drilling his thumbs into his eyes, he battles the voice from within. Melony approaches him from behind, placing her hand on his shoulder to comfort him.

"She's just a teenage girl. She'll wise up and come ba...." Melony is unable to finish her sentence when Karl rapidly turns on her, backhanding her so forcefully that she falls into and over the living room end table.

The world spins as Melony lies on the floor, head throbbing from the impact. She sucks the air, wincing, her mouth tasting like an old penny. Her breaths come in shallow gasps as her body trembles, not just from the shock of the blow, but from the sickening realization that Karl did this to her—that he'll do it again.

Karl's eyes darken, the muscles in his face contorting into an animalistic monster. Bending forward, hovering over Melony, he grabs her. Lifting her up by the throat, he brings her face within an inch of his. His growl sounds guttural, through gritted teeth. He slams her against the tile at the edge of the kitchen entryway, her head lobs forward and back as it smashes against the floor. Melony's dizzy, feeling faint from the blows.

"She's mine!" Karl shouts as he slams her back down then releases her limp body and stands up calmly.

The depravity of emotions as he stands confuses her, and the detachment in his eyes enhances her fear. Standing over her with a possessive smile and slit eyes, his voice lowers. "You'll bring her back to me... or you'll wish you had. Do you understand me?" His smile is tight and unsettling.

A drop of her blood drips down Karl's cheek. He moves his hand to the wetness and rubs at it with his fingertips, sniffing the blood. Relaxing his shoulders, his eyes roll to the back of his head in pleasure. Melony, still trying to stop the room from spinning, sits up. Leaning with one hand on the floor for balance, she makes the mistake of threatening Karl.

"I'm calling the police!" she shrieks with more fear than courage behind her statement.

Karl inhales deeply, pausing with calculating eyes. He drops into a low squat and cradles her chin in between his bloody fingers. He turns her head to reveal the reddening mark swelling on her face.

"No… you won't. We both know that I'll do much worse to little Clara if you try. It wouldn't be my first time evading the cops from slapping a *bitch* around. Don't think you're special darlin'." His sinister smirk sends chills down her spine. She tries to pull her face out of his hold, but he pinches down tightly, making her chin smart. "Now, you be a good girl and get me a new drink since you spilled mine." His eyes move to the shattered glass on the floor behind the end table.

Getting up slowly and shakily, she proceeds to make another drink. She doesn't know what else she can do.

Chapter Twenty-Eight

Walker Harris: For Walt

A knock at the door rattles as I'm showering. I rush through rinsing and jump out. I run to the door wrapping a towel around my waist, hoping to God it's not my PO for a random inspection. Sadie and my sister will be coming by later to move Clara in. It's not *illegal* for Clara to move in; my parole specifies avoiding Karl, not my family.

I shift my shoulders, the physical discomfort rolling down my back. I don't want my parole officer to start digging, for any reason. I open the door to Sadie and Clara, arms full of bags and boxes.

"Did you have to live on the fifth floor with no functioning elevator? Jeez…." Sadie huffs, out of breath. "Nice towel." Sadie raises her eyebrows jokingly as she pushes past me. "I'd say you should be a gentleman and grab some of this stuff… but I don't think anyone wants you to let go of the towel." Both Sadie and Clara begin chuckling.

I smirk at Sadie, and she returns the favor. Noticing my thoughts are a little too flirty, I straighten my back and clear my throat. I need to practice restraint.

"You can put your stuff in my room; I cleared out part of my closet for you." I point to the room off the small living space. I glance down at the towel spreading apart, I adjust it trying to avoid drawing attention. "I'm gonna get dressed, I'll be right back." I slip into the bathroom. Putting on deodorant, I gaze down at the light grey sweatpants and a black tee shirt sitting on the sink counter. Banging on the bathroom door startles me.

"Dang it, Walker! Hurry up! I got to pee!" Sadie shouts as she smacks on the door.

I chuckle softly to myself, thinking *'She's too damn comfortable'*. I open the door swiftly, catching her closed fist mid-knock on my chest.

"Can I help you, Miss Thomas?" I say in a formal murmur. Sticking her finger in her mouth and sticking out her tongue, she pretends to gag.

"Ew, gross, Walker's pretending to be a gentleman... how disturbing." Clara giggles sheepishly over by the couch as she pulls out a few of her belongings out of a duffle bag.

My eyes dart from Clara to Sadie. She feels my eyes and transfers her weight, turning her face away. She nudges me out of the bathroom and closes the door behind her.

Clara, not making eye contact, makes a quiet, nonchalant observation. "You like her, huh?" she asks rhetorically without so much as a glance.

"I don't know what you're talking about." I try to refrain from smiling, but the corners of my mouth rat me out. I grab my jaw to hide the uncontrollable smile. "Sadie's with a cop and I'm fresh out of prison. *We're just friends.*"

Clara smiles, peeking at me from the corner of her eye. She pauses her unpacking to face me. "I like Sadie. She's funny... and nice. Qualities *you* don't have." I stick my tongue out at her as I nudge her arm. She playfully shoves me back, eyebrows furrowing. This behavior must hurt something deep down.

"Hey, Walker…." She sounds like she's struggling to ask something.

"You don't have to… I know. I never blamed you. Not even for a day. I'm glad to see you're… well… as well as someone can be, considering." A rush of air escapes her mouth. The tension in her shoulders release allowing her body to relax.

"I thought about you every day… I'll never forgive myself… even if you did." Clara grabs a pile of clothes out of the duffle bag and heads off into my bedroom.

I stroll past the living room into the small kitchen. Turning from the sink with a glass of water in hand, I almost run into Sadie. She startles me, forcing water to fall to the ground.

"Damn it! Sadie, what the hell are you doing?!" Both of us bend forward to pick up the cup that fell to the floor and our heads bounce off each other. With my head spinning, I stand up. Sadie grips her head, laughing.

"I startle you, so you beat me with your hard head?!" Her laughter warms me, and I smile.

Rubbing her head, she grabs onto my upper arm to stabilize herself. Her chuckles slow, but her grip on my arm remains. Our eyes pull away from her hand on my arm, slowly locking eyes. The tension in the air robs me of my breath, my body tingles with anticipation.

I lean in, unable to resist temptation. She leans in as well, with a dazed gleam in her eye. I pull up and rest my lips against her forehead instead. "I'm sorry, I couldn't help myself." I mutter under my breath. The last thing I want to do is ruin her happy relationship with sexual tension.

Sadie jumps back abruptly, the moment over. "Oh! Umm…. I don't know what came over me." She hesitates, her glimmering eyes begging me to interrupt her—to stop her from dismissing this moment we're sharing.

I place my arms behind my back and nod my head slightly.

Her eyes still longingly looking into mine.

Clara walks into the living room, clearing her throat to get our attention as she stares at us with a smirk on her face. "Sooo… what's up with you guys?"

Sadie leaps back, like we were fucking in the kitchen and Garrett walked in. She couldn't get away from me fast enough, clearly ashamed of her advances. I'm glad it didn't go any further; I wouldn't want to be someone she regrets.

Sadie stands straighter and tries to shrug off the entire exchange. She's pretending it never happened. Not going to lie, it hits my ego—her immediately dismissing the thought of being with me and tucking it away to the back of her mind.

Shifting in place, I grab a kitchen towel, cleaning up the mess before going to my room. I nod to Sadie and Clara as I walk past each of them, saying goodnight.

I'm glad Sadie's able to dismiss the heated moment between us. Unfortunately for me, it'll be impossible. I'll spend the night imagining the feeling of her trembling skin beneath my lips. The longing look in her eyes. Her soft hands grasping my arm, making my mind wander to other places I'd like her hands. Going to bed flustered is difficult, but my sister sleeping on the couch makes it easier.

Cold shower for me in the morning.

Looking in the mirror, I feel out of place. I don't feel prepared to be surrounded by a life that forgot about me a long time ago. I stand in front of the mirror, buttoning up my short-sleeved collared shirt.

Clara strolls into my room. "Look at you, all dressed up and somewhere to go." She's smiling ear to ear. "Excited to see Sadie again? You seemed pretty *excited* to see her last night," she says in an insinuating tone. I roll my eyes.

"You don't know what you're talking about. Sadie and I are *just friends….*"

"For now," Clara interjects, still smiling like the Cheshire Cat. "You're just going to deny you've got feelings for her? I mean… hell… *I* do, too; she is amazing."

"If that's what's best for her, damn straight I will. I'm going to let her be happy." I say as I push past her to my closet. I put on the dress shorts that I thrifted for today's party.

Clara lowers her voice to imitate me as she jumps into my line of sight, demanding attention. Her eyebrows furrowed; she tries to pull off a stoic look. "I'm *Walker,* and I'm a *man* who knows what's best for all women! I make the decisions because I'm a *big man!*"

"Hilarious… no, really… you should be on SNL." I pause to slow clap, sarcastically un-entertained.

"In all seriousness, Walker, it's her choice. By not telling her how you feel, you're taking away her right to choose. Isn't that wrong to do to her?"

Clara has a point. I consider telling Sadie the truth as I finish getting ready and Uber to the other side of town.

Arriving at the party feels like arriving at a red-carpet event. There's hired valet available to those who drove themselves, gigantic floral arrangements with sparkling tinsel framing the entryway, where staff are chauffeuring guests through the foyer to the party. In the backyard, there are huge white tents with enough seating for a large wedding.

People gather in small groups throughout; some holding drinks, others cocktail plates. There's a band off to the side with a handful of children dancing to the upbeat music. Towers of patriotic floral arrangements are scattered throughout the yard, and decorative pieces float atop the water of the in-ground pool.

The smell of grilled chicken wafts from one tent, which houses the buffet style food and built-in bar that already exists as a backyard lawn ornament. Staff in blue attire with red accents bustle about with trays of appetizers and signature cocktails. The bar is crowded, and it isn't even noon yet.

A familiar voice comes echoing behind me. "The mayor is standing right over there with his wife, talking to the gentleman from the DA's office. Get a picture of him before he leaves this party! If our family's Fourth of July party is going to be featured in the paper, I want *that* to be the picture!" Diane snaps at two gentlemen, each holding a professional camera.

They stand in her presence for a second too long, and Diane shoos them off. "I'm not paying you to look dumbfounded! Go take pictures!" she mutters under a smile as some guests are shuffling past.

Her eye catches mine, and she approaches me with a forced, tightly pressed smile. "Oh, um… Harris, isn't it? Walt Harris! So glad you decided to show up." She looks me up and down with a sharp, critical glare in her eyes and pursed calculative lips.

Sucking through her teeth, she shifts her weight to one hip. "Dressed… in the best formal attire I'm sure you have available to you." She wears a politician's smile, the kind that doesn't quite meet her cold, green eyes—a stark difference from Sadie's burning warmth.

She clearly doesn't like me… without even knowing me. Richard approaches us from behind Diane before I can respond to her *kind* words.

"Hey, look who showed up against better judgment!" Richard smiles as he outstretches his hand. "How you doin' son? Taking care of yourself, I hope."

He's such a genuinely kind man. Every inch of Sadie looks like Diane, but her soul comes from Richard. I reciprocate the handshake warmly.

"Thank you, sir. It's nice to see you under better circumstances." His eyes flinch, remembering what happened to his little girl.

"I can't agree more. Make sure you get yourself a drink and some food. The company is…." He pretends to fall asleep, snoring, and snaps his head back *awake* with a chuckle. "But the fireworks will be worth it." His smile fades as he turns to Diane, who's unamused by his comments.

She shrugs his apologetic arm off her shoulder and straightens her dress.

"Yes, well, I believe the company to be well suited for this *status* of party," she says, flexing her head away from both of us. Flashing a look at me out the corner of her eye, she mutters under a shallow exhale. "For the most part." She then takes a deep breath and spins inwards to the house. "I need to go ensure that the food is in order… enjoy your time, Walt." Diane feigns hospitality as she walks away, calling me by the wrong name.

Richard doesn't catch the comment, distracted by someone he works with. He catches up with him, leaving me behind. I turn my sights to the open bar. If I'm going to be involved in more conversations as lovely as this one, I'll need a drink.

I shuffle through several groups of people, awkwardly standing a step outside the gathering. With my free hand in my pocket, I nod. I pretend that I know the premise of each conversation, secretly hoping that no one asks my opinion on stocks or financial gains in property investments.

A slight sweat works up on the nape of my neck. The combination of drinking and the sweltering Kentucky summer heat soaks the collar-line on the back of my neck. I tug at the fabric, running my hand between my shirt and skin. Deciding to cool off in front of one of the ceiling fans under the white tent, I saunter over. Sadie and Garrett bicker as I enter the tent. Unseen, I step to the side and listen in.

"He's in love with you; you're an idiot if you don't see it," Garrett huffs, adjusting the watch on his wrist. She sighs without a response, looking down at her freshly painted red nails. "You knew? You just don't care… is that it?"

Rolling her eyes, she glances up from her nails to Garrett intensely staring at her. "I want us to work." She avoids answering the true question Garrett was asking, looking over her shoulder at the crowd of people off in the distance.

"Do you love him too?" he asks without hesitation, gripping the table like he's bracing for impact.

She turns her attention to the hem of her dress, picking at it. Her emeralds flicker up to meet his eyes and back down to the dress.

"I don't know how I feel…." She hesitates when a gentleman enters the tent beside me, bringing their attention to me. I act as if I stumbled into the tent with the other gentleman.

"Hey, how you guys doing?" I ask as I approach them.

She sits up, rolling her shoulders back. Her half-hearted smile reveals the conflict she's feeling inside. Garrett huffs, leaning back in his seat and crossing his arms stiffly over the other.

"Bored. Glad you came." A sigh of relief hugs her words.

Garrett shifts, lifting his chest and pushing his shoulders back. Seeing her eyes widen excitedly as I sit, his jaw clenches and lips tighten. He puts an arm around her, leaning on the back of her seat.

"We're as good as we can be in this heat." He smiles unauthentically and hooks Sadie toward him to kiss her on the cheek.

She winces at the force of the kiss and leans away. He catches her in a one-armed embrace, stopping her from pulling away. I smirk, attempting to ignore the flaunting of Sadie like a kid showing off a toy at the park.

"Yeah, it's pretty hot. Gotta love July."

He forces a chuckle and nods in agreement. Sadie inches away from Garrett, rubbing the side of her face that he wet with his lips. He stretches his arms out as he stands from the chair.

"Imma go see if I can sneak some dessert out of the kitchen. Want anything, babe?" Garrett asks Sadie. *Doesn't he know that she's not fond of sweets?*

"No, I don't really like dessert. I'm good, thanks."

Garrett huffs. "I didn't know that. You never told me." His smile returns as quickly as it faded, and he stands over me. Putting his hand on me, he grips my shoulder too tightly for it to be pleasant. "Keep an eye on *my girl*." Releasing my shoulder, he pats firmly and meanders off.

My attention returns to Sadie, fidgeting with the length of her dress. Awkward silence fills the air as I move into Garrett's now empty seat.

"Hey, I want to talk to you about something…." The thought of revealing my true feelings causes a lump to grow in my throat. My mouth dries when our eyes meet, and my mind trails off as I zero in on every inch of her face.

She decides to talk first. "He knows I don't like dessert. I've never eaten dessert," she sighs, glancing away from me. Her eyes show contemplation, weighing her feelings. With her thoughts growing too heavy, she heaves a breathy exhale.

"I know," I respond, realizing that this conversation is shifting to complaining about her *boyfriend*. I huff, annoyed that I could be absent minded enough to listen to my little sister's advice. She knows how I feel, she said it herself. She's choosing him, as she should. "Hey, where's the bathroom again?" I ask, standing up.

She gazes up at me, smiling pleasantly. "Inside, across from the dining room. But if that one's occupied, you can use my bathroom. Up the stairs and down the hall to the left."

I nod and abruptly walk off, leaving our conversation behind me. The first bathroom is locked. I wait a few minutes, but no one exits. Not wanting to wait much longer for the liquor to strong-arm my bladder, I move on to the upstairs restroom. A red velvet rope lined the bottom of the stairs with a small sign reads *OFF LIMITS.* Stepping over the rope, I scale the stairway.

Finishing up in the restroom, a loud thud bangs against the wall of the restroom. Someone's in the hallway leaning on the shared wall.

As I leave the restroom, I look to see who made the thud on the wall. It looks like Sadie and Garrett are intensely making out, but after a second glance, I notice it's Diane pressed against the wall. Garrett's nestled in the crook of her neck, holding her up in the air with her legs wrapped around his waist.

I stumble back, unsure if I'm actually seeing what I see, or if the alcohol has me hallucinating. I rub my hand down my face, as if they're a mirage.

Garrett hears my presence and turns his head to face me. Dropping Diane, he turns to me with his pants unzipped. He clearly planned going further than what I witnessed. "Please don't tell her… this is… it means nothing."

I shake my head, unable to put words to the second-hand betrayal I feel. "Listen, don't ruin today. Let me tell her. Give me… a few days. No use making yourself the villain."

He's right. The bastard's absolutely right. If I tell Sadie, I'll always be the guy who told her that her boyfriend's cheating on her… *and with her mom.*

"By Monday, if I see her and she doesn't know… I'll tell her."

He nods his head, zipping up his pants. He steps past me, going down the stairs. Diane, avoiding eye contact, stands against the wall, adjusting her hair in the hall mirror across from her.

Giving Garrett the time to tell Sadie isn't for him. It's for Sadie. I don't want her to experience the humiliation of others finding out before her. She might not believe me anyway, considering it's her own mother and her long-term boyfriend.

I sigh, pulling Diane's attention off herself. "This is disturbing… even for you *Darlene*." I know it's not her name… and not the time to make a verbal jab, but I had to… *for Walt*.

Chapter Twenty-Nine

Sadie Thomas: Maybe I do

Garrett comes stumbling out of the house with no dessert. "What the heck? Did you scarf it down inside?" Giggling under my breath at my own joke, but then I notice Garrett's disoriented pale face and beet red cheeks. "Hey… you okay?

What happened?"

He peers around at the party and back to me, visibly struggling to maintain his composure. Inhaling sharply and blowing out his exhale, he wipes the back of his hand across his sweat-beaded forehead.

"Garrett?" I ask, standing up to meet him and reaching for his flushed cheek.

He grabs my wrist as I reach, pausing for a second and then brings my hand up to cup his cheek. His whole body liquefies as we make connection. Shoulders slack and posture caves as he sighs.

"I'm okay… maybe heat stroke. I'll be fine." He flashes his teeth in an insincere smile before rubbing his wet forehead into my hand, making me cringe.

"Ew! What the hell! You're gross!"

He laughs at my reaction, shaking his curly black hair, releasing drops of sweat into the air like a wet dog shaking dry. I turn away giggling, but something inside feels strange as unease settles in my stomach.

Something about his words feels off, like he's hiding something. My throat tightens from the disorientating shift in emotions. I've never felt this way about Garrett before. I smile, but a pang of hurt and confusion sits idly underneath my skin. Anticipation brewing for another shoe to drop.

Walker emerges, but instead of rejoining us, he heads straight to the bar. He spends the remainder of the night drowning himself. Garrett, holding my waist, shuffles me over to a group of his colleagues to chat about pensions.

I stand with a quaint smile, but out of the corner of my eye, I study Garrett, searching for any sign of what spooked him. His carefree laughter and boasting with friends feels natural, but night and day compared to moments ago. I bob my head and laugh when others laugh but bury myself inwards to consider what caused the shift in him.

"I'm going to get some water, I'll be back." Garrett, midstory-telling to a work acquaintance, acknowledges with raising his hand and continues talking.

My mind concludes that I need to talk to Walker. I wonder if he saw whatever spooked Garrett. I'm also curious why he's avoiding me. Something happened inside... I need to know what.

Approaching the bar, I find Walker chugging back a glass of beer before the foam fizzles out. He slams the beer down, holding a double shot of rum in the other hand.

"Are you drunk?" I ask.

He twists his head just enough to acknowledge my presence then back to his drink. His shoulders are slouched, propped up on his elbow with his hand clutching at his disheveled hair. I hesitate at his side, looking at him with a mix of concern and judgement, tilting my head. He scoffs and mutters something like *'you're wasting your time'* under his breath as he takes a sip.

"You shouldn't be here. Go socialize." I push through, planting myself in the seat beside him. "I don't fit here either.

I'm not built to be he…."

Walker stiffens, the disgust melting into a downturned face. He huffs at me, dismissing the words as I say them. His bloodshot eyes roll to the back of his head dramatically.

Walker interjects, slurring his words as he aggressively makes his pronouncement. "The only person that doesn't belong here is *me*." Walker's red teary eyes lock onto mine, heavy with something unspoken. His jaw clenches, a distant hurt buried in his hollowed blue eyes.

The silence between us stretches uncomfortably. I swallow hard, uncertain how to bridge the gap between us. This isn't him… it's not Walker.

"What do you mean? We're the same… I thought that… well…." I stutter over my words, unsure how to act with the cold stranger I'm talking to. Walker stands slamming his drink down. I've never seen him so heartless.

"You're delusional. I'm an ex-con with no future. And you're a doctor. You're born into *this*." He swings his arms around, referencing the lavish party surrounding us. "You belong here. We're not meant to exist *together*!" Walker yells, laying his feelings bare for everyone at the party to see. As he storms off, he cocks his head over his shoulder and whispers in a melancholy tone, "In *any* form of existence."

Tears swell in my eyes. My chest heavy with hurt, I take a steadying breath and use the back of my arm to wipe them away. Leaning out of the seat to stand, I grab his half-finished drink and throw it back.

The bartender asks if I want another. I must look distressed. I nod violently and chug down the two swigs of that drink too, wincing at the burn as I swallow. I smooth my red dress with blue flowers, preparing to go back to Garrett, who's laughing with a group of lawyers now. I dissociate as I approach them, feeling Walker's presence on the other side of the yard, I fight the urge to glance at him.

He's wrong… he's meant to be in my life.

The automatic outdoor lights click on as the sunlight disappears. The fireworks display that my parents spent thousands on will begin soon.

Everyone gathers around the portable stage the band performed on, where my father stands with a microphone in hand. Swaying with a drink in his hand, he slurs, "Hey, everyone! I, ah… wanted to welcome y'all… and… thanks for coming. I was asked to gather everyone for an announcement…. but first…. I want to make my own little announcement." Dad pauses, taking a drink. He stumbles back a step, trying to tip his head back to empty his glass. "Miss Sadie Thomas, come join your dear old dad on the stage, please." He staggers forward, gazing around the crowd looking for me.

He knows better than to put me in the spotlight, though being drunk doesn't allow much room for remembering. I stumble onto the stage, cursing under my breath as I lean into my father.

"The hell are you doing?!" I mutter in his ear, hoping the microphone didn't pick up my voice. He smiles at me sloppily and pulls me under his arm, facing me to the audience.

"My intelligent daughter is preparing to go on a journey! And I'm so blessed to be a part of it. When just a short while ago I thought that I wouldn't be able to be here for all of this." He places his fist over his heart, choking back tears, reminding me of his heart attack earlier this year. The difficult memory combined with the stench of scotch radiating from him burns my eyes.

I'm *going on a journey?* What kind of Hallmark bullshit is this? Dad takes two steps forward and spins me to face Garrett, who snuck up behind me onto the stage. The band begins playing a slow song behind me. Before I can process what's happening, Garrett gets down on one knee.

Gasping and disoriented, I gaze blankly around at the faceless bodies surrounding the stage. The music, although soft, is deafening from where I stand next to the speakers. My gaze falls on Walker, whose eyes are wide and mouth open ajar. I hesitate, hoping Walker will say something. But he doesn't... because he doesn't want me.

A thunderous crack splits the air and whistles as fireworks erupt, making me flinch. Gasps ripple through the crowd, gawking at the bright colors exploding in the night sky. Diane's shriek cuts through the stunned silence like a knife.

"Dammit Greg! *After* she says yes!"

My head whips toward her. Seeing the excitement on her face feels wrong. I cringe, still trying to process the commotion. I glance back at Walker to find him walking away. The blur of noises and people fall into the abyss I shove them into, and I decide to be practical.

Instead of following my heart... I'll stay with what's comfortable.

I nod, smiling a pitiful smile, eyes saddened. Garrett hops off the ground, embracing me with a tight hug. Looking over his shoulder the light of the fireworks, give off hues of red and blue against the white tents. The fresh pain of loss sucker punches my gut, stealing my breath away. Loosening the hug, Garrett leans me back in a swooping kiss. Tears form in my eyes, but not from happiness.

Chapter Thirty
Walker Harris: Unwilling Secrecy

I rush into my apartment, slamming the door closed behind me. I lean against it, trying to catch my breath. The entire ride home, I clutched my chest, forcing my emotions down as deep as they could go.

The fucker said he'd tell her! Instead, he proposes! He proposed in front of everyone.... The man deserves to have his face caved in.

Anger boils, threatening to spill everywhere. I can't afford to go back to jail for a parole violation if I beat this prick. Breathing hard, my mind spirals out of control.

Clara leaves the bathroom in pajamas and looks ready for bed. "Hey… wait… what's wrong? You okay? You look like you're gonna be sick." She approaches me, putting the back of her hand to my forehead. I yank away from her touch, feeling volatile.

"I'm fine." I storm to the kitchen sink and rinse my face, hoping to cool myself down rapidly. I pause, hovering over the sink for a moment to pat my face dry before proceeding to the couch. Clara follows behind me silently and sits beside me.

"Did you—" She's making connections, assuming I'm upset from rejection.

"No." I cross one arm over the other, leaning back into the cushion, my shoulders sinking into the foam padding. She stares at me, waiting for me to continue.

"But… why…." Her words fluctuate.

She's leaning toward me, trying to meet my eyes. I glare at the television, muted, flashing an advertisement.

"She's engaged."

Clara's eyes widen. Her mouth falls open. Swallowing, she drops her chin to her chest and twiddles her thumbs.

"Oh…." Distant words followed by silence.

Images of Garrett proposing to Sadie and being promiscuous with her mom blend in my mind. If I tell her now, she won't believe me. She'll think I'm just trying to cut her out of her engagement to lower her standards to my level.

"I caught Garrett upstairs going at it with her mom…. Her fucking *mom*." It's eating away at me, and I need someone to agree with how awful a person Garrett is. He had me fooled, always doting on Sadie. I didn't realize he was doting on her mom, too.

"You're serious?! And she still said yes?!" Clara exclaims.

She doesn't realize Sadie doesn't know. Come to think of it, I didn't stay long enough to hear whether she said yes. She could've said no. I just assumed that she'd say yes.

"Well… I didn't tell her." Perplexed, she freezes.

"You do realize the woman you love is marrying someone who's cheating on her… and you… what… don't want to hurt her feelings?" She's waving her arms above her head, trying to prove a point.

When I shrug dismissively, she crosses her arms, furrowing her brows. Clicking her tongue, she shifts before sitting back down. "Tell her. She deserves to know. I guarantee Garrett won't tell her." Clara waits for me to come to my senses and agree with her decision.

"I don't want to tell her. I could just let her be happy.

Garrett's better for her... anyway... she won't believe me over him."

Clara winces, twitching away from the words, she folds inwards over herself. "Sometimes silence doesn't help. Sometimes people wrongly go to prison or end up in a marriage they don't realize is a prison." Her baby blue eyes fill with remorse. Shoulders slouching, she brings her knees up onto the couch to her chest. The guilt she's feeling is palpable, bringing on a sinking unease.

*If I don't tell her... I've chosen **for** her.*

"You're right. I'll tell her." I put my hand on her back to comfort her, but she flinches at the unexpected touch. Her eyes flick to mine and soften. The corner of her lip quivers, twitching to release a small grin.

I smile encouragingly. The pressure of guilt squeezes my words. "I'm sorry, I didn't... I mean... I'm sor—"

"Don't be. You saved me." Clara puts her hand on my arm, interrupting my sorry excuse for an apology.

"Not soon enough." I choke out as I move in my seat.

I shake my head, hoping to shake away the weight behind those words. I clear my throat, ending the conversation... for today.

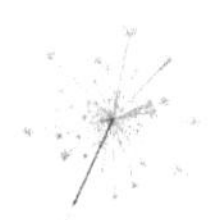

I stand at the front desk, staring at Sadie's hands flipping through papers she's sorting. Daniel had congratulated her weeks ago when we came back to the shelter after the party.

She wears his ring. It's safe to say that he hasn't told her. Either that... or they worked through it. I plan to tell her. There are moments that I *want* to tell her. Especially with Garrett showing up every day to see her. Each time he strolls in, he glances at me. His eyes show calculative, computing whether I will tell her.

I open my mouth to say something, being just the two of us here. When I go to speak, rocks form in my throat. I'm unable to utter the words Sadie needs to hear; out of fear of losing her but also struggling because of this dividing wall built between us. She's not talking to me. This isn't a one-way street. I draw in a breath and shut my mouth firmly.

She won't believe me, anyway.

Even if he did tell her some of the truth, his fidgeting and flighty behavior tells me that he hasn't told her everything. I'd tell her now, but so much time has passed. The longer I wait, the more uncomfortable I feel.

Each day drags into the next, blurry and weightless. I move, I talk, I exist… but there's nothing of substance behind it. I get an empty, sinking feeling that I've become part of Garrett's lie, and I don't know how to claw my way out.

Chapter Thirty-One
Karl Reed: Backseat dealings

I let myself slip. Beating Melony, although pleasurable, isn't smart. She's flightier, which makes her a risk. Even plying her with the usual romantic endearments isn't pacifying her like it has in the past.

Taking the last sip of the beer, I contemplate my next move. I know Walker needs to be removed from the picture. The guys at the bar I egged on only raised alarm bells. I crack another beer open, tossing the bottlecap on the floor. Melony's at work.

Telling everyone. She knows Walker's right. About everything. They'll come for you. Because of him.

I growl at the voice, which gets louder with every sip I take. Some drink to quiet the voices. I drink to quiet my inhibitions. The paltry amount that I do has slowed my ability to plan my next steps. Not wanting to go to prison is the largest hurdle. But if I don't do something about Walker… I'll be locked up.

Hitting Melony forces me to expedite my planning. It's a matter of time before she tells someone. She's scared, and she'll search for security. That's what made her such an easy target in the first place all those years ago. Her darting eyes, the insecure tick of giggling softly under her breath as she apologizes for someone else's mistakes. The way she tucks her hands in her scrubs to conceal as much of herself as possible. The slump in her shoulders she carries around, like she wants to fold over herself to hide. The layers of makeup coat her insecurities like a mask she washes off every night.

The perfect target. The easiest prey. The meek rabbit ducking in and out of its hole.

It's her own fault, really.

If you don't want to be hunted in a world of predators, don't act like prey.

I grin, recollecting the thrill of the hunt. The mask of a dumbfounded man enamored by a woman's beauty. Everything she was searching for. It's a pitiful excuse to act like a complete idiot. Such a ridiculous concept.

I browse through the local gun show's event times in the newspaper. I don't have where and when planned, considering I don't know where Clara is yet, but I've determined how.

I'll get Walker alone and torture him, *because why waste the opportunity*, and then shoot him. I need a gun, or the plan that's forming is all for naught.

Glancing at the time, I sit forward to chug my beer. The local gun show started a few hours ago, and I don't want the crowd to die down too much. I shake the pocket of my cargo shorts, jingling the keys to ensure I have them. Before heading to the car, I scan the room, noticing that there's a notepad magnet on the refrigerator. I write a brief note to Melony, hoping to get back into her good graces so she'll keep her mouth shut. Just a bit longer now, and I'll have it all planned out.

Walking into the Ice Park Complex for the gun show required going through local law enforcement checks. Not having a gun speeds up the process. Browsing the weapons lining the tables arouses my endorphins as the smoky acrid fumes tickle my nose. My grin grows with each step I take. Glancing around, I study others' faces to match the energy of those around me. I don't want to appear suspiciously happy, though the general population is visibly intrigued.

It doesn't take much perusing to come across a .9mm handgun; easy to conceal and commonly used. Picking up the gun, the metal feels cool to the touch. Small compared to my hand, but able to serve the purpose in mind.

"You seem pretty interested in that one. You shoot often?" The older gentleman behind the table asks politely, eager to make a sale.

I mimic his level of enthusiasm. "It's a hobby I'm looking to pick up. A buddy of mine shoots and says I should start small." I lift the gun, insinuating that the .9mm will be my starting gun.

Another customer at the other end of the long table heckles, complaining about the poor service. The gentleman pauses to glance down at them briefly before turning back to me with a clipboard with a stack of forms and a pen on a chain.

"If you want to buy it, you'll need to fill this form out, and we'll get you set up. Just the background check and… ugh… excuse me a moment, sorry," the salesman apologizes as he shuffles off to cater to the noisy, impatient prick at the end of the table.

Steal it. No one's looking. Run.

Shaking my head, I set the gun down. I glance at the paper filled with personal information questions and peer up to the cameras in the complex, rotating around, noting that they are at all corners of the room. I huff, annoyed with the risk of getting caught, and turn to walk away.

Cameras make it more difficult.

Before I leave to go back home, I use the restroom. A lean man with jeans and a tan button-up shirt approaches me from the stall he was quietly sitting in. His face worn and covered in sores.

"I saw you eyeing that handgun in there. You didn't want it?" His grin stretches tightly over his lips. His eyes overflow with poor intensions.

"Not my taste," I reply nonchalantly, adrenaline kicking up my heart rate at the thought of this going south.

He digs at an itch on his arm with his head tilted to the side, as if something crawls beneath his skin that he can't scratch. He flashes his decaying yellow teeth.

"Listen, I need cash fast. I got a dealer that I dipped on and need his money now. I saw you in there looking at the gun like I look at a hit. You want one like it? Tan Buick in the back of the lot. Twenty minutes."

I peer at the bathroom exit as he leaves, then at my phone. *I can knock out a beer in twenty minutes*, I think to myself as I proceed to my car.

Chapter Thirty-Two

Clara Harris: Deepest darkest comes to light

Carrying a cardboard box to the complex dumpster of my old journals and plushies, I weigh the options. Walker's been hurting for weeks. His now monotone voice that's hardly present anymore—it's difficult to watch. He's been through so much in life… why can't our family catch a break?

I gulp, attempting to push the darkness back in its cage. All the therapy in the world but coexisting with Walker and his pain filling every crevice of the apartment creates more dark days lately. Slipping back into a reclusive depression feels impossible to avoid.

Chills race up and down my spine as a creak from up the alley echoes off the buildings, drawing my eyes. It's broad daylight, but monsters lurk during the day too. A cat digging in the trash down the alleyway hops out and scurries away. Releasing the breath I held, I turn back to the dumpster to throw away my journals. I wish I could throw away the memories inspiring the dark contents within them. The deepest, darkest thoughts I've ever had, smashed between a front and back cover.

Him coming back has me constantly looking over my shoulder. Why would he come back? Hasn't he taken enough from me?

My hair stands on end as I remember the feeling of his fingertips tracing my skin. I cringe, turning my head to the side reflexively. A slow, rocky breath shakes as I blow out. The goosebumps on my skin and chills running the length of my spine don't dissipate.

The same thoughts that build my nightmares I'm plagued with every night—waking up eyes wide, grasping my throat. I grip my throat, digging for air.

I always feel a deep urge to scream, but I can't breathe, much less scream. I shake my head, forcing a gulp to push away the tightening sensation. Knowing that Walker is across the park at the shelter reassures me. The eerie feeling pushes me to head to the shelter for security. Throwing the last of the contents away with the box, I walk around the building to the public park.

Strolling through, my eyes dart in every direction. Walking slowly, I spiral through the dark corners of my past. Each step feels heavier than the last, as though the earth itself is trying to swallow me whole. Flashes of Karl blurs my thoughts, bringing on a rush of paranoia I can't catch hold of.

Seeing the shelter in the distance helps to give grounding to my fears. I wrap my hand around the base of my throat, feeling the breaths rise and fall. My eyes flicker side to side, searching for anything green. Green trees. Green park benches. Green streetlight. Green grass. Green shirt on the random lady walking her dog. I take intentionally slow breaths until my breathing evens out.

I'm accustomed to panic attacks. I've had them every night since the day my peace was ripped away from me.

Passing by Sadie's red car, a sense of reassurance helps to further slow my breaths. Walking into the shelter, I wave to Sadie.

She smiles at me, her face scrunching in confusion. "Clara? What's going on? Everything alright?"

Green, the color of Sadie's eyes fluttering over me, assessing for any sign of duress requiring her help. Her white floor-length skirt catches my eye as she twists to return to the front desk. I follow her, searching for the words to explain why I came to visit.

"Is Walker here?" I ask, scanning the room for him.

Sadie chuckles a singular sarcastic sound, and her smile falls. Her ring glimmers in the sunlight coming through the large window. She follows my gaze down to her ring.

"Oh, yeah! You haven't seen it. Isn't it so pretty?" She shows off her two-carat, oval-shaped diamond engagement ring. She's forcing a swooning tone, even though she never seemed to care about these types of things.

She's playing the part, but for who? She sees that I'm not swooning over her ring with her and shifts her emotions in a calculative way. "He should be back soon; he went with Daniel to pick up donations. Is there something I can help you with?" She flashes her teeth, genuinely wanting to make a difference, reminding me of the Sadie I met a couple months ago.

Realizing that Walker is gone, I decide to do the decent thing that no one else had the gall to do. I was silent once, and it wrecked someone's life; I'm not doing it again.

"Actually, I need to talk to you… in private." I grab her hand to brace her for the pain that's coming. "I'm sorry." A guilty frown pulls the corners of my mouth down. Empathy causes me to clench my eyes shut, preparing myself to be Sadie's foundation while she processes the news.

"Why? Why are you sorry?" Sadie stammers.

I struggle to meet her eyes but force myself to do so for her sake. *She deserves to be told.* My hands tremble, wishing the news didn't exist—that people who are inherently good only receive good. Unfortunately, that's not the world we live in.

My heart pounds as I look into Sadie's eyes, struggling to find the right way to say it. "I... there's something you need to know about Garrett." I pause, biting my lip.

Sadie arches her eyebrows.

Chapter Thirty-Three

Sadie Thomas: Everything comes out in the wash

Trigger Warning: Chapter contains suggestions of violence and homicide

"I loved you!" I shout, shoving Garrett out the front door. He stumbles back, hands outstretched, begging for my forgiveness. "You're lucky I don't call the cops to have you removed. I bet that'd be pretty embarrassing at work! Now go!" I take the engagement ring off and throw it at him. "We're done!"

Slamming the door shut isn't enough to satisfy the rage coursing through me causing me to smack the door repeatedly until I'm out of breath. I press my clammy head against the cool painted door, my breaths ripping through me rapidly and squeezing my eyes shut. My father approaches from behind, gently grabbing my shoulders.

"What'd the door do to you?" A soft chuckle resonates the sentence.

I turn into him, burying my head into his sweater vest. He pats my back with one hand and tucks a strand of hair behind my ear with the other. "Oh, Sweet Girl… I'll tear the damn thing off its hinges if it hurt you this much."

I force a sad laugh. He's trying to lighten the sorrow with humor. I just… I can't find anything humorous with the betrayal and disrepair swirling about inside.

"He cheated on me. Someone told me… they saw him… he admitted to it. It's been going on for over a year… A YEAR!"

Dad stiffens under my touch. His muscles tense and the comforting back pats turn to clutching. His heart thudding faster against my ear.

"Well, what sort of man asks a guy to marry his daughter while sleeping with some tramp."

My eyes shoot open wide. Realization strikes me that I'm not the only victim in this predicament—I'm about to destroy my parent's marriage. He pulls back when he senses my body go rigid and watches my eyes transform from heartbreak into guilt.

"It… it's mom… he was with mom." Calling her mom is like gargling acid.

Dad's eyebrows raise, anger slipping into denial. He shakes his head, not saying another word as he retreats to his office. He pours himself a drink so he can sit and ponder whether he believes it to be true. Whether his wife of almost thirty years had an affair.

I'm indignant, how could Garrett do this! Not to mention… he proposed in front of all Dad's colleagues. If it were a regular breakup, they could've concealed the scandal from everyone. But now it's breaking off an engagement.

I peer down the hall, hearing the clinking of his bottle of scotch shaking against the crystal glass. My eyes cave in empathetic sorrow. Everyone will know. Had Walker told me, I would've never said yes. The humiliation my father is about to go through would never happen.

The word *infuriated* isn't strong enough. Walker shouldn't

have kept this from me. He said he was my friend! The anger snowballs within, urging me to drive to the other side of town to confront him. To demand his apology and explanation.

As I leave the house, Diane closes the driver's side car door with a shopping bag tucked under her arm. Her eyes catch mine, a moment of guilt flickers across her face before transforming into distaste. She upturns her nose in the opposite direction as she starts for the house.

"That's it? You fuck my boyfriend and you're going to act like I'm the one that's vile!" Anger pushing me to attack, I straighten and lock my knees to prevent violence.

"He came to *me*, Sadie. Maybe if you knew how to handle a man...." She trails off with a shrug, her lips tighten into a firm line, and eyebrows raise.

I scoff as my hands hover over my forehead. "You're not right in the head! Clinically insane if you think that you're in the right here!" She stops walking, standing at the bottom of the steps looking up to me. "I used to excuse your comments—your jabs at me. I'd say to myself, *'She's broken and wants better for me but doesn't know how to say it.'* But that's not true, is it? In your eyes, I'm nothing more than an extension of you. A trophy to show off when I succeed and a shame to hide when I don't. A pawn to use—"

"Now, Sadie, you're being irrational... that's not—" Diane interrupts.

"It's not?! You use people! You used Dad until there's nothing left but a shattered shell of a man sipping scotch in the only room he feels safe in! You used me to make yourself feel better. Whether it's tearing me down or showing me off, you come out looking great. I'm done! Keep your comments to yourself. Don't speak to me again." I spit my words in an aggressive hiss, cutting ties with the woman who gave me life. Tears stream down my face, and I'm not sure if it's heartache or rage fueling them.

I turn shoulder as I walk past her to my car, she's only one out of three people I'm after today.

"Walker Harris! Open this door now!" I bang on the door to his apartment, hand reddening from the force. I huff at the lack of response and kick the door. "I need to talk to you! You can't avoid me! This ends now! Come out!" The door cracks open. Walker squeezes through, side-stepping out of his apartment, closing the door behind him.

"I know why you're upset. I want you to understand how deeply sorry I am that—"

"Sorry? Because you're a shit friend or because Clara told me?!" I interrupt. My snippy retorts spill out with my rising temper, my words, clipped and accusatory, are loud enough for the world to hear.

"You're mad because I didn't tell you." Walker's voice shakes with the weight of what he's trying to tell me. "I should've told you. I was going to... I didn't... I couldn't lose you," he hesitates, trying to work through what he's going to say.

He inches back, trying to control the emotions threatening to pour out of him. His hands shake, but he forces them into his pockets, probably hoping I wouldn't notice.

Clearing his throat, he continues, "I'm selfish. It's not that I don't care. I just... I didn't want to be the one who destroyed everything." Avoiding eye contact, he turns away from me, facing the decorative painting hanging in the hall.

His reaction confuses me, which simmers my rage. "What the hell are you talking about? How would *you* be the one destroying everything?" I cock my head to the side, trying to connect the missing pieces that are trapped behind words that aren't said.

"It figures. You're too good of a person to understand. Too selfless to see why someone would hesitate revealing information for selfish intentions." He pauses for me to figure out for myself what he's trying to say, but my puzzled look reveals how lost I am. "Ugh… I have to spell it out for you, don't I?" He tries to look annoyed, but I can sense his nerves. "I… have… feelings… for… you." Enunciating every word doesn't make it easier to process.

I knew deep down that Walker had feelings for me; but until he said it out loud, it was just speculation. My heart pounds hearing him pronounce his feelings for me.

"But… if you *like* me… wouldn't you *want* to tell me… so I'd leave him?" Something isn't clicking. It only makes sense that he'd want us to break up. My mouth stays open slightly, trying to process the inner workings of Walker's twisted point of view.

"Because I'd lose you!" His eyes dart around the hall as he refuses to make eye contact with me. He opens his arms wide. "Not to mention… you guys separating means… I'd have no excuse to keep my feelings to myself… which scares me." He shoves his hands back into the front pockets of his denim jeans, turning away from me completely.

"Your feelings scare you? So, you let me say yes?! That's bull-shit, Walker!" My patience runs thin.

"I'd be the guy to ruin your relationship. The guy who ruined your parents' relationship. The guy to burst the bubble." He glances up from his feet to meet my eyes for the first time since I got here. "No matter what, I'd lose you. I was trying to figure out how to tell you without losing you."

I fall quiet for a moment. He's not wrong, but he also isn't right. "I can see that… but not telling me and I find out from someone who might as well be a stranger hurt."

He flinches at my words, his eyebrows tensing with regret.

"I'd never hurt you intentionally. I was trying to figure out how to... I care... I just...."

Walker's intensity struggling to break free halts my breath, and the tension in the air pushes in on us—a magnetic force so strong I have to fight to stay upright.

"Well, yeah, we're friends." Sadie says, as she cocks her head to the side.

He grips his chest, like a pain rushes through him, exhaling heavily. I reach my hand toward him for comfort but stop halfway. He follows my eyes down to my hand hovering. The sound of his words transforms from sorrow to cheerful. I can hear the smile in his words.

"No... we aren't friends," he replies, quiet and stern.

I'm still looking down to where my hand once hovered, as he draws closer. The warmth of his presence melting me. Heat runs in my veins, burning as it spreads. Chills cover my skin. His breath tickles my forehead.

"Wha...what?" My cheeks flush from his proximity. His hands trace the skin of my forearms, leaving a blazing path. My mind blanks, believing for a split second he's breaking off our friendship. His lips skimming my forehead corrects that thought.

"We're not friends, Sadie. If I were your friend, my heart wouldn't break from your pain. If I were just your friend, I could breathe when you weren't around," he whispers softly.

"So, you like... *liiike* me?" I hesitantly ask. My breath hitches, chest tightening in at his flirty smirk. Every inch of space between us seems to shrink until his presence is all-consuming. Intoxicated, I shake my head and pull away.

"No... not really," he replies with a sarcastic undertone, taunting me. His fingertips have made their way to the edge my shoulders.

I sheepishly reply, "Oh...." I'm unable to respond with the smothering tension clouding my mind.

His smirk spreads into a huge toothy grin. He snickers under his breath as he exhales. He pulls away, toying with my body's yearning for his closeness.

"I've always struggled voicing my feelings. I make jokes because I'm nervous or uncomfortable." He takes another step back, and instinctively, I move forward. His eyes soften. "You've become everything to me. Every glance at you makes me smile. My heart skips a beat every time you laugh. My hair stands on end when you're close. Breathing the air close to you calms me —makes me feel like I'm home." His piercing cerulean eyes drill into me, his smile fading in the silence of my stare.

No one has ever spoken to me like this. "I… I don't understand…." My eyes widen as words evade me. I want to respond with more, but the utter dismay has me frozen.

"How can you *not*?! Sadie Thomas, you're beautiful. Not just your looks. But how your face scrunches when you do math. The way your eyes light up when you see how you helped someone. How earnest your heart is. The nervous tic you have of biting the inside of your cheek when you don't know what to say next. I can tell you try to make everyone happy, and for some odd reason that actually makes you happy too…."

Looking me up and down, he takes a step, the edge of frustration in his voice eliciting an uneasy feeling. I step back, collapsing the space between my back and the hallway wall.

"Don't get me wrong, you are an absolutely beautiful woman head to toe…." He peers down my body with a sensual longing in his eyes before dragging his slowly back to mine. "But your looks are breathtakingly incomparable to *who* you are as a person. Every minute I spend away from you makes me feel like I'm underwater, choking to come up for air."

I part my lips to speak. His eyes trace my lips, pausing me in my tracks. I press them back together firmly as he stares. "Tell me you don't feel the same. If you don't, I'll go into my apartment and never bring it up again." He leans away from me, just an inch, allowing me space to think.

"I… I… I can't…." I stutter, struggling to process how I feel. I should let him walk away, but my body pulls toward him.

Guilt claws at my throat. I'm not ready for this… not after everything with Garrett… but every touch from Walker makes it hard to remember all the reasons why I shouldn't.

"You can't love me, or you can't *let yourself* love me?" The options sound so similar. I turn my head away slightly, facing my flushed cheek to him. My face pointing to his apartment, I study the gold-plated number on the door.

"I shouldn't…." The realization that I do love him calms his face. He leans over me, placing his hands over my head on the wall. I gulp as he locks me in. My heart races as he grins devilishly.

"There are lots of things we shouldn't do, Miss Thomas…." Leaning down into me, he's able to sense my trembling anticipation. His lips press against my ear, almost as if it were a kiss. "Tell me to stop, and I will…."

He drags his lips down from my ear to my jawline. My breathing staggers and a faint squeal leaves my lips. He pulls back, assessing me with concern. He rapidly realizes it's nervous excitement and his eyes dilate. For a heartbeat he pauses, just long enough to give me one last opportunity to say I don't want this.

I've never wanted anything more. I lean my hips into his and with that motion his arm grabs me around the waist. Pressing himself into me, pushing me against the wall. His free hand grasps my head, fingers intertwining with my hair. Rushing in to kiss me, his lips crash against mine. My arms wrap around his neck, pulling him to me, filling every space we aren't touching.

I can feel every inch of him pressing into me. My body melts into his, like we were built for each other. His tongue slips into my mouth as the kiss deepens.

A faint creak echoes in the hall, too soft for me to care. Walker obliges my urgency to continue for a second more before another squeak sounds from the end of the hall. Walker's head snaps up. Frozen, his eyes widen at a shadow moving into view.

A gun glints in the dimly lit hall, pointing directly at Walker.

Chapter Thirty-Four
Walker Harris: Let us live

Trigger Warning: Chapter contains graphic depictions of sexual and physical violence, graphic depictions of sexual assault, and gun violence

Karl stands at the end of the hall with a handgun pointed in our direction, eyes blackened with rage and sweat beads at the start of his hairline, his gait staggers as he stumbles down the hall to us. I put my hands in the air as I sidestep in front of Sadie.

"Wh-where is she?! You're keeping her from me!" Karl spits at me, his hands trembling.

Sadie's pressed up against my back, trembling and softly whimpering. Her body heaving with disheveled breaths, she sobs, overcome with fear.

"Shut the fuck up!" Karl jabs at the air in our direction, taking two lunging steps rapidly toward us.

Reactively, I flinch toward the door behind me. I don't want to turn my back to Karl, so I put my arm down behind me, reaching for her. She grabs my arm like a lifeline, hugging it tightly. Never taking my eyes off Karl, I try to comfort Sadie.

"Take a deep breath... I got this," I whisper. Her terrified whimpers cause a lump in my throat.

Nothing will happen to her... *over my dead body*. She needs to calm down... I've dealt with guys like him in prison. The worst thing you can do is match their energy level.

Halting just a few feet away from us, Karl's eyes lock onto mine, wild with rage. "You ruined everything! My Trinket... She'll be mine again *when* you're gone." My eyes search our surroundings for anything to subdue him. Everything I come up with puts Sadie at risk.

"Listen... let's talk about this... you and me. Let Sadie go and—"

"Nobody's leaving...." A sinister smile contorts his face into that of a wild beast, eager to inflict pain.

He closes the space between us, pressing the gun to my chest firmly. The metal of the barrel leaves an indentation in my skin. Standing tall, I refuse to cave. Too much is at stake. "Don't be rude... invite me in." Karl's eyebrow twitches in excitement, baiting for me to crumble.

I turn sideways, moving Sadie as I rotate and use my free hand to open the door. My eyes trained on Karl's hand as he flicks the end of the gun toward the apartment. We cooperate cautiously, ambling toward the living room. The small lamp casts a dim, ominous glow on the vinyl flooring. The gray walls feel crushingly close as we enter. What was once my haven has transformed into another jail cell.

Karl shoves the cool metal to my lower back, incentivizing my cooperation. He guides me to sit in the olive-green armchair that's diagonal from the chestnut leather couch and takes the seat next to Sadie. She folds away from him. Karl studies Sadie with piercing, calculative eyes.

He draws a deep breath through his nose, as if he can smell the fear radiating off her. He sighs, intoxicated with terror coating the room in a thick film. Silence smothers me as my eyes bounce around the room for any out. I reposition in my seat, causing a creak. Karl whips around, pulling focus from Sadie to me.

"Do you feel powerless? Helpless.... inferior?" He slurs his words, spewing spit as he stammers his cocky, rhetorical questions.

His calm demeanor is more unsettling than the volatile anger. His face relaxes, a twinge of a smile peeking through. Facing the gun towards the ceiling, he puts his hands up. He pretends to be me, mocking my fear. Realizing that we aren't laughing at his teasing, he sighs and switches his crossed legs.

Turning his attention back to Sadie, he leans to her, inhaling the air around her—capturing her scent. He grips a lock of her hair between two fingers, twiddling it back and forth. He brings it to his face, sniffing. My stomach churns, unable to pull my eyes away.

I wait for an opportunity to present itself. Then it dawns on me... the only idea I can conjure up. He asked if I'm *humiliated.* This is about *ego. If I taunt him enough, he could slip up and I can charge.*

"Clara was only a child. You're sick...." I bury my fear, forcing an over-inflated confidence to take center stage. I lean over the arm of the chair, planting my feet on the floor assertively.

Recognizing the power move at play, his smile diminishes to a thin line. Stiffening at the challenge, he pushes back with anger taking hold in his eyes.

"Shut up," he says, unenthused with the insult. He begins to refocus his eyes on Sadie when I continue.

"Who goes after little girls? You're weak. Sad, really...."

Karl, frustration building, stops pointing the gun at me as he brings his hands up to cover his ears, shaking his head in denial.

"I said, shut up! Shut up! *Shut up!*" Karl stands, continuing to shout at me in a panicked rage.

"A pathetic excuse for a man!" I enunciate every word, loudly and direct. Each word jabs deeply, twisting the inner-workings of his mind.

He pulls the gun from the side of his head, waving it as he drunkenly tries to focus his aim.

Before he can settle his line of fire, I charge him. Gripping the gun with both hands, I fight to pull it free. Sadie jumps over the back of the couch and crouches down behind it, shielding herself. I struggle with Karl, stumbling about. A cracking whip sound thunders suddenly through the room, creating a ringing in my ears.

He shoves me, forcing me backwards. My head bounces off the end table as I fall to the floor. A burning sensation throbs on my lower left side. My hands trembling, I reach for the source of the hurt. A warm, thick liquid coats my fingers, slicking my hands.

He shot me.

My vision blurs, disoriented, with black throbbing around the outer corners of my sight. I lose track of the wound under the blood-soaked shirt, attempting to apply pressure through the faint feeling clouding my spatial awareness.

He turns his attention to Sadie, who's still hiding behind the couch in hysterics. Through my troubled vision, I see her crouching down, covering her ears and squeezing her eyes shut. Her body vibrates, petrified.

"Hello, Walker's plaything." Karl toys with Sadie, like a cat playing with a mouse.

Sadie glances over as I drag myself toward her. Blood from the top of my head drips into my eye, further clouding my vision. Karl follows Sadie's pleading eyes toward me. He lets out a low, maniacal laugh, and stumbles over to me. Using the wall closest to me, he balances himself into a squat. He hangs his head to the side to ensure we are eye to eye.

"Look at your hero, Sadie... look at him now," he speaks to Sadie, but stares at me.

The acidic scent of gunpowder mixes with the copper smell of my blood, concocting a pungent odor. Nausea sloshes stomach acid, bringing some up to my mouth. Gripping my hair, he forces my head up, showing my face to Sadie. "Look at him!" He spits at the ground in front of me. Dropping my head, he stands, swaying as he tries to balance himself. He staggers back to Sadie; her soft sobs propel me to her.

I have to get to her. In my disoriented mind, I think that I'll make a difference. Even with my limbs growing heavy and my core tingling, numb, I believe that I can stop him.

He uses the couch to squat down to Sadie, who is curled in a fetal position. As he balances himself in a low squat, she jumps up, lunging toward him. Catching him off guard, he falls onto his back. She stomps on his hand with the gun, hoping to knock it free.

Being focused on the gun, she doesn't anticipate him to punch her with his free hand. She falls to the side . She scurries to get up, *to flee,* but Karl gets to his knees faster than she can stand and rips her to the ground by her hair. "You little cunt! I was gonna let you die quick, but now...." His shift from a predator taunting his prey to blind rage shakes every inch of the apartment. Sadie rolls up, preparing to fight again.

Karl pistol-whips her. This doesn't stifle the fight she's putting up, it only creates more erratic movements. Kicking, clawing, screaming and flailing, she manages to make contact more often than not.

Karl is infuriated and tired of the struggle. He tosses the gun off to the side and grabs both sides of her head and repetitively smashes her head against the vinyl floor. Her body falls to the ground limp, and blood pools under her head, gathering her blonde hair into a matted knot that's tinged deep red.

The moment we shared, not even an hour ago, ruined in blood.

A tingling, burning sensation spreads throughout my body as I drag myself to her.

Karl stands up, panting. He brings his fingers up to his face, smelling Sadie's blood that coats them. He picks up and drops Sadie's arm, confirming she's unconscious. "Fuck… she's like a wild fucking animal!" He turns his head to me, noticing that I'm still conscious… barely.

Trying with all my might to focus, I'm able to meet Karl's eyes. He's looking up from under his eyebrows with a demonic grin. I know whatever he's about to do can't be good. I push myself forward again, fighting to keep my breath steady.

He kneels to her, staring into my eyes my vision fades with each throb that pulses through me. He traces his hand along her body as the familiar sound of police sirens echoes in the far distance. My head falls to the floor, unable to push any further. I slip into the darkness that pulls at me with forceful hands.

CHAPTER THIRTY-FIVE
WALKER HARRIS: IT'S ALL MY FAULT

Trigger Warning: Chapter contains suggestions of homicide and violence

The faint sound of mechanical beeping repetitively alarms in my ears. Slowly, the sound grows louder and louder. I blink, opening them in a squint from the sunlight glowing through the window. Letting my eyes adjust, I focus on the television off in the distance.

Once my vision is clear, I survey my surroundings. White is everywhere I look. White blankets cover me. White walls surround me. White rolling table holding a white foam cup. A whiteboard with bold black words written on it. The date is what catches my attention. I've been asleep in this hospital bed for four days.

Raising my arms in the air is difficult against the resistance of gravity pulling them back to the bed. After much effort, I bring my hands up to my face. My hands are dyed red but scrubbed of blood. I attempt to lift my head and glance down at the rest of my body, but both my left side and head throb intensely, causing my head to bob in disorientation. After the pain from moving my head, I decide to do my best to sense with touch, sight, and sound.

The soft cotton consistency of the hospital gown clings to my neck with a drawstring. The medical tape and gauze encasing my lower abdomen feels scratchy and wrapped firmly. My fingertips trace the bandage, wincing at the flashbacks of the gunshot wound. Memories of what happened flood to me in fragments, as I struggle to piece the timeline together.

An image of Sadie laying limp on the floor brings on clarity.

Sadie! Is she alive?

I pull myself up into a seated position, only to be met with an alarm from the bed and an automated voice requesting me to get back in bed. The nurse comes rushing into the room.

"Look who's awake!" The nurse, with a name badge reading Maggii and shoulder-length black hair, exclaims enthusiastically as she adjusts her face mask on the nose. The navy-blue scrubs are a stark contrast to her pale skin. She smiles at me as she walks around the bed to press the buttons on the side rail to stop the alarm. She stands on the side of the bed, studying me as she awaits my response.

"What… happened?" The words scrape out of my throat, raw and dry. I wince at the sharp discomfort. My mouth feeling like dust; I forcefully gulp, hardly able to swallow. The nurse places her hand on my arm, the warmth helping to ground me.

"You don't remember? You've had two surgeries for a gunshot wound. You're through the worst of it, though." Maggii smiles reassuringly. I try to sit up again, but she raises her hand to stop me. "You can't get out of bed just yet." She glances at the nursing assistant wearing black scrubs as she walks into the room. "I'm gonna call the doc. Stay with Mr. Harris, he'll probably have some questions."

With a nod from the nursing assistant, the nurse strolls out of the room. The nursing assistant steps closer to the bed, tucking a curly strand of her red hair behind her ear.

Her brightly colored hair pulls focus from her round face. "Two detectives came earlier today, but you were still asleep. Do you remember what happened before the ambulance brought you here?" The nurse's assistant is either nosy or making conversation.

I shake my head. I remember bits and pieces, but I'm still putting together the puzzle. Besides, if I tell anyone about what happened, then that leaves Karl in the hands of the justice system. He's already gotten away with hurting people I love once, I'm not about to let them handle him again.

Karl will die. I'm going to make sure of it.

Everything he's done to our family and Sadie... he's not walking away from this.

The nursing assistant frowns at the lack of details, empathy filling her eyes. "Well, what's the last thing you remember?" she asks earnestly curious, folding up her notes sheet.

"I remember being with Sadie... and then—" Flashes of what truly happened contort my face, but I let her believe it's from pain as I grab my head. "Then, I woke up here. Is she okay?" Her frown remains, but her eyes shift into a pity-filled gaze. She shakes her head sadly but stops when she realizes that she'd have to give me recounts of what happened.

"The trauma must be blocking your memory. You were also out for several days; your memory might come back in spurts. Sadie's not awake yet, that's *all* I can say."

I sigh in relief, knowing what happened could've killed her. He could've killed both of us.

The guilt of Sadie being there in the first place forces a knot in my gut. I press my lips firmly together, swallowing hard to prevent the nausea from overcoming me. She would've never been here... laying somewhere in the hospital... trying to survive.... *if it weren't for me.*

"Did they catch whoever—the person who did this to us?" I

question, pretending to be ignorant of who they needed to catch.

The nursing assistant turns at the sound of someone entering the room. A man shuffles into the room with a woman following close behind. The man wears khaki dress pants and a white button-up shirt with the sleeves rolled back. His hazel eyes calculating as he studies my facial features. He leans against the wall across from my bed while the female detective steps forward. Her black hair is slicked back into a tight ponytail, pulling her caramel skin taut. Her smile, snow white up against her mauve lips.

"Hello, Mr. Harris. My name is Detective Gonzalez, and this is my partner, Detective Magley. We're from Lexington Special Victims Unit. Can we talk for a minute regarding the events that brought you here?"

"Special Victims Unit. Isn't that for…. rape victims?" They glance at each other hesitantly.

Realizing that I might not really recall everything that may have happened causes me to thrust forward, pushing through the pain. Vomit threatens to tear out of me, and I cover my mouth.

"We handle all sorts of cases. We're here for your account," the female detective continues, pressing for me to give information in place of receiving.

Pushing myself to be okay, I gulp back stomach acid. Wincing at the pounding in my head, I squeeze my eyes tightly.

"Who would do this? Did you catch them?"

Detective Magley leans forward off the wall to answer my question. "No… we haven't. Can you describe them? Was there only one?" He takes out his phone to record the conversation.

I take a deep breath, trying to bring forward a visual of Karl in my head. A shiver races down my spine, cringing at the mental image.

"I… uh… maybe in his forties… white and shorter than me,

but not by much. Average build... but with a gut." I recognize that I'm describing Karl completely and that I need to throw a wrench into the investigation. "He had longer brown hair with a brown beard... it's fuzzy though maybe he was blonde." Wanting to shift the conversation in a different direction, I continue speaking. "I vaguely remember someone coming into the apartment. I must've left the door unlocked after letting Sadie in." I rub my forehead, dizzy from moving my head back and forth between the detectives.

Detective Gonzalez comes forward. "Can you talk to a sketch artist if we send someone up here?"

I nod my head slowly, closing my eyes to help stabilize the spinning. She repositions her stance as the nursing assistant walks in, dragging a vital machine on wheels behind her.

"Sorry to interrupt... need a set of vitals." She smiles at each detective as she passes them to get to me.

"We're done for now, anyway. Thanks for your time. If you remember anything at all, give us a call." Detective Gonzalez places a business card on the rolling table.

I force a polite smile. Detective Magley nods at me in thanks as he follows his partner out of my room. I sink down, out of the upright, tense position. The nursing assistant tilts her head; a puzzled look presses her eyebrows together.

"I don't do well with cops," I mumble under a huffed breath as I cleave the interaction from my mind. "How long do I have to stay here?" She giggles at my question as she wraps the blood pressure cuff around my arm.

"You realize you haven't even walked yet? Let's see how you do with a few things first," she snickers.

Getting discharged from the hospital after a week of pushing to leave was serene, but I can't bask in the freedom. I have a mission in mind that I've been building since I woke up. Clara coming to visit daily was my saving grace.

My apartment is roped off, being that it was a crime scene. For obvious reasons, she didn't want to go back to stay at my mother's home, so Sadie's dad was kind enough to allow Clara to stay in a guest room at their house. Sadie's father was at the hospital every day and noticed Clara visiting both Sadie and me, which is how we stumbled into this arrangement. It's the safest she can be, at least, until I can get out of here and kill Karl.

My plan is loosely structured and poorly thought out, but the end objective is very clear. His death won't bring peace. I doubt I'll ever truly recover. But after going for the people I love twice, I won't risk a third time.

I ponder whether Karl is ballsy enough to stick around when Clara pulls up in Sadie's car. Richard agreed to let her drive it while Sadie is still in the hospital, which is more than generous.

"Sorry I'm late… how long you been out here waiting for me?" She parks the car off to the side in the patient drop-off zone and gets out, rounding to the passenger side and opening the door.

I hobble over, still unable to stand up straight from pain. The pain pills filled at the hospital pharmacy rattle in the brown paper sack I carry. "Not long at all."

She grabs the plastic patient bag off the ground, her hands shaking anxiously. I can sense that she wants to help, but knows I'll snip at her for not letting me do stuff for myself. I make it to the door, holding onto the frame as I hand Clara the paper bag. "You look better than yesterday," she says reassuringly. Her words carry forced enthusiasm, and guilt-filled dread covers her face.

Her hands tremble as she gets her seatbelt on. Her eyes

follow mine to her shaking hands. She sighs, clenching her fists to force away the quiver.

We drive to my apartment, not a single conversation between us. The sound of wind ripping past the car combines with the hum of the engine and the transmission shifting gears. The tense anticipation of seeing the apartment since *that* night is palpable between Clara and me.

Turning into the small side parking lot, both of us exhale a held breath. Parking the car, there's a brief pause before Clara turns to me.

"You ready?" she asks as she pulls the keys from the ignition.

I nod, and we head up the five flights of stairs, which takes longer than expected from the frequent breaks. Standing outside of the apartment, my heart races. Sweat drips down my back from the combination of climbing the stairs, pain, and the uncertainty of what we might encounter.

Clara puts her hand on my shoulder, encouraging me to take the leap and enter. We open the door to a horror scene, standing in the doorway gawking at the dried splotches of blood on the floor. The outline of my legs with smear marks from where I dragged myself across the floor takes up half the living room—a perfectly rounded circle of crusted blood where Sadie's head once laid. Clara gasps as scenes of what happened are easy to conjure.

"This was meant for me, wasn't it? You said he came for me.... it's.... it's my fault!" Cries edge into shrieks as her breathing buckles. She gasps at the air, only for a moment. The next second her face stills, relaxing to show no emotion. Her eyes distant and empty as tears dribble down her cheeks. She stares blankly at the dried blood on the floor.

"This isn't your fault. He's sick. Twisted. He should've died seven years ago. I would've gone to jail for life, but it would've been worth it to keep everyone safe." I struggle to grasp the right words to help her, limping over to comfort her.

She flinches away from my touch. Wrapping her arms around herself in a protective self-hug, she turns away from me.

"Can I go?" she pleads. Without waiting for me to respond, she steps to the door and out into the hall.

I glance back at the blood crusted floor before returning my gaze to Clara. I nod, limping over to the couch alone and sitting. Clara closes the door behind her.

I don't blame her for not wanting to stay here. I don't want to stay either, unsure if cleaning the blood up will be able to rectify the guttural feeling of being on the brink of death. Flashbacks replay in my mind on repeat.

I'll kill him…. for everything he's done, *everyone he's shattered…* no matter what.

Chapter Thirty-Six
Walker Harris: Free of pain

Trigger Warning: Chapter contains graphic depictions of suicide and murder

Aggressive banging on the door brings me out of a deep sleep. Worried that it's Clara in danger, I rush to door, as fast as the pain will allow. I yank it open to reveal Garrett.

Many days' worth of beard overgrowth and black sunken in eyes tell me he hasn't been taking care of himself. The stench of alcohol and cigarettes melted into the over-powering scent of a vanilla-based cologne. The relief that it's not Clara in danger showing up on my doorstep releases the tension in my shoulders.

I sigh before I question his late-night visit. "Why are you here?" I inquire, not having anything left to say to him. "I didn't tell her, if that's why you're...."

Garrett leans against the doorframe, exhaustion dragging down his face. He interrupts my assumption. "I know you didn't. Sadie told me who told her. I'm not here for that." His shoulder slips from the doorframe, and he catches himself with one hand, gripping the top trim of the door to stabilize himself.

I can't tell if he's drunk or exhausted.

"Then why?" I cock my head to the side.

Garrett's eyes peer past me to the stains on the floor. His legs, already unsteady, buckle at the sight.

"Who... who did this to her?" His voice cracks, and tears threaten to fall as he sucks in air to choke back the distress. "She's not... awake... she's...." His voice cuts out as his emotions take hold of his composure. He falls to his knees, and I stumble back.

"Jeez! Are you okay?" I exclaim.

His sobs stifle off, forcing composure as he stands back up to face me.

"Fuck, no! I loved her!" he shouts, frustrated that I'm not following his erratic behavior.

"Love," I correct him in a level tone, clipping off the end of his sentence. He pauses, studying my face. "She's *still* alive." I shift in the discomfort of his silent stare then turn and hobble to the couch. Garrett stumbles behind me, flinging the door shut behind him.

"Barely! It's all my fault. Had I not been with... had I not... She would've never been here with *you*," he sneers the last word, following me to the couch. Remorse floods me as he jabs, hoping to shift the blame he feels. "Who did it? I need to know!" His eyes bore into me.

"I told the police—" I start to give him the same story I gave to the detectives, but before I can get far enough into it, he interrupts.

"Don't give me the bullshit you gave them... I *know*... I fucking know that you know. I want to kill him! For what he did to her... I'll kill the sick son of a bitch. Tell me now or I'll add you to the list!"

Garrett isn't stable. The burdening hurt he's carrying is too much to bear. I can empathize with him; guilt overwhelms me as well. If I were only quick enough... if I came home soon enough. *If I were strong enough.* Everything boils down to my not being *enough* to protect the people I love.

"I don't know, Garrett! If I knew, I'd tell the detectives. I want him to rot in prison." I fake confusion and frustration behind every enunciated word.

Suspicion still dances in his eyes, but he stands and starts toward the door. Either he's concluding that I won't delve any deeper, or his exhaustion is taking hold of him. As he opens the door, he rotates toward me to utter his last remarks.

"I'll find him. When I do, he'll die." The calm deviation in his mood leaves twists my stomach.

At least we're on the same page for once.

Standing on the curb at the public bus-stop, the orange and purple hues of sunset hold my gaze. As I near my mother's home, anxious about my plan, I contemplate whether to drive away. Even with having every reason to rid the world of Karl, I still don't know if I have the resolve.

My mother left for work, but Karl's car sits outside. I can't determine if its gall or stupidity that motivates him to stick around. Reviewing my plan, my body shakes with anxietyinduced adrenaline. I inhale deeply, making my jagged breaths even.

Closing my eyes, I imagine my mother's house from years ago, hoping that not too much has changed. In the past, Karl would be passed out by now in the recliner. Whether he's different seven years later, I haven't a clue. Based on his behavior at my apartment, he doesn't appear to be a recovered alcoholic.

Cursing under my breath, I rock myself forward out of the

car. Pushing myself toward the door, I drag my feet, struggling to overcome the dread of crossing a line that I can't return from. I approach the side of the house, hoping my mother's hidden key location hasn't changed. When I lived here, the key sat in the unlocked windowsill of the kitchen.

I thrust myself through the overgrown bushes that sit below the window. The branches scratch at my skin, leaving a burning sting behind with each reddened scrape. I reach the window, worried that the struggle is a sign to turn around. I shimmy the stuck window up and blindly feel around for the key before sliding the window back to its original position, and I fall backwards, landing on my butt. I huff a burst of air as I bounce off the ground. Taking a harsh breath, I grimace at the pain in my core. The unkempt grass tickles my palms, intertwining in my outstretched fingers.

I should just go home.

Images of Clara and Sadie take turns flashing in my mind, and I launch myself off the ground, moving to the kitchen side door. The screen creaks as I slowly draw it open. I hesitate, allowing my eyes to adjust to the dimly lit kitchen. The television in the living room blares but is drowned out to the tune of Karl snoring. As I creep through the kitchen on the balls of my feet, I'm alert, my focus fixed on the living room.

I round the corner of the wall that divides the kitchen and the living room to see Karl laying back in the recliner. Standing face to face with a sleeping beast, roaring snores belt out of him. I swallow memories of the last time I stood in this house. The clock hanging in the living room across from the entryway chimes on the hour, snapping me back to reality.

Karl's leaned all the way back in the recliner with his legs up. An empty rum bottle sits on the floor near him, a gun sits on the coffee table. I lift my hand holding the knife, preparing to end him. My hands shake with anxiety as I struggle with conflicting thoughts.

If I kill him... I'm no better than him.

He deserves *to die.*

As I battle with the inner demons plaguing me, movement catches my eye near the kitchen.

I jump back and jerk the knife in the direction of the threat. A smaller, dark silhouette appears in the threshold of the kitchen.

I hiss under my breath, "What the hell are you doing here?!" My words are direct and demanding. Her flattened emotions pull her face stiff.

"Why are you?" A monotone statement, her distant and lifeless eyes peer to my hands at my sides.

I push the knife behind my back, shielding Clara from my motive. I can't follow through with this now. *Not with Clara here.* She's already been exposed to a lifetime's worth of trauma.

I walk around the recliner, meeting her at the kitchen entry. Her eyes focus on my previous spot before returning to me when I cease movement. She retreats a step back, drawing out her steps and arms slowly.

Metal glints at her side in the light casting off the television. I clutch her wrist, pulling up her arm to reveal a butcher knife. She doesn't try to conceal it. My eyes dart to hers, unfazed by the urgency on my face, she stares through me. She's here with the same objective.

Her detached emotional state raises alarm bells in my mind. I pull the knife from her hand without resistance.. Her arm drops before she turns down the hall to her room. I hurry into the kitchen, returning the two blades into the knife block and proceed to the hall, following her.

Before I can, a series of knocks tap at the front door. My eyes widen, fearing Karl will sober up at the sound of the knocking. Clara doesn't flinch as she enters her old bedroom and closes the door behind her.

Holding my breath, I glance in Karl's direction, keeping

perfectly still. A moment passes, and another snore thunders from him. I sigh in relief.

I open the front door to Garrett... *again*. In uniform, he stands on the front doorstep. Professionalism evades him when his eyes meet mine.

"What the fuck are you doing here? You can get in so much trouble." When I don't respond, he leans back, gesturing for me to exit the house. I turn to ensure that Clara isn't out of her room before sauntering past Garrett. "I could arrest you right now, you know that?"

"Then do it." My voice quivers. "How'd you know it was me?" I walk to the edge of the front porch and sit down. Garrett follows and sits beside me.

"Neighbors called about suspicious activity. I recognized the address and was close enough to take the call." He pauses, looking me over. "He did it, didn't he?" Garrett asks rhetorically. I put my head in my hands, burying my eyes in my palms as I nod.

"He hurt Clara too... all those years ago," I state in a hush.

He sighs, glancing back at the house, and returns his gaze to me in silence.

"How?" Garrett asks, studying my face while he waited for a response.

Guilt makes it difficult to sit in my own skin. "A knife. I put it back. I couldn't." I stare down at the dirt below our feet through the bleak light the house lights cast.

He nods again. "I don't know what you want me to do, Walker. You can't be here, you had intent, and if it were anyone else, you'd be in the back of my car." I close my eyes tight, accepting my fate. "I haven't called it into the station yet. I could, if you report him to the detectives, say it's all clear. Karl needs to go to prison... not you."

My fists ball up, squeezing tightly at the poor options I have laid before me. "Not good enough… he deserves to die," I growl through clenched teeth.

Silence falls between us as we sit for a minute, processing the night's events. Crickets chirp in the summer evening chill, emphasizing the tranquil quiet that night offers.

"And it's your choice to make? Are you so sure it's justice, and not revenge?" I want to agree with him like a sensible person would. "I wanted him dead, too… but that's not my choice to make." Avoiding his eyes, I continue to stare at the ground beneath my feet. I shake my head, disapproving of my own actions.

"I feel just as out of control as I did seven years ago. I can't let him get away with this aga—" Before I can fully utter *again*, Garrett is placing his hand on my shoulder, reassuring me.

"We won't." I meet his eyes, his smile reassuring.

He's cleaned up and looks mentally sound. Leaps and bounds from the last time I spoke to him. He must have processed what happened and came to the same conclusion he helped me find.

POP!** Pause…. **POP!

Garrett's eyes widen to saucers. We both spin to the sound inside the house. Jumping off the porch onto his feet, Garrett removes his gun from the holster and flips the safety off.

"Is anyone else inside?!" Garrett demands in a stern voice.

I nod, pulling my attention from Garrett to the house. My legs weaken with the fear of losing my sister.

"Clara!" I shout, trembling with dread.

I take two disorienting steps toward the house before setting off into a wobbling sprint. Garrett grabs me, holding me back. Desperate to know if she's safe, I fight to get free. *I have to see her.*

He struggles to keep hold of me, calling over the radio attached to his shirt. "10-33! Shots fired! I repeat… shots fired!

Requesting immediate backup. Officer 627 on scene. Not waiting for backup!" he shouts over the radio.

"10-4 Officer. We advise you to await backup." Garrett releases his radio and looks down at me struggling against his grip.

"Wait here. It's not safe." He grabs my shoulders and turns me, forcing my eyes to meet his. "Wait. Here. *Do you understand?*" Clear and under control, Garrett commands me.

My eyes flick between him and the house. I nod rapidly. Taking my word for it, he drops his hand and cautiously approaches the house.

"10-17. Repeat 10-17. Back up in route. Wait for backup. Don't engage." Garrett opens the door carefully, scanning the room before straightening into a calm stance. He cautiously enters the house.

Chapter Thirty-Seven
Unchosen Fate

Trigger Warning: Chapter contains graphic depictions of suicide and murder, graphic descriptions of a crime scene

Entering the house, Garrett observes a spray of blood across the living room wall. Blood pools around Clara, flowing down from the gunshot wound in her chest to her neck. Her body lay sprawled across the coffee table, her head hanging limply over the edge. He rushes to her.

"Clara?! Clara, can you hear me?!" Placing two fingers on her neck, Garrett doesn't feel a pulse. On the floor under her right hand is a handgun.

Karl has a single shot to his head. His mouth gapes open, looking asleep.

Garrett thinks to himself, *the lucky bastard got to die peacefully.* He moves about the crime scene delicately, assessing both Clara and Karl. The guilt of not fully assessing the scene sits on his shoulders as the sound of backup rings through his ears.

Turning to the front door, Garrett notices Walker standing in the entryway, his breaths heave, shuddering through him in violent gasps. Sobbing to himself as he stares at the sight of his sister. Swallowing hard, the pain in his chest constricting tightly. His body trembles as he analyzes the aftermath surrounding Garrett.

"Walker. Hey, you have to go... *now*. You can't be here." The police sirens grow louder as Garrett shakes his body aggressively trying to snap Walker out of it.

He blinks in dismay, struggling to grasp the realization that his sister is dead.

Why didn't he see the signs?

Why did she act so normal... so... happy?

Trying to convince himself that she's not dead, he stares at her pulseless body. Garrett shoves him away from the scene. The growing intensity of the sirens encourages Walker to snap out of it. He rushes off, leaving his little sister behind. Garrett, walking into the kitchen, notes a suicide letter hanging on the refrigerator door.

I can't pretend to be normal anymore. I can't escape him. He won't hurt anyone else. I won't hurt ever again. I'm sorry.

    -Clara

Leaving his mother's house, Walker catches the last scheduled bus to the hospital where Melony works. He knows that someone else would tell her if he didn't, but news like this should come from him. Walking into the hospital, he recalls the last time he saw his mother. The pain of her wanting to forget his existence incomparable to the excruciating pang of loss he feels now.

Walker approaches the nurses' station, heartbeat thrilling in his ears. A heaviness takes hold of him. He grips his gut, trying to settle the discomfort. Waves of grief wash over him as he draws closer to Melony, who's sitting at a computer.

Melony focuses on the chart in front of her and doesn't notice Walker standing at the counter.

"Mom?" Walker says in a shaky, broken voice. The hurt is impossible to hide.

Walker's face takes on a greenish hue. She pauses before looking up, unable to believe her ears, dragging her eyes upward slowly until she meets Walker's.

"What… why are you… Walker?" Struggling to find the right words to say, she stutters in disbelief. She's thought about this day for years but didn't truly believe it would ever happen. She steps out of the nurse's station into the hall where Walker stands.

"We need to talk." Hurt cracks each stuttered word.

Melony looks him up and down, thinking that he'd been hurt. When she sees that he isn't, she glances down the hall to the elevators.

"Let's go sit. You can tell me about the problem over there." She puts a hand on his back, showing him the direction. He hunches over in pain as he hobbles. "You're limping?" A concerned look takes hold of Melony's face, drawing her eyebrows inward.

After spending seven years trying to detach herself from Walker, at the end of the day, he's still her son. Nothing could ever remove the deeply rooted maternal love. At the end of the hall, to the right of the elevators, is a seating area.

"I was shot. That's part of what I wanted to tell you about." As they walk down the hall, Walker begins to tell her everything —what happened seven years ago leading up until tonight.

Hoping she'll understand the pain that Clara went through and why she thought there was no other escape. Melony stops fidgeting, focusing on Walker as he nears the end of his story.

"Clara... she's.... she didn't make it, Mom," he chokes on his words, barely able to breathe through the knot in his throat. The weight of his words heavy, pushing on his chest, squeezing his lungs. A sharp, twisting ache settles where his heart sits. He tells his mom about what happened tonight with Clara.

"No... no, she... she can't be... she was better! Not Clara... no..." Stumbling over her words. Bringing her hand to her mouth to cover it in dismay. She shakes her head as she twists in her seat. After writhing around in the discomfort of the words he utters, she decides to stand. Melony's breathing accelerates, gasping as tears build in the corners of her eyes. "It's not true. It *can't* be."

"She's... *dead.*" Walker forces out, the breath surrounding his words harsh, clipping his words. He leans forward, gasping like he's been sucker punched in the gut. Adrenaline leaves his body in spurts, causing dizzying nausea. He clutches his gut, begging his body to keep it down.

"No!" she shrieks, an agonizing cry heard throughout the ward. Melony grips Walker by the shoulders, her fingers digging in as if she can make the truth disappear. Her body shakes with disbelief.

Walker can feel her pain like an electric current running between them. Her legs buckle, and she collapses onto her knees, crashing down. Her hands cling to Walker as a lifeline, subconsciously searching for anything to ground her. Bunching his shirt in her rigidly clasped fists, her body rocks with each breath. The quiet violence threatening to overtake her. Guilt meets heartache—rage meets denial.

The elevator behind her dings as the doors slide open. The police uniform is the first thing visible, and Walker's body tenses.

Garrett turns his head to them. He's come to notify next of kin of the deceased. Garrett's eyes trail down from Walker to the floor where Melony fights for each sharp breath. Eyes softening in regretful compassion, he parts his mouth to speak. A hoarse catch in his throat diminishes the words, rendering him silent.

Sucking in a deep breath, trying to clear his throat, he draws Melony's attention. "I... I'm so... sorry for your loss, Ms. Harris."

Melony's last name is snuffed out by her wails. She flings herself off Walker, forming a ball on the floor as she sobs, clawing at her throat with each gasping breath. The loss of her child too much for her to process. The guilt of not seeing her pain, not intervening when she could've. The guilt for believing the happiness Clara projected. It's all too much for her to bear.

"I should've known... I'm her mother... I should've known!" Her voice cracks, bellows of desperation and remorse booming off the walls down the hall.

Walker drops to the floor, folding over his mother.

Embracing her tightly, he cradles her as she sobs.

Chapter Thirty-Eight

Walker Harris: Destined Silence

Sitting in the late-summer sun in a black suit forces perspiration to build on my lower back. I pull at the sleeve cuffs on my wrist, the starched fabric soaking with sweat. In a black floor length dress next to me, Mom sniffles. Her pallor skin highlights puffy, red eyes and nose.

The brightness of a cloudless sky contrasts the feelings swirling about inside. Clara's casket lay closed at the front of the crowd, and people I've never seen come forward to pay respects. Most from the high school—other students and faculty uniting to show solace.

The funeral director stands to the right of the casket, squinting at the summer sun shining in his eyes. Clara's school picture, expanded on a canvas, is propped on an easel with flowers draping around it. The mature dogwood trees to the left bend the sunlight, forming shadows on the ground. The dark green colliding with the remaining white flowers, which fall to the ground petal by petal. Muted conversations dispersed in the gathering of strangers.

"You know she killed herself," one older, audacious woman

wearing a dramatic black hat whispers to the younger, rounded lady beside her.

Mom clamps down on my arm, also overhearing the conversation behind us. I tense every muscle, restraining myself from verbally attacking this insensitive woman. The lady receiving the gossip gasps as the woman hisses *shh*, reminding her to be quiet.

The lady who gasps responds, "It can't be *that* surprising. Wasn't she the girl who had to be locked in a psych ward?" Others' eyes pull to the two women.

My jaw strains, rigid as my teeth crush together, threatening to shatter. Nostrils flaring, I adjust in my seat, pleading with myself to shake their words off. Making a scene won't rid me of heartache.

"Yeah, poor little thing was screaming for help," the woman in the black hat huffs in a disappointed tone. The younger woman clicks her tongue.

A creaking sound from the chair as the round woman repositions herself breaks the silence. "Well, you know how the saying goes: healthy hearts sing, broken hearts scream." *I can't take anymore.*

I whip around to face the two gossiping shrews. "Unless they're silenced to make awful people like *you* more comfortable," I interject myself into their terribly timed fabrication of empathy.

The woman with the black hat blows out a dramatic scoff.

Following the funeral, I visit Sadie daily. I want to be there when she wakes, but walking into the hospital sends shivers down my spine. After everything that's happened, and all the time that's passed, hope is bleak. The staff at the hospital all insist that she's improving, but every time I come, she looks *exactly* the same; beautifully frozen in a deep sleep.

Entering the elevator, I press the button to get to floor two. It takes a minute for the elevator doors to close and the elevator to move.

It's been a month since the attack, and she still hasn't woken up. With everything that's happened since I was discharged, the attack in my apartment feels like a lifetime ago, yet images fill my mind every time I lay my eyes on Sadie's face. Her eyes widened with fear, pleading for me to save her. The look that haunts my dreams. I wish it were something I could forget.

As I pass the nurses' station, I overhear the doctor speaking to a nurse. The conversation compels me to stop after hearing Sadie's room number.

"Hey Jackie, you have room nineteen, right?" He pauses; she must've nodded. "I know she's getting ready to discharge to LTAC... but has anyone discussed the pregnancy with her parents yet." My stomach falls through the floor. My eyes saucers in disbelief at what my ears heard.

"No, the hospitalist hasn't told them yet," the nurse replies solemnly, sighing with her words in disapproval that everyone is avoiding telling Sadie's parents the somber news. The doctor snorts.

"There's no excuse! I won't sign off on this discharge until the parents determine if an abortion is warranted." He snarls his words, anger at the hospitalist falling to the nurse.

In a sympathetic tone, the nurse responds, "If it were my daughter in a coma...." She pauses to process the unfathomable hurt. "I don't think I could abort the only piece of her I have left, even if it's the result of her being—" The nurse abruptly stops as she exits the nurse's station, nearly running into me.

"Oh goodness! I didn't see you there!" the nurse exclaims, jumping up and shouting in surprise.

I'm unable to move, the weight of the newfound information weighing down my feet.

She turns her head, studying my appalled eyes. "Something I can help you with?"

My jaw locks at the thought that she could be carrying *his* child against *her* will, sending waves of terror through me. I thought this was all over—that we reached the capacity for horrible events. But that's life, I guess… just when you think you can take time to heal, the rug is ripped from beneath you.

I open my mouth to speak, but I'm cut off by the nursing assistant shouting from down the hall.

Standing just outside of Sadie's room, the nursing assistant in black scrubs beckons the nurse. "Jackie! Come quick!" Taking exacerbated breaths of excitement, she leans forward to catch her breath for a split second. "She's awake!"

Acknowledgments

First, I would like to recognize my husband and children. Without the amazing family we've made together, I wouldn't have the passion and admiration for life that I do. I love you, and even though I know with or without this book you are proud, I wish to further that pride. You inspire me to be the mother and wife that I am. Furthermore, you support and encourage me to be myself within that. I cannot thank you enough for the love I receive.

Secondly, I would like to thank my mom and dad for always reading my work growing up and giving encouragement even when it was terrible. I cannot thank you enough for pushing me to be the best version of myself, not just as a writer, but as a person.

Thirdly, I would like to thank my Nana for giving me such love for reading. Since I'm an auditory learner, she would read to me extensively to aid my comprehension of school material. Had I experienced that alone, I probably would not have developed such a deep passion for reading. Nana has always supported me and listened to me in all of my ideas, my current reading, and throughout school. Thank you from the depths of my heart for being everything I could ever want in a grandmother and more.

Finally, I would like to thank all of my family and friends who have not only encouraged me in writing this particular work, but each and every piece leading until now has formed me into a writer. From friends who edited my writing to cousins and friends who read my work with enthusiasm and excitement for the next part of whatever I worked on, I received much support. True friends are hard to find, and I have been blessed along my walk of life with you. Thank you for being a part of my life and helping me become the person I am today.

<u>Mentionable Individuals Who Helped with Unspoken Destiny:</u>

Fellow Writers Who Helped Me Keep Going & <u>So Much More</u>: Black Dahlia & S.B. Ellie

Editor & Proofreader: Mallory Day & Refine and Format, Spite and Spine Ink

Developmental Editors: Mira Young, Maddison Jade

Indie Author Revolution: For giving me a home in the writing community, a family of fellow authors, and friends I couldn't imagine life without.

Erin Silva is a former cardiac nurse who turned stay-at-home, homeschooling mom of three—and a proud military spouse. She now channels her passion for helping others into writing romantic suspense with a dark, emotional edge. When she's not writing or answering questions, you'll find her planning home-school lessons, managing the chaos of extracurriculars, and embracing the beautiful mess of motherhood. In addition to writing, she volunteers as head of public relations for The Indie Author Revolution, a nonprofit organization.

instagram.com/Erinmsilva19
tiktok.com/@Erin.m.silva.author